Blazing 2

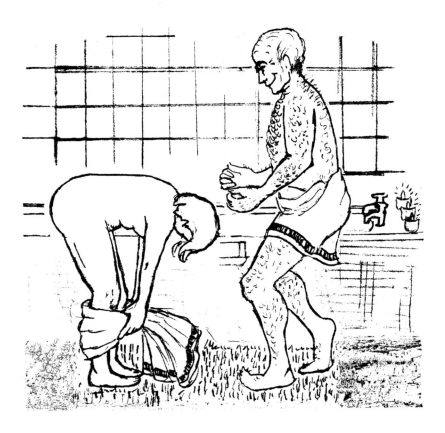

by

Angela Ashley

Magpies Nest Publishing

First Edition
Published by Magpies Nest Publishing 2004.
Printed and bound by BemroseBooth Limited, Derby.

Further copies may be ordered from:
Magpies Nest, 5 Old Hall Drive, Ulverston. LA12 7DG
www.magpiesnestpublishing.co.uk
email: embers@magpiesnestpublishing.co.uk

ISBN 0-9548885-2-9

Contents

Chapter one

A granny in search of an orgasm

In my mind's eye, I could see the ecstatic looks on the face of the pretty naked female as her lean, handsome, virile lover makes his erotic manoeuvre down her hot moist body. I can feel him kissing her throat and breasts, licking her belly button, slowly mouthing her body as his lust takes him further and further south to where my imagination is being led. Although the lover's dark curly head disappears from the screen, the girl's expressive face, her sighs and moans, tell me that he's reached his target for tonight. Mm, hot stuff on late night television and very informative too.

Things were not so when I was young, or if they were, I never knew about them. When I went to see our doctor just before I married Roger, he informed me of a certain procedure to ensure a more comfortable wedding night. It was most embarrassing. I just sat there having a man tell me what I should do with my fingers to stretch a membrane I didn't know I had. Except for the name of a messy contraceptive gel, that was the only sex education either of us received. Not exactly exciting stuff. Was that all there was to nuptial bliss?

I smiled at my recollections of our wedding night. There had been no preliminaries and no foreplay. It had been a tiring day and Roger, unable to control himself, went straight in for the kill. It was a single push lasting a few seconds, nothing more. But it was so very powerful — the symbol of our love and desire to be united for ever. Of course, I dare say Roger might have seen it differently, not so much a covenant of love as a lack of control on his part. But, even so, it was a very special ritual and symbolised our wedding day vow that God had joined us together and no one would ever come between us.

"Hello, Alice, I haven't seen you for ages."

Torn from my nostalgic reminiscing of fifty years ago, I looked up to see Tony Bradshaw, a friend of Roger's, smiling at me.

"Hello, Tony," I said, surprised to see him. "I've been around. Where have you been, the Bahamas?"

"Actually, yes, for a whole month. I won a little money and decided to get myself a tan," he replied beaming, his flashing white teeth contrasting with his golden-brown skin.

"It certainly suits you," I said, looking at him more closely.

I thought him to be incredibly handsome for a man of his years. Tall, broad-shouldered with an athletic build, he was looking exceedingly healthy; whatever he'd been doing on his holiday, it couldn't have been just boozing, eating, lying on his back and thinking of England. He was wearing a blue jersey, which brought out the colour of his sparkling azure eyes and his immaculate trousers reflected the sun-bleached white of his hair. Together with his magnificent tan, he looked like he'd just stepped from a millionaire's yacht in the tropics; I must admit, I wouldn't have minded being there with him.

"Do you mind if I join you?" he asked, in his soft cultured voice.

"Not at all," I answered politely, and smiled at all the jealous glances coming my way from the blue-rinse pensioners at the table near by.

While he was sitting down, I took off my blazer and put it on the back of my chair. I was getting hot. Whether it was the heat inside the room or the warmth of Tony's presence I couldn't really say. I dropped something out of a pocket and I bent down to pick it up. Tony bent over too and we nearly bumped heads. I laughed nervously like a silly girl. I noticed him glancing down my cleavage; he couldn't help it really, it was just under his nose. I must admit I was thrilled he wanted to look; after all, I'm no spring chicken.

He beat me to it and coming from under the table, he put the retrieved coin in front of me. "You might need to spend a penny sometime," he quipped, those luscious lips curling into a smile.

I beamed appropriately at his little joke and shyly slipped the coin into a trouser pocket.

The waitress came with my snack and took Tony's order for coffee. She hovered over him a while, ostensibly waiting to see if he wanted anything else but, by the way she was looking at Tony, more likely wanting to give him a coded message of her availability for service any time. He gave her one of his charming smiles. "All for now, my dear," he said, with just a hint of a wink. "I'll let you know when I'm hungry." She went away content.

Tony looked at me and raised an appreciative eyebrow. "You know, you look pretty good yourself. What are you doing these days?"

"Not a lot. I still paint. I've joined the local artists' group." Not wanting to make out I was another Grandma Moses, I added, "I do a bit of voluntary work, the usual household chores and I look after the grandchildren occasionally. You know, that sort of thing." I thought it all very boring stuff to a man like Tony.

He was quietly gazing at me as though summing me up. I found it rather disconcerting. Had he sussed out my attraction to him? Out of nervousness I blurted out a reminder of my marital status; "Oh, yes, and I do Roger's typing for him. But of course, you know that already since you're on the same committees."

He smiled at me most engagingly. "As a matter of fact, I thought he typed the minutes himself. I didn't know you were his little slave."

"He can't use the computer," I told him, but feeling I was letting Roger down, I quickly added, "Of course, he probably could if he tried but I don't mind typing the minutes for him, plus his letters, e-mails, and anything else he needs doing."

"I'm sure he appreciates it, I know I would," he said softly, looking at me with such intensity that it was getting acutely embarrassing. I was in danger of blushing — at my age!

I remembered he had a wife called Edith. "Oh, I expect you get your wife doing all sorts of things for you," I replied, giving a nervous little giggle and wondering why I was feeling and behaving like a silly teenager.

"I'm afraid not. Edith's left me. One reason for me to spend a bit of money before she takes the lot."

"I'm so sorry, Tony, I had no idea. Roger hasn't said anything."

"Really?" He raised an eyebrow. "Well, it's nice to know I'm not the centre of gossip, makes a change." I wasn't sure whether he was pleased or sorry.

I recalled some of the lurid stories that spread around about Tony and his various women friends. His reputation for having the largest and most creatively used piece of masculine equipment turned many a head and other bits of a woman's anatomy in that direction. I wondered if Edith had walked out on him because of another woman. I didn't have to speculate for long.

"My fault actually; she caught me with Susan Briggs in a nice little hotel restaurant. Susan was dressed all sexy and looking like a lonely man's best friend — his faithful bitch. She was goggling at me with her big soulful eyes and pawing at my legs." He gave a bit of a laugh. "When Edith saw us go upstairs to the bedrooms, she suspected the worse."

I was amazed at what he was admitting. "I'm not surprised. You're not telling me that Susan was going upstairs to give you a big lick on the cheek?"

The mention of a faithful bitch had brought up memories from my childhood and of how my sex education relied almost entirely on the activities of our spaniel Flossy. She had co-operated with her Casanova suitor by allowing him to get at her in a most improbable manner — coupling through a hole in the fence! Flossy's yelps brought us hurrying to the scene. We found her bum to bum with her mate on the other side of the fence. It did nothing to improve my sex education. I guess a man would have to have a serious case of stem wilt to get himself into that position. I was smiling at the memory when Tony's voice broke into my thoughts.

"Do you really want me to tell you what we were doing?" he asked, lowering his voice to a sexy whisper.

I looked down and blushed at my erotic thoughts. The truth was I did indeed want to know what they were doing, and if their cries of ecstasy reached beyond the bedroom door.

"So you see, my dear, I'm free and easy," he said airily without waiting for an answer. Coming swiftly to earth again, he sighed deeply. "Though I must admit I was used to having my dear Edith around even if she didn't care for the sort of thing I enjoyed with Susan."

"Presumably you still have Ms Briggs to bring you consolation?"

I couldn't believe this conversation I was having with Tony. I had never talked that way with him before, or with any other friend of Roger's for that matter. What was happening to me?

"Susan was put off seeing me again. Edith hit her with her handbag." He grinned. "Unfortunately, it was more like a leather shopping bag. Don't know what was in it but it knocked Susan over. I had to take her to the hospital for stitches."

"Good heavens! Poor woman, she got more than she bargained for out of the affair."

"I gave her a bit of compensation, much to Edith's annoyance. I think my wife wanted her to go to court for it."

He didn't say any more on the subject because his coffee arrived. I would be willing to swear that the girl had tucked her skirt up shorter; the split at the side was at a very handy level. When I saw the saucy smile on her face I wondered if Tony had discovered that for himself — accidentally of course. I reproved myself for my naughty thoughts. I put them down to Tony's sexy reputation. No doubt the girl's grin was merely wishful thinking. But it made me wonder if Tony's reputation was based mainly on speculation and unfounded rumour. Then someone passing the table spoke to him. Tony introduced the newcomer and, standing up, politely excused himself while he went over by the door to have a word with his friend in private. The ladies close by were watching them like a bunch of vultures. I heard a Mrs Loud Mouth say, "That's Clara Franklin's husband," and the others smirked and nodded their heads knowingly. No doubt their friend Clara was about to be torn apart, well chewed, swallowed down by tepid coffee and thoroughly digested — to be passed on to others in a most unpalatable form!

I began looking out of the window thinking about Tony's love life and wondering what he was like in bed. Were the stories true? Then I forced myself away from bedroom scenes; they were too disturbing for comfort. But what was happening outside was no better. I found myself watching a young couple in a doorway opposite the café erotically entwined in a bit of love-play. She was wearing a skimpy top and a skirt that was barely above the bikini line and reaching only to her thighs; he was dressed in a vest and the tightest of jeans. The girl's arms were tightly around the young man's neck and he was gripping her buttocks and pulling her up to him. They were kissing mouth to mouth with tongues, and rubbing each other's erotic zones with their bodies. I felt sexually moved and my voyeurism disconcerted me. Tony's voice again broke into my thoughts.

"You see, Alice, everyone's at it these days. Young folk do it openly but if we oldies did that in public they'd take us off and put us in care!"

I had to laugh with him, but I soon sobered up and diverted my mind. "I'm really sorry about Edith. You've been together a long time."

"That's true, but you know, she hasn't been a proper wife to me for many years — if you know what I mean?" But not expecting an answer, he added, "She wasn't keen on it before she went through the menopause and afterwards, well, she just dried up — in more ways than one."

I thought how lucky I was to still be on HRT and I began to appreciate my know-it-all Roger a bit more. I recalled his insistence on my seeing a doctor when I started having problems after my last operation. I looked up and saw Tony watching me closely.

"I'm sorry, I think I've embarrassed you with all this talk. Perhaps you think like Edith and you're taking my criticism of her personally."

"Oh, no, Tony, please don't think that. Actually, in a way, I'm enjoying this little chat."

He was looking at me very intently. "Really? Then you're not offended and we can still be friends?"

I had never been Tony's friend; he was a friend of Roger, not me. But I'd always found him jolly and pleasant to be near. To be truthful, I thought him very sexy and wished a bit of it would rub off on to Roger. I wondered how old he was. He certainly looked quite youthful but I knew he'd been retired a few years.

"I'm not at all offended, please believe that." I assured him. "I feel flattered that you're able to talk to me the way you're doing."

"Is that so?" he said with a sexy half-smile. He took hold of my hand. "You know, Alice, I've always liked you. You're smart, intelligent and, if you don't mind my saying so, quite sexy."

I was flabbergasted. I was also very flattered. Thrills ran through my whole body but the conversation was going in a dangerous direction — I might end up as Susan's replacement! With Tony's hand holding mine, it seemed like a delightful prospect. Swept with a wave of guilt at my sensual longings, my cheeks began to colour more deeply.

"I've done it again, haven't I? I've embarrassed you," he whispered, sounding a little concerned.

I smiled nervously. "Of course not."

"You look incredibly lovely when you blush," he murmured softly.

It was such a corny thing to say, normally I would have laughed in response. But he was looking into my eyes so intently that I felt bewitched by his words. My hand, which he was still holding, was glowing from his touch and I knew my heart was beating much faster in response to my disturbed emotions.

He gave me one of his flashing smiles and said briskly, "But I apologise; put it down to my randy state having just lost both wife and lover."

Before I could recover enough to answer, he gave my hand a little squeeze and let it go. "I must be going now — an appointment with my solicitor. I'd love to see you again, Alice. Lunch perhaps? Or maybe we could go to a tea and dance session at the Vic? You do dance, don't you?"

"I used to but I think I've forgotten how." My feelings of guilt rose to the surface. "But I don't know, Tony, there's Roger to consider."

"Does he consider you? From what I know of him, he's always busy with something or other." How true that was, especially when it came to sex. When Tony saw my embarrassment, he quickly added, "Tell you what, I'll ask him about it when I see him at the next meeting in a couple of days. Anyway, I'll give you a ring."

As the prospect of dancing with Tony sunk in, my nerves started playing a rumba throughout my body. Trying to keep my excitement from showing, I merely smiled in acknowledgement.

Standing up, he said pleasantly, "Cheers, Alice, see you again sometime," and leaving a fiver on the table to cover both our coffees, plus a handsome tip for our obliging waitress, he left the café.

There was no doubt about it, my little encounter with Tony Bradshaw had stirred something in my knickers and I was feeling a potent mixture of guilt and sexual excitement. I turned my mind back to the thoughts I'd been getting earlier that morning and pondered on the coincidence of meeting Tony so soon afterwards.

I suppose it's natural for a geriatric like me to be continually getting pictures in my mind of an hourglass with the sands of time running out, and to get thoughts of what is and what might have been. I contemplated my fifty years as Roger's faithful, loving wife and of my devotion to our four sons and their ten children. Some would say, it had been a happy and fruitful existence and they would be right, but I knew something had always been missing in my marriage and it was causing me an inner restlessness.

Late night television had opened my eyes to the ecstatic joy that was possible from sexual encounters. Writhing in the pleasure of oral delights was something totally unknown in my experience. And I was being constantly amazed at the full-throttle intercourse that produced shouts of ecstasy from both of the partners, and it set me wondering why it had never been so for me. I began feeling a sense of loss for what I had never known. There was no doubting Roger's orgasmic pleasure from our nuptials; surely it was time for me to experience similar rapturous joys from our union.

I knew my childhood experiences had brought about deep-seated inhibitions. I'd had grinning old men touching my breasts as I walked past them, making me feel sick and totally embarrassed. I'd been humiliated by having a man's hand grip my bottom while bystanders smirked at my cry of shock and shame; and I'd suffered a traumatic incident in the park when I was just a kid. Hardly surprising I came to see touching as being associated with indecent desires and therefore a shameful and squalid activity.

I had problems throughout my teenage years with boyfriends wanting to fondle my body. It always ended with them dropping me in frustration. When I was almost eighteen, I had actually allowed a boy called Dennis to feel my knickers area through the thickness of my clothes, not for my pleasure but to please him. I really liked him and was afraid of losing him. But I lost him anyway because he said that his studies were suffering because of the sexual tension he was under. He left me feeling wretched and ashamed of what I'd allowed him to do.

To make matters worse, the following day, a smirking scruffy man came up to me and asked if I'd enjoyed the night before. I was mortified, especially as I had an inquisitive friend with me.

"What's he talking about?" she asked.

Before I could answer, the revolting, disgusting, Mr Scruffy Peeping Tom grinned and piped up, "I saw you by the river in the moonlight," and sniggering, went off; no doubt to spy on another unsuspecting couple.

I was only glad that I had not done as Dennis had requested — put my hand inside his trousers. It wasn't entirely for moral reasons that I had declined his generous offer; I thought it a horrible and absolutely disgusting thing to do — most unhygienic!

Thinking about my education, I realised it completely lacked anything to do with sexuality. We were supposed to have sex lessons at school but we didn't get any further than the division of single-celled animal life. We did search the biology books hoping for further enlightenment but all to no avail. Maybe our teachers were afraid of polluting our minds, or were worried we would put theory into practice. But more likely they were too embarrassed to enlighten us on the mysteries of copulation — we might ask questions!

Giving birth was another hush-hush subject not to worry children with, that is, if it could be avoided. After all, the question might well arise as to how the baby had got inside a tummy; never mind how it got out. Watching Flossy give birth to her pups gave me some clues but giving birth to a baby in a similar way was a very scary thought. No, babies were far too big. Having long dismissed the gooseberry bush theory, the doctor's bag lie, and the stork delivery system, most of us came to the logical conclusion that babies, however they got inside a tummy, would have to be cut out.

When I was thirteen and started my periods, I nearly fainted with shock — my pee had turned to blood! Without explanation of what it was all about, I was provided me with protection for my clothing. I had never heard of sanitary towels for such a purpose. Hardly surprising, if they were ever mentioned at all, it was by using their initials! Compact towels, 'a boon to ladies when travelling', was the only advert I ever saw and that was only on the dispenser in the ladies' toilets. I must admit I had no idea what a boon was and, when I was a kid, I never had a spare tuppence to find out. I saw periods as being no different to bitches being on heat, and I was forever fearful the boys would catch me out.

When the Americans came over to help us win the war, grey rubber things like deflated sausage-shape balloons appeared in parks visited by Yanks and their good-time girls. Some boys would blow them up until they burst. I heard one girl say that Yanks put them on their private parts and we wondered why. It seemed ridiculous anyway; I had once seen a man peeing up a wall and it was with a wrinkled object only a few inches long. It was some time before discovering answers. Even when I was going out with Roger, I thought it was a huge Swiss penknife in his mac pocket that came between us when he was kissing me. But I formed the impression, from hearing adults talking, that whatever the Yanks and their girls did in the park was a morally bad and disgusting thing to do, and that rubbery sausage-like skins had something to do with it.

Returning to the present, I sat pondering my situation. Tony had certainly stirred up my emotions. I had believed that true love and marriage would make clean all that seemed squalid and ugly, yet even in my precious moments with Roger, I carried the burden of deep-seated guilt. I was now truly mixed up, feeling bad about being sexually moved by another man and yet, more than ever, my natural desires were crying out for fulfilment.

Roger too had brought into our relationship a total ignorance of the finer art of making love. His upbringing regarded sex as something not vital, except for producing children and he'd always been satisfied with a minimum amount of contact. After all, he was a busy person. A quickie once a week, fortnight or month was enough to keep his engine from rusting up and nicely ticking over. Our marriage wasn't without its loving moments, but if that were all any woman got out of sexual activity then I just could not comprehend why anyone would pay large sums of money or ruin their lives, and the lives of their families, to get it.

Deeply aroused by my encounter with Tony Bradshaw, I resolved to discuss sexual matters with Roger and let him know how I was feeling about our love life. But I knew it would be difficult to talk to a man who thinks he knows it all and who has fifty years of marriage under his belt and four sons to prove his masculinity.

A familiar female voice interrupted my thinking.

"Hello, Alice, you look deep in thought."

I looked up and saw Jean Smith, the town gossip.

"Quite right, Jean. Thanks for waking me up. I must get back home, lots to do," and ignoring her plea to stay and chat, I rose to my feet and went to pay the bill.

"Cheers, Jean. I'll see you some other time," I said as I left the café, while knowing I'd do my best to avoid her.

For the rest of the day, I wrestled with how to approach Roger. All the time I was thinking about sexual matters, Tony Bradshaw kept popping into my mind and I found it very disturbing. At my age, to get fanciful notions about a sun-tanned Casanova is quite ridiculous. I set to work doing Roger's typing knowing that trying to make sense of his handwriting would need deep concentration.

In the evening, I sat with Roger while mending his work-shirts. They needed the frayed collars turning. He would be happy to go on wearing his old clothes for messing about in until they dropped off his back, but I have some pride even if his is in short supply. The least I can do is to make sure his rags are neatly held together.

As I tried, for the umpteenth time, to get the thread through the needle eye, I casually asked him, "What do you think about all this sex on television?"

Either he didn't hear me or he was avoiding the question. Since he was doing his usual trick of watching a documentary whilst studiously reading one of his journals, I decided to ask him again but a little louder.

"Roger. Do you think there's too much sex on television?"

"You don't have to shout, I'm not the one who needs a hearing aid," he said testily, looking up to watch an excavation going on in an ancient burial ground.

"Then answer my question."

"What was it?"

"Sex, what do you think of it?"

"Sex? We've been doing it for fifty years; I don't have to think about it. Isn't it time we had our drinks?" He went back to reading about the latest in engineering technology.

"It's only half past nine," I protested. I tried a different tack. "Unless you want to go to bed early," I said, in what I hoped to be a sexy voice. I wanted to stir something in his pants even if I couldn't reach his loftier mind.

"No, there's an interesting programme on after the news bulletin. But I'll have my chocolate now," he muttered; now concentrating on the bits of old bones being carefully examined by experts. "Just look at that," he said intrigued, "a ritual murder. Spike straight between the legs — fascinating!"

I gave up. His mind was on other things, even if not totally unrelated. Apart from which the horrible killing had put me off. I would have to do something to draw his attention to what we were missing, but how?

Roger may be in his mid-seventies but he's far from being old and decrepit, although dressing like a tramp around the house and garden may suggest otherwise. He's a very active person and always has been. He's continually engaged in improvements to the house and keeping the garden in good nick. He has his clubs and societies and is an officer or member of various committees. He enjoys going to lectures on any engineering subject and helps organise many of them. He plays a mean game of bowls and fills up the rest of his time in his extensive workshop. Between all these activities he makes sure the weekly crossword is completed and his entry form filled out for that prize which constantly eludes him. Hence, the difficulty of my task. But I've always been a very determined woman when things are important to me and I do not give up easily.

Convincing Roger of what was missing in our marriage was going to need cunning as well as tact. Concentrating on physical impact, I decided to try suggestive undies that "temptingly reveal the path to erotic satisfaction" or so I was led to believe from an advertisement. I let the matter brew in my mind overnight.

In the morning, I looked in my building society passbook and decided how much I was prepared to spend on pretty but useless titillating knickers and bras. I went to a specialist shop in town armed with twenty pounds. After a brief look around, I decided to return later with fifty pounds.

While waiting to be served at the building society, I changed my mind. Fifty pounds was a lot of money that would keep me in knickers for years. But the whole point of buying new knickers was to have Roger get me quickly out of them. Determined to succeed at this self-appointed objective, I took out one hundred pounds instead, and with a deep sense of guilt at my extravagance, I returned to the lingerie shop to view their collection of gorgeous lacy tempters.

A smart middle-aged well-corseted lady came along to see if I needed assistance.

"I'm just looking for something pretty for a friend," I cheerfully lied.

She fixed me with her beaming smile. "Was it something in particular? For a special occasion maybe?"

"She's feeling a little depressed," I lied again, adding in a conspiratorial whisper, "She thinks her husband is going astray and she wants to lure him back. I want to help her, you see."

The assistant nodded knowingly. "I quite understand, madam, it's a common problem. What size is your friend?"

"I'm not exactly sure but my clothes fit her very well," I said, pleased with my acting skills.

"Unless you're thinking of something simple like a nightdress, I'll need to take your measurements."

I pointed to a rail in the middle of the shop. "I was thinking of something like those red lacy things hanging up over there."

"Well, let's measure your bust and see what cup you'll need." She suddenly realised the slip. "Ah, that is, what your friend will need, of course."

She had me sussed all right but to spare my blushes and get a good sale, she was content to keep up the pretence. Taking me to a fitting room with a tape-measure at the ready, the dear understanding lady was very thorough taking measurements and I was quite impressed. I usually bought my undies off the shelf from a leading chain store and I wasn't used to such personal attention. We returned to the chamber of erotic delights.

"There are some blue silk sets over here that would really bring out the colour of her eyes," she informed me, smiling sweetly. "That is, if they are just like yours."

"They are very pretty, but I'm not sure." It wasn't really my eyes that I wanted Roger's attention drawing to.

"Do look around, madam, we have a fantastic selection. All the 38c bras have a yellow label. It would be best to try on them on as they do vary a little." She softly whispered, "If you wish to try on the knickers it will have to be over your own. I'm sure you understand. Hygiene and all that."

Smiling, the helpful assistant left me to it. She was now keeping a keen watch on a pair of young teenagers just entering the shop.

I felt very self-conscious looking at wired, low cut, see-through bras, and wispy knickers that barely covered the palm of my hand, but if I wanted my desires to find fulfilment I had to get on with it.

The pair of teenagers with pierced eyebrows, nose, tongue and navel, giggled as I held up a bra. I heard one of them snigger, "Hanging baskets to grow her melons in."

The garment was two sizes too big. I put it back and looked for the yellow labels. Quickly gathering together a handful of garments I headed for an empty cubicle to be out of sight. I also needed to get some idea what these things looked like on — I didn't want Roger to think I'd bought him something fancy for his greenhouse.

I took off my clothes down to my knickers and looked at myself in the mirror. My breasts were all right. They didn't look like the firm round ones I'd seen in sexy TV programmes, but they suited Roger. He didn't care much for pudding-basin breasts anyway; he always said that he liked my dumplings.

I pulled down my knickers just to get a look at what bits I wanted to teasingly cover. My tummy flesh looked like the skin on a rice pudding tipped sideways. I had an operation to get rid of my reproductive units and hitch up my waterworks some years before, and it left my loose stretch marks draping down like a waitress's apron. I was hoping the firm lace would control and hide some of it.

I pulled my knickers up and tried on a thong. With having good buttocks there were no loose bits there, just tight muscles. At the back I would look pretty good but at the front my 'apron' would just flop around.

I tried on high-legs. That was better; even over my knickers I could see they would make my legs look longer, and there was sufficient body on them to cover and tighten-in the worst of my tummy. For sexiness, there was that teasing bit between the legs just asking to be pulled aside. I decided it was the style to suit my plans and discarded the rest.

I tried on the matching bras to each of the knickers. The narrow strap ones cut into my shoulders but they had the better fitting cups. I looked in the mirror and tried to see myself through the eyes of

Roger. I decided he would prefer the ones that would push up my breasts and give a deep cleavage — he's a bit of a breast man. Three were cut low enough to excite him with the exposed maximum, whilst titillating him with the hidden minimum. They had matching knickers in the same colours. I decided to get three sets: red, black, and white. Then I looked at the price tags.

I asked to have the black set put aside and went back to the building society to draw out just enough to enable me to get the red set as well. I thought I would have to wait until pension day to get the white set.

As I entered the shop for a third time, the assistant looked up with a welcoming smile. She carefully wrapped the purchases in pretty paper. "Your friend is going to be very pleased with these, madam." Speaking very softly, she added, "They should keep her husband at home."

Although feeling most embarrassed at our coded messages, I smiled and nodded. She then gave me a little wink and whispered, "If it doesn't work, tell her to put a little itching powder in his pants. No rival woman will want a man that's always got a hand in his crotch."

Mental pictures of some poor sod being tormented silly in his nether regions were not pleasant. For some reason, Tony's smiling sun-tanned face had popped into my mind. Now feeling a mixture of guilt and doubt as well as sensuous excitement, I returned home with my little parcel. By the time I turned into our street, the clouds had lifted and I was beginning to feel younger. I walked up our flower-bordered cobbled drive with a lively step, despite the joints that were getting a little arthritic. Our creeper-covered white house glowed in the summer sunshine. A state of euphoria was creeping over me; would tonight be the night? I wondered.

Roger was busy in the garden trimming the hedges. I made him a cup of tea and we sat down in the gazebo while he had a little rest.

"Did you get what you wanted?" he asked me between slurps of hot tea.

"I bought a few pretty undies. A bit extravagant I suppose. I don't really need any; the ones I've got are perfectly good. I just fancied something pretty." I was rather hoping he would start thinking of lacy knickers and what was inside them.

"Oh, I don't know, you deserve a few little luxuries," he told me with a gentle smile. "I don't mind you spending a few pounds if it cheers you up a bit. Do you need some money? Would a tenner pay for them?" He started digging into a pocket for cash.

"Not quite," I said, thinking how horrified he'd be if he knew the real cost. "Thanks for offering, but I don't want you to buy them. What makes you think I need cheering up?" I felt pleased the conversation was moving in the right direction.

"You always buy something you don't need when you're bored," he replied, looking past me to see which trees needed attention.

So as to be eye to eye, I moved straight in front of him. "There is something I really do need, Roger, and only you can give it to me."

"I say, Alice, look at that bird in the oak tree. Is it a woodpecker?" He was now standing up and looking over my head.

"Where? Oh, I see it. Yes, I think it is." I was getting more frustrated by the second. "Roger, did you hear what I said to you?"

"Now is that a male or a female? What? Oh, yes, there's something you need. Buy it from our joint account." He watched the bird fly off and let his eyes stray over our magnificent old deciduous trees and well-pruned shrubbery. "Ah, nothing like a garden to keep you fit and happy. Now I'd better get back and finish that hedge," he said as he handed me his cup. "I've got a lecture tonight," he reminded me. "Don't be late with the meal, I have to get there early."

Roger went off down the garden, humming to himself while I went inside to get started on the pastry, thinking of the best way to introduce him to the new sexy me.

There was no chance to talk over the meal; he was listening to the news before dashing off to his lecture. I insisted on kissing him before he went out. I sniffed his deodorant and put my nose into his armpits.

"You sexy beast," I said, snuggling up to him.

"Not now, I'm late already," he said impatiently. "I'll see you at half-past ten; you can do your doggy imitation then."

Well, at least he didn't laugh at my little attempt to be seductive. I decided to have a bath later and get ready for him coming back home.

As I lay relaxing in the warm bubbly water, I thought about some of the sexy things I'd seen on television when Roger was out at some of his late meetings. Occasionally, the programmes were on when Roger was in. At first I would turn to another channel, especially if any of the family happened to be at home with us — it was so embarrassing to see couples engaged in erotic behaviour when my children were present. But after leaving it on when we were alone I got used to it. Roger would be reading anyway.

I was intrigued with the things they did. We only had normal sex; at least, we thought it was normal. He might touch me a bit and I might touch him, but not usually; he liked to get on with it and then get off to sleep. I didn't think we could physically manage a lot of what they did on TV but some methods and positions looked quite possible for a couple of geriatrics to adopt, even if they might prove a bit of a strain on our mildly arthritic joints.

Oral sex was something different. On the TV I'd seen a man's head between a woman's thighs and a woman bobbing her head up and down within her partner's groin area. Well, it could mean only one thing — close ups made sure of that. I wondered what it must taste like. I wondered if it was really hygienic. Suppose couples hadn't washed for ages? I guess you had to be fond of smelly cheese in those circumstances; we only ate hard mature Cheddar, so I wouldn't know.

I suddenly remembered Roger telling me fifty years ago about a picture he'd seen where a man and a woman were licking each other and I had been utterly disgusted. But hygiene was much better these days and perhaps we were missing out on something good. I wondered how I could broach the subject. I'd heard such things were in certain magazines but I doubted I had the courage to go into a shop and buy one.

I wondered what my sons would think of their mother, an old lady, thinking about sex, let alone practising it. When I was a youngster I didn't think middle-aged parents engaged in sex any more; certainly not grandparents — it just wasn't decent. But why wasn't it? Because we have old wrinkled bodies? We are all the same in the dark. It just might be more difficult, that's all. But in spite of my reasoning, the familiar sense of shame at thinking erotic thoughts and desiring sexual satisfaction refused to go away.

I stepped out of the bath and dried myself, trying to ignore the wrinkles. I dusted with a small amount of fine talc and put on just a little perfume. I held up the extravagant black undies, torn between using them and taking them back. Decision made, swiftly cutting off the labels I put them on. I had to admit the knickers looked a lot better on naked flesh than over my panties. I fastened the bra on the tightest fastening and adjusted the shoulder straps to a comfortable level. I was very pleased with the results. My breasts were rounding up over the low cup giving a deep attractive cleavage. My nipples, showing through the lace, were hardening into stiff peaks as I became sensually alive. I was already imagining doing things to Roger that would set him on fire and both of us sharing in the best sex ever — as seen on TV!

I slipped on my dressing gown just as I heard Roger's car coming up the drive. I could feel the lace against my skin and it was firming my nipples even more. Would Roger notice? I was actually feeling moist down below and, thinking it to be a good sign, my excitement increased as I hurried to the door to greet my darling husband.

"Hi," he said, as he came through the door, "I won't bother with a drink tonight, I had a coffee at the meeting and I don't want to be up half the night."

"How about a nice relaxing bath?" I said with thoughts of what might happen afterwards.

"At this time of night? No, I just want to get to bed."

"Oh, dear, I am sorry."

"Good meeting though; lots there tonight. I saw Sid. You know, Alice, he must be nearly ninety but doesn't look it. Jim was there too, and Les and Bill who used to work for me. I haven't seen any of them for ages. The place has gone to pot since I retired. They say it's all computers now," he added in disgust. He threw off his coat for me to hang up. "Had too much coffee, must get upstairs."

I put his coat on a hanger and hung it in the hall cupboard. "I'd better come too or I might wake you up later on."

"Doubt it, I'm jiggered." He was pulling off his shoes at the foot of the stairs. His nose sniffed the air. "You smell nice, been out?"

But before I had chance to reply he was halfway up the stairs and out of his clear-hearing range. At least, he would see me in my undies as he was getting undressed — that might wake him up. I picked up his shoes and put them in the hall cupboard.

While waiting for Roger to emerge from the bathroom, I sat at my dressing table brushing my hair. I knew that getting a wash and cleaning his teeth would make him more alert. I was right. Before long, he came briskly into the bedroom and slipped smartly into bed.

I walked over to his side of our king-size bed and slipped off my dressing gown, letting it fall to the floor. The soft glow of the bedside lamp was flattering to my ageing skin and was giving a gentle shine to my silver hair. Surely the total impact of perfume, semi-nakedness and seductive black undies would do something to move him in the right direction? I waited nervously for his reaction but it wasn't forthcoming.

"What do you think?" I said, in what I thought to be a sexy manner.

"About what?" He answered with his eyes closed.

"Open your eyes and see."

Squinting, he opened his eyes. "Can't see properly without my glasses."

"I'm wearing my new undies. Put your glasses on and look."

"Can't it wait until morning? he mumbled grumpily. "Get to bed, you're keeping me awake."

I gave up. Disconsolately, I took off my pretty things and was about to put on my long-sleeved nightdress when I had a sudden thought. He might not want to look at me but he couldn't avoid smelling me. I slipped into bed naked and snuggled up to him.

"What's this? You don't usually come to bed with nothing on." He put an arm around me. "You smell nice too. Where did you go tonight?"

"Nowhere." Trying to be sexy, I rubbed up to him. "I've been waiting for you to come home."

He got the message. "Oh, I see. Don't know if I can make it though."

He slipped off his pyjama bottoms and climbed over my body, pushing my legs apart. It didn't take him long to get a bit of a rise. He pumped away for almost thirty seconds, grunting with the pleasure of it. Finally, he collapsed on top of me, his volcano having erupted and spent. Rolling over to his side of the bed, he was soon fast asleep. I lay quietly weeping, utterly frustrated at my inability to gain the satisfaction I had so ardently sought and completely unable to communicate to Roger my true feelings.

Chapter two

Various encounters

I woke in the morning feeling tired out. I went to the bathroom for a pee and to wash away Roger's spillage from the night before. I hate being smelly in that area, or in any place for that matter. I had a wash all over while I was at it and went back to the bedroom. I wondered whether to get dressed or put my nightdress on and go back to bed for an hour. In the light coming through the curtains I could see my black undies on my dressing table stool and they made me feel depressed. I thought of all the money I'd wasted and that made me feel sick with disgust and self-hatred.

Roger was stirring. He looked at the clock with half-open eyes. "What time is it?" he asked, his voice rough from sleeping with his mouth open.

"Seven. Are you getting up or do you want a cup of tea in bed?" I asked him in a rather offhand manner. I wasn't feeling in a loving mood.

He was already climbing out of bed to go to the bathroom to relieve his bladder. "I think I'll take a shower — a bit glued up," he answered, oblivious to my sour humour. "Won't come back to bed, I'm going to that exhibition in Manchester with Fred."

He trotted off to the bathroom and I heard him coughing up his usual build up of overnight phlegm. I picked up the pretty black lace undies, thinking perhaps I should frame them and hang them on the wall. They would add a touch of femininity to the rather masculine feel of the room. It had been that way ever since Roger had fitted his own very angular built-in furniture. My bottles of perfume and feminine touches did little to soften the effect. The room had Roger written all over it.

The undies were too expensive for an old geriatric like me to wear in the daytime; they wouldn't do much good for my silhouette anyway. It was all very depressing. I sighed and went to talk to Roger. He was about to get in the shower.

"Do you need any help, Roger?"

He was busy adjusting the temperature of the water. "I can manage thanks." Just before he pulled the shower door closed he remembered, "Oh, weren't you going to show me some undies or something? Put them on; I'll have a look when I get out of here."

I was thrilled. Not only had Roger remembered my little purchases, he wanted to see me wearing the sexy things. I went quickly to the bedroom like an excited youngster. I slipped off my dressing gown and put on the lacy garments. I dabbed on a little perfume and brushed my hair. I considered using a little make-up, but I rarely use it and it didn't seem appropriate first thing in the morning. Anyway, it was certain other bits of my anatomy that I really wanted noticing.

While Roger was in the bathroom, I went downstairs and quickly made some tea and took it upstairs with a few biscuits. I had to be in the bedroom waiting; Roger must not get dressed before he'd viewed me in my new undies. I heard the bathroom door open and I stood posing by the big wall mirror.

"I've put my pyjamas to be washed," Roger announced regally as he entered the bedroom stark naked, Little Willie dangling unceremoniously from its bushy undergrowth. Then he saw me standing there. "Very nice," he said appreciatively. "I'll just put my glasses on so I can see you better."

I stood in hopeful anticipation, trying to hold my tummy muscles in while keeping my shoulders well back to show off my breasts to best advantage. My rice pudding-skin apron was tucked up and being held quite firmly inside the lace panel of the knickers. There was no spare fat or anything else showing over the buttock and thigh area. My breasts were reaching out over the top of the wired bras in a most provocative fashion. I thought the whole effect was certain do something for him.

"Wow!"

I was almost quivering in girlish anticipation. "You like them? You don't think they were a waste of money?"

"Nothing is wasted on you, my love," he said, his tenderness rekindling my love for him.

He came to within a few feet and stood in front of me. I could see he was aroused; a man can't hide that sort of thing. Soon Roger would be at his peak of manly perfection.

"Turn around and let me see the back view."

Utterly thrilled by the way things were going I turned to face the mirror. He came close and put his arms around me. I loved the feel of his thick body hair against my naked flesh. He slipped the straps from off my shoulders and held my breasts cupped in his hands. "Beautiful," he murmured and kissed the back of my neck.

He unfastened my bra and let it fall to the floor. "That's better, I always prefer you with nothing on."

He slipped his hand inside my knickers. "Take them off, they get in the way," he demanded, but in a gentle sort of way.

I happily slipped them off, but while I was bending he cheekily slapped my bottom. I hated the manoeuvre; it reminded me of being slapped by a lecherous male at the swimming baths when I was a young girl. But now was not the time to complain.

He pulled me up hard against him. "Lovely, much better. We should do this more often," he whispered, rubbing his freshly-shaved cheek against mine.

I just knew we would get somewhere this time. I was sexually excited and deliciously alive, ready for anything Roger was about to do. Unity of ecstasy was in sight.

"Mm, now then," he mumbled.

My heart was racing, my breath panting, and my mind suspended waiting for Roger's next move to complete our act of love.

"Better drink that tea before it gets cold." Switching off his sexual impulses, he glanced at the clock. "Must get dressed, I'm meeting Fred at the station in thirty minutes. Damn it, I was going to walk but now I'll have to drive there."

I wanted to scream. I could have howled with frustration but somehow I managed to keep cheerful. After all, I didn't want to deter Roger from acting on impulse at some other time. I forced a smile and said, "Well, what do you think of my new undies then?"

He was now busily pulling on his underwear. "Fine, very pretty, but you look better in nothing."

"You think they're a waste of money then?" I asked him, now feeling very bad about spending so much on something Roger so easily dismissed.

"No," of course not. If they make you feel better then it's worth it. What does a few pounds matter? We can afford it," he said grandiosely.

He put on his trousers and came over to kiss me. "Come on, cheer up. Go and put the kettle on, I'll be down in a minute."

I'd had my orders and so, putting on my dressing gown, I went downstairs to get his breakfast ready. By the time he came down, his tea, toast and cereal were awaiting his consumption.

While he munched and slurped, I took my tablets and put on a new HRT patch, all the time thinking of how to approach him with my problem. I asked tentatively, "Roger, was it all right for you last night?"

He picked up his paper to look at the headlines. "Was what all right?"

"You know, what we did." I was annoyed that I now had competition for his attention.

He looked over his paper and said jovially, "You mean when you seduced me and kept me awake when I should be getting my beauty sleep? What a temptress you are!"

"Was it all right for you?"

"Of course, it always is," he assured me. He put down his paper for a moment. "Has this got something to do with your little purchases?" But before I could answer, he picked up his paper again and said from behind it, "You know you don't have to dress up to turn me on, you're fine as you are."

I allowed him to get on with his reading; after all, he only had a few minutes before he had to dash off. I let my mind wander to the first day I met him, thinking of how incredibly good-looking he was in his youth. At that time his hair was dark, thick and wavy and he had dense long lashes framing his brown eyes. His heavy eyebrows and his constant need of a shave made him look very masculine. His mouth was softer in those days and his lips tended to curl slightly at the corners. At least they did when he looked in my direction. He was wearing a scruffy looking raincoat that would have done justice to a crime novelist's description of a private investigator's disguise. He also wore an old scarf that appeared to be itchy; he would occasionally flick his head sideways as if trying to get rid of a fly. But when he spoke, his voice was deep, very rich and easy on the ear.

"Damn! I nearly forgot," exclaimed Roger, destroying my precious picture of him. He had finished his last spoon of cereal swallowed down by the rest of his tea, and was now reaching for my eye drops.

As he put the drops into my eyes, I whispered tenderly, "I love you, Roger," and tears induced by memories of our first meeting, mingled with the eye drops.

"Of course you do. We love each other. Fifty years together must prove something. What's the problem, love?" he asked tenderly, while I dabbed away the surplus teardrops. "Worried about getting old?"

His concern touched my heart and I began to feel bad about my desires. I said uncertainly, "No. Well, not exactly."

"Look," he said, taking command of the situation, "you go and get your hair done, it always cheers you up. Meet a friend and have lunch out. I have to be off now. We'll chat when I get back tonight."

He kissed me and dashed off. I watched him go, love clouding my vision. I stood admiring his energy and enthusiasm. Always so strong and virile, and yet five years older than I am. He never had problems getting it up either, even if it wasn't a daily event; but that was nothing new. I sighed, frustration beginning to build up again. I knew it would be a week or two before he would exercise his conjugal rights again. That morning had been something special and I'd so much wanted us to complete it in a unity of body and soul. Oh, yes, he might do a bit of kissing and cuddling from time to time but the main event, as he often called it, would wait until his need was great.

I couldn't understand it, if I achieved the sort of ecstasy he obviously did I would want it daily. But after much pondering, I thought that maybe deep satisfaction reduces longing and brief topping up sessions were enough until overtaken by a deep urge. I had urges frequently, but even when Roger was in a co-operative mood they let me down during the final moments. Perhaps it was as well that we hadn't gone any further that morning.

My reasoning led me into thinking there was something wrong with me. It was pleasant enough to be touched but it didn't get me anywhere. I longed for him to unite us and for me to feel the fullness of his presence. Certainly, the joining of our bodies gave me some satisfaction, but it did nothing else. Was I devoid of sensation in that area? Perhaps it would make no difference what Roger did. Maybe I was incapable of feeling anything special. Well, I knew I felt pain if very little else. Four difficult births and a pelvic floor operation made me very aware of an alive and active nervous system!

I sat with a cup of tea, again thinking about my early days with Roger. From the first day I met him, when we started to catch the same train, he would try to sit opposite me. Every time I glanced up, I would find him looking at me and disconcerted by the intensity of his gaze I would shyly turn away my eyes and look out of the window.

He always carried a little case with him, which he placed on the luggage rack above him. When it was quiet I could hear a ticking noise coming from that direction. It was the clock inside his case that broke the ice. Imagining a bomb in the case, I looked up and started smiling at my absurd thought. He must have known what was in my mind because he gave me a big smile. I smiled back, and from that moment my fate was sealed. Eventually he sat next to me and started up conversations. After a few weeks he asked me if I would go to the pictures with him.

That first date with Roger went very nicely. I wore a beige slim-fitting woollen dress with an embroidered net insert at the neck reaching down to reveal a small amount of lightly-veiled cleavage. The fine-knitted material clung to my figure, as was the fashion then. When I took off my coat in the cinema Roger gave me a very admiring look, which made me feel good about myself. He was looking good too; his smart brown suit and a pale beige shirt went well with his colouring. He held my hand while we were watching the films, and I felt relaxed and comfortable by his side.

On leaving the cinema, we walked a little way before he took me home. It began to rain so we stood under an empty bus shelter. Suddenly, he lifted my chin and kissed me. It was our first date and I hadn't expected anything of the kind. His lips were very soft and gentle and I loved the feel of them on mine. His kiss was somehow satisfying even if it wasn't earth shattering. We didn't say anything, just looked into each other's eyes, and then he walked me to my door and said goodnight.

Smiling at my thoughts of long ago, I stood up and walked to the sink to wash the breakfast pots. I looked out of the window and thought how blessed we were to have a pleasant home with an acre of garden. I delighted in the sheep-scattered green fields beyond our wall and the misty mountaintops just visible above a wooded hillside. From living in a bedsit for three years, we had gradually worked our way up the housing market to our handsome part-slate four-bedroom home complete with two bathrooms — a luxury never dreamed of fifty years ago. True, some might say our furniture, bought as we expanded, was somewhat eclectic and lacking coordination. But we were brought up in an age where things were made to last, not in today's throwaway society. At least, our carpets and curtains are all relatively new and, being carefully chosen, bring colourful harmony to the mix of furniture styles. With a good husband and loving family, I had no right to be discontent. In a pensive mood, I let my mind drift again to when I was nineteen and courting Roger.

He attended evening classes three nights a week and went home at the weekends. We met up on Friday nights only and always followed the same pattern as on our first date. I wasn't sure how he felt about me. I didn't even know if he went out with other girls back home. Of course, we didn't talk in the cinema and there wasn't much time afterwards. We didn't seem to have much to say anyway, it seemed enough just to be with each other.

My sister told me that the daughter of Roger's landlady had told her that he wasn't the serious sort. According to her, I'd better not get emotionally attached to him because he had let a girl down badly at home. The poor kid was put in bed for a week suffering from depression because of him. I said nothing to Roger but what I'd heard had put me on guard. I was determined not to end up as one of Roger's cast-offs.

I took up square dancing with my friend Rosie and we went to lessons at the local dance hall. It was great fun and neither of us was short of boys to dance with, but one in particular sought me out as a regular dance partner. David was a very pleasant boy and easy to talk to. He was very ordinary looking: medium height, slim build, fair hair, and grey eyes behind wire-framed glasses. But I wasn't after a young man to walk out with, and I didn't see David as a prospective boyfriend anyway. I never mentioned Roger because he wasn't relevant to any of our conversations. At that time, I considered my artistic career to be my future, not getting married to become someone's doormat.

David was a very committed Christian. He was exceedingly disturbed when it came out in conversation that I had not been baptised. I said that surely there must be more to being a Christian than saying a few words and getting splashed. But he really cared about my salvation and told me about the Church of England baptism service. I was already a believer as far as I was concerned and I didn't want involvement in formal religion. I came to see David as after my soul for God, certainly not as wanting me for himself in any way whatsoever. He was always correct and a perfect gentleman.

David asked me if I would partner him on a course he wanted to go on; it was for learning to teach country dancing. I had the time and I enjoyed dancing with him, so I was willing to accept. We met in town after work and he invited me to have a coffee and cake with him. I wanted to pay for my own food but he insisted and since I was helping him out, I accepted.

Roger brought it all to an end.

One Monday, I met David as usual at the coffee bar and we sat talking as we normally did but I could see that he had changed. It wasn't long before the bombshell fell.

"I've met Roger."

That was a shock. I tried not to show my discomfort. "Oh, yes?"

"You didn't tell me you had a boyfriend." He sounded more sorrowful than angry.

"Should I have done? I just see Roger on Fridays — nothing serious."

"That isn't how he sees it."

I was both pleased and confused to hear that information. "That isn't the impression he's given me. Anyway, how did you get to meet him?"

"A friend works at his place and your name came up and he knew we were dancing together. I went to see Roger today during the lunch break. I asked him if he was serious about you and he said he was. He was upset that you hadn't told him about me."

"He knows I come dancing," I said, feeling defensive. "He doesn't like dancing. He's never seemed serious about me so why should I tell him that I have a partner to dance with?"

"It matters to him and it matters to me."

He sounded deeply aggrieved and I was beginning to feel like some kind of two-timing Scarlet Woman. "But, David," I said, "it isn't as if we're going out together, we're just dancing partners."

"That isn't how I see it. I like you a lot," he said, looking at me with pain showing in his eyes.

The situation had taken on a new twist. I had no idea that he regarded me as a girlfriend. I didn't want him to think ill of me and that I had been stringing him along. "Look, David, someone told me not to get serious about Roger. He let someone down badly. He's older than me. You know, old enough to go steady with a girl, but he's not the marrying sort."

"But I am, Alice."

I was staggered. How could he talk of marriage? I had never once thought about him in that way. He had never kissed me or given any intimation of his feelings towards me. I looked into his troubled face and felt utterly wretched. Clearly he loved me and I had, in his eyes, just been using him for my own purposes. I saw him as a friend, a dancing partner, and we got on very well together. But all the time he saw it as a growing boy-girl relationship.

Returning my thoughts to the kitchen sink, I finished off the dishes and went upstairs wondering what had happened to gentle David. Would my life have been very different with him? But I didn't love him and I could never have married him. I changed the bed with my mind still in the past.

What David had discovered had clearly ruined our dance partnership. I knew that from then on he would be dancing with others and I would be lost without him. Why did he have to take our relationship so seriously? I was selfishly angry. But more than anything I was furious that the two of them should meet behind my back and discuss me as though I were some sort of commodity — deciding between them which of them should have me. No doubt David was being very courteous towards Roger; willingly stepping down rather than be the cause of a relationship breakdown. But did I have no say in the matter?

I made my protest to David. It didn't have to be that way. Roger had never shown any sign of commitment, whatever he may have told him. It was only a casual relationship with no strings attached on his part.

He took my hand and said tenderly, "I've told you, he doesn't see it that way. But if he doesn't want to marry you, Alice, I certainly do."

I looked at him and saw a kind of hope through the pain that he was suffering. I was touched but I just couldn't fancy him that way at all. The fact that he went behind my back told me that he believed in male dominance and although I needed that for dancing, I wasn't going to let someone take over my life. I was on a ladder to success and I didn't want a man to hold me back, not even Roger.

The finality of my relationship with David came when he told me that henceforth, although we would meet in the coffee bar until the remaining dance training sessions had finished, he would no longer pay for my coffee and cake. I thought that a bit mean since I had offered to pay for my food in the first place, even though he had invited me there. I didn't have time to go home before meeting him at the training centre near his place. If buying a coffee and a cake constituted ownership, I was glad he wasn't my boyfriend. But I was very cross with Roger.

"How could you go behind my back?" I demanded of Roger when he met me later.

"I didn't, he came to see me."

"But you discussed me as though I were a prize cow!"

"Nothing of the sort. He just wanted to know if I was serious about you. You never told me about him. I'm the one who should be angry."

I was furious that he should put me in the wrong. "I don't see why, we only go to the pictures together. You're not serious about me. I've been warned about how you treat girls."

He was staggered and wanted to know what I was talking about. I told him but he casually dismissed the gossip. "Oh, that was a girl who thought more about me than I did about her. I don't know why. We didn't go out together as such. I never told her I loved her or anything like that."

"Huh! You've never said how you feel about me either. We've only been out a few times. How could you say you're serious about me?"

"Because I am."

"You could have fooled me. Now you've ruined things. I'm not going out with David, I only see him to dance with. Now he won't dance with me any more all because of you."

"I'll take you dancing," he said with incredible confidence.

I was most unhappy at the idea of a beginner replacing the expert David. "You can't dance," I told him sharply.

"I'll learn."

But Roger never did learn to square dance. Moreover, he refused to wear plimsolls and so he skidded along the floor, knocking others over on his way down. The dance hall became more like a bowling alley. He didn't care that he totally embarrassed me in front of David and all the other dancers. Eventually, I refused to go with him again. I taught him ballroom dancing instead; but he remained a disaster on a dance floor.

He didn't do too badly in my mother's empty back bedroom. We had a training manual and an old wind-up gramophone to aid us. It was hard graft getting him to pay full attention but he seemed to master the rudimentary steps of the dances I was familiar with. I have always admired Roger's confidence though. At our first proper dance he had no qualms about trying out his budding skills; he headed straight for the floor and started off — wrong foot first. I sucked in my breath as pain soared up my leg and said patiently, "Wrong foot, Roger. Try again."

Before long we were off but he was out of time with the music. The dance was a foxtrot and he was trying to perform a quickstep so we got our feet tangled up. We eventually managed by doing a bit of a jog-along. The only disconcerting thing was his habit of seeing a space and racing for it. This was to be a habit I never managed to get him out of. He has always been happy doing his own thing on the dance floor. I have always been the miserable one by refusing to dance with him unless the floor is chock-a-block with other dancers. He has two left feet and no sense of rhythm, and is totally unable to be in harmony with a partner. He has no finesse and I should have known his manner of making love would be very little different.

Bringing my mind back to the present, I picked up the black undies and burst into tears. I saw myself in the mirror — just a pathetic old woman in search of an impossible dream. Wrinkles, grey hair, varicose veins, body elastic no longer able to hold up or hold in — like ageing knickers' elastic of days gone by. I laughed hysterically as I thought of all the knots that got tied in the elastic of those old navy-blue school bloomers. But, although my flesh has succumbed to gravity, just like the bloomers, what I am is essentially the same. I began to understand why movie stars resorted to surgery. I sighed; there would be no such aid for me; my problem lay elsewhere anyway.

I washed my face and put on a little make-up. I refused to give in to misery, old age or self-pity. I put on my usual bra and pulled the straps up a little to raise my breasts. That gave me a better shape under my blouse. I left open the two top buttons to reveal a slight cleavage. I put on my close-fitting pair of trousers that tended to make me look slimmer. What I saw in the mirror made me feel better about myself. With no sensual garments tarting me up, I was just me — seventy but vibrant with life. I slipped on my blue blazer and went out, determined to continue in my search for fulfilment. My first stop would be the local newsagent.

I walked down the hill into town, careful not to trip over the uneven rough paving stones the council had recently had laid to give the place 'atmosphere'. Ironic really, tarting up the town to give it an ancient appearance when some of us senior citizens were doing our best to keep young and healthy — falling over knobbly slabs would not help us in our quest. I went into the shop at the bottom of the hill and looked along the many rows of magazines. My eyesight wasn't good enough to see what was on the top shelves and I couldn't have reached up there anyway. I pondered what to do. A young girl came up to me and asked if I needed help. "No thanks," I said embarrassed, and left the shop feeling utterly defeated; tripping on one of the rough slabs but coming to no harm.

I went to my usual café so that I could sit and give the matter some thought. I saw one or two people I knew but I wanted to be alone. I smiled and gave these acquaintances a pleasant greeting, but when they asked me to join them I said I was expecting to meet someone and left them to chat to each other. I found myself a small table tucked away in a corner. The waitress came and I ordered coffee and a toasted teacake. At a time like this I needed comfort, never mind the calories. I sat looking out of the window, giving my ankle a bit of a rub whilst pondering my dilemma.

Across the road I saw the young girl that had been with her partner the day before. She seemed to be waiting and I wondered if the boy would turn up. I saw him arrive and they threw themselves into each other's arms. Before long they were kissing and petting. My mind went back to my own girlhood and to my first love. He was the boyfriend of my best friend Carol.

In the park I watched them lying under the willow tree with his body wrapped around hers. Eric was kissing Carol and my heart was breaking. I wandered away, as I always did, to visit the wishing tree on the little island in the middle of the lake. As I crossed over the first bridge I stopped and looked down into the water at my own reflection. I sighed; Eric had said that he would kiss me when I was twelve but who would want to kiss a girl like me when Carol was around? Pangs of jealousy pierced my heart.

One day, I went with Carol to the lido. I didn't know she had arranged to meet Eric there. She wasn't supposed to go with boys but I didn't mind being her alibi. I came out of the changing-room and saw Eric in his swimming costume as he lay on the decking. He was taking in the sun while chatting up Carol. He may have been thin but to me he was just right.

After a little while, a certain something fascinated me and I could hardly take my eyes from looking at the unusual sight. It wasn't the interesting bulge in his groin region, that phenomena could have been anything; after all, I had a pocket in my navy school knickers so why shouldn't he have one in his swimming costume? No, what attracted me were little black hairs, like curly bits of wire, peeping out from the legs of his cossie and also sticking up through the material in the region of his bulge. I found them quite riveting — how did they do it? His hair must have been very stiff indeed. I looked at the dark hair on his head, chest, arms and legs but none of it was that stiff. I found it fascinating, absolutely fascinating. He saw me looking at his personal area and grinned. I looked shyly away. There was so very much for me to discover about boys.

It was after the lido visit when Eric kissed me. I never thought it could happen. I had been waiting for Carol under the willow tree when Eric arrived early.

"Come on, Alice, now's your chance," he said.

"What for?"

"What you've been waiting for."

I couldn't believe he meant kissing. "Waiting for?"

He grinned. "This," he said, and pushed me on my back, kissing me just like he kissed Carol.

It was my very first kiss. I didn't know what to expect but it wasn't unpleasant, although the taste of onions was a bit off-putting.

"I saw the way you were looking at me at the lido," he said grinning, but before he could say more, Carol appeared. She gave me a hard look and so I left them to it until it was time to go.

Just before we left the park, he whispered, "Meet him tonight outside the cinema near your house."

I thought he loved me and wanted to be with me, just me, without Carol around. I waited and waited, going over many times the funny feel of his lips on mine. I didn't mind the waiting because I just knew he wouldn't let me down.

Would we go to the back row and cuddle up together on a double seat, like all the courting couples did? Would he bring a bar of Milk Tray for us to eat? I had sixpence left out of my pocket money, so should I offer to buy us ice cream at the interval? Suddenly, he came into view. The sight of him coming along the road filled me with excitement and it was with joyous expectation that I listened for his first endearing words.

"Hello, Alice, there's something I want to ask you."

I waited with baited breath for the words I wanted to hear — words that would linger in my mind — words that would make me feel special, just like Carol. I smiled and said shyly, "Yes, Eric?"

"I need a pair of used knickers for a bet with the boys. Will you give me yours?"

My heart sank. The rotter! How could he? Of course, he could never ask Carol but why did he ask me? I dropped my head as tears rolled down my cheeks. "No," I muttered.

"Damn it!" he said, and walked off without even saying goodbye. I went home and cried myself to sleep.

I was suddenly brought back to the present.

"Hello, Alice, we meet again," said a familiar cultured voice. "Do you mind if I share your table?"

My heart raced with excitement; Tony was standing over me, the whole of his handsome face — eyes, cheeks, mouth, and the dimple in his chin — caught up in his disarming smile. He was dressed all in black, just like the man you used to see in the TV advert for chocolates. His straight back, broad shoulders and slim waist were emphasised by a broad belt slotted through his fashionable low-cut fitted trousers. His tan looked gorgeous, his hair shone silver white, his blue eyes sparkled and his muscles bulged beneath his tight-fitting shirt. What a man, or so he seemed after thinking about that weedy teenager, Eric!

"Please do, Tony, I'm glad to see you," I said, unable to hide the real pleasure his presence gave me. I felt the same excitement as when I was twelve and waiting for Eric; it was most disconcerting.

Tony slipped the white jacket he was carrying over the back of the spare chair and sat down. The waitress came to him immediately to take his order. Smiling at him coquettishly, she went to get his coffee. Three women, who'd been waiting ages, were furious when the waitress walked past their table to serve someone else, that is, until they looked our way and saw Tony. They smiled at him and then turned into a little huddle, rapidly talking to each other while glancing in our direction. Tony acknowledged their smiles of recognition with a wave of his hand, and then he turned to where I had been looking when he came into the café.

"I see our young lovers are at it again."

"Things were so different when we were young," I replied demurely, looking out at the kissing couple. Even at that distance I could see they had their tongues in a loving embrace. The boy's hand was now pressing the lower half of her trunk up hard to his groin area. Erotic sensations caused my heart to beat faster. I sensed Tony was watching me and I quickly turned my head away and picked up a menu.

"Decided on an early lunch?"

I wasn't sure whether he was amused at my embarrassment, or trying to make conversation for my benefit.

"I thought of coming sometime this week," I lied.

"I know a lot better places to eat. Perhaps you'll let me take you out sometime?"

My heartbeat rate increased. "Thanks, but I am rather busy."

"Have you thought anymore about dancing?"

"Quite a bit," I said truthfully, thinking of my reminiscing that morning.

"Does that mean you'll consider coming this Friday?"

"I'll think about it. It all depends on Roger."

I could see him trying to catch my eye so he could work his magnetic charm on me. I couldn't help but wonder why he was asking an old girl like me with so many sexy younger women to choose from. Was I some kind of challenge to his male ego?

He took my hand and said softly, "Live a little, Alice. There's nothing like a tango to regenerate a weary heart."

Phew, I was getting hot. Regeneration, Tony style, was a delightful prospect. The grinning waitress came with Tony's coffee, and while she was giving him the 'glad eye' I pulled my hand away. But his touch had already swayed my decision in his favour. I realised the dangerous path I was treading when I foolishly looked into his eyes.

"I don't know about a tango, but I'd love to dance with you, Tony."

The look he gave me in return sent a thrill down my whole body. I knew we were giving each other coded messages and I had to disentangle myself. I changed the subject and asked him about his recent holiday. Then I talked about our caravan holidays and the coastal paths we had walked. But every time I looked at him, he was captivating me with his 'bedroom eyes' and his devastating smile.

A friend of Tony's arrived; evidently he was meeting him there. Tony introduced us but I stood up to go, saying I had to get back. I was glad to be able to get away even though part of me was under Tony's spell and longed to be near him.

Tony stood up and kissed my hand in farewell. I noticed women looking in my direction, jealousy written all over their faces. A few had raised eyebrows, but I refused to feel guilty. Even so, I deliberately turned my thoughts to Roger. With determination I put on my blazer, walked to the till to pay up and, with eyes watching me, I walked out of the cafe. With Roger uppermost in my mind, I was on my way back to the paper shop.

I knew exactly what I was going to do; I rehearsed it over and over in my mind so as not to hesitate when I entered the shop. I went up to the counter and said, quite brazenly, "It's my husband's birthday tomorrow and I want to give the old codger a surprise to liven him up. I want one of those sexy magazines you keep on your top shelf."

"I'll get one for you," said the young man with a pleasant smile. He didn't even raise an eyebrow, which made me wonder if oldies were regular customers for top shelf titillaters.

He went with me to the magazine stands. "We have all sorts. How far do you want to go?"

"All the way." I grinned nervously at my boldness.

"Right. They don't go any further than this one," he told me, getting a magazine from the furthest position on the top shelf. "It's rather expensive, do you want to glance at it first to see if it's what you want?"

The thought of being observed looking through a pornographic magazine was absolutely horrifying. "No thanks, if it's expensive, it must be good."

With other customers looking on with grinning faces, I gave him the money and quickly left the shop with the well-wrapped magazine tucked tightly under my arm as if it might try to escape. I just caught a woman's comment before the door closed behind me.

"I hope she knows what she's doing. She'll give the poor bugger a heart attack." The following laughter faded away as I hurried up the road.

When I arrived home, I hung up my blazer and put the kettle on to boil. I sat looking at the wrapped-up magazine as though it were Pandora's Box. I felt very diffident about looking through its pages now I actually had it in front of me, but I could hardly give it to Roger to look at if I didn't know what he was going to see. I took it out of the several bags that covered its shame. Wow! If that was on the cover what was I going to find inside?

I made the tea and poured myself a cup. I started turning over the first page when the front doorbell rang. I nearly jumped out of my skin! Heart racing, I snatched up the magazine and, as if it was about to burn down the house, I looked for somewhere to dump it. The bell rang again. I was going around in circles. Where? Where? Where? With the doorbell ringing again, this time with more urgency, I finally shoved it under a seat cushion of the sofa in the living room. I tried to calm myself while making my way to the front door.

"Hi, Alice, sorry to disturb you. I guess you must be busy." It was my friendly neighbour, Barbara.

I closed the front door and led her to the kitchen. "Not very. I was about to have a cuppa; would you like one?"

"Thanks, mustn't stop long though, I'm meeting Clive for lunch," she said cheerfully. Barbara was certainly dressed for the occasion. She was wearing a smart beige trouser suit with a low-cut pink blouse showing a very attractive deep cleavage.

I offered her a chair at the kitchen table. "Tea okay?"

"Please. No sugar, I'm trying to lose weight."

"Your Clive gets about more than Roger, where's he gone today?"

"It's his band. He's getting involved with the afternoon dancing at the Victoria Hall," she answered, putting milk into her cup from the jug on the table. "The band's been practising all morning; they'll need to, it's ages since they played for ballroom dancing."

I poured the tea into her cup. "Strong enough for you?"

"That's fine."

The mention of afternoon dancing had made me feel a little guilty. I knew I wanted to go dancing with Tony, but was that all I wanted to do with him? I tried to concentrate on Clive.

"He must really enjoy what he's doing. How long has he been playing in a band?"

"He started as a teenager fifty years ago, but it's ages since he's done any professional work."

"Would you like a biscuit?" I wanted an excuse to eat one myself.

"No thanks. Actually, I only called to see if I dropped an earring here the other day."

She was giving the biscuits a longing look. I had to admire her restraint.

"I haven't found one but then I haven't been looking. Where do you think you might have lost it?" I hoped it wasn't in the living room.

"Well, since I was sitting on the sofa, perhaps it's gone down by the cushion." She rose from her chair. "I'll go and look."

"No! Stay here and drink your tea before it gets cold," I insisted, putting my hand on her shoulder to sit her down again. "I know the places where things can slide."

"I'll come and help you."

"No need, I'll only be a minute," I answered quickly. Before she could get up again I was off into the living room like a scolded cat.

I went straight to the sofa, took out the magazine and put it on the floor underneath. I lifted the cushions and put my hand down the sides. Nothing there except biscuit crumbs and fluff. Then pushing my hand hard down the back I came across a condom in its little packet. I wondered how on earth it got there, and came to the conclusion that it must have slipped from someone's pocket when they had been visiting.

"Found something?" Barbara had come into the room while I had been distracted.

I turned around to face her. Laughing, I said what I had found. "But no earring I'm afraid." I hoped that would be the end of the search.

"Perhaps it fell under the sofa? Do you mind if I have a look?" she asked, getting ready to do a bit of pushing.

"You look under the chair cushions. I'll look under the sofa," I insisted, and laughing to hide my embarrassment, I added, "There's probably dust there."

"I'll give you a hand to move it," said Barbara brightly. Before I could object, she had pushed the sofa right back, revealing the magazine in all of its naked glory.

"What's this?" she asked.

Not wanting to see the look on her face, I had my eyes half closed. Before I'd found words to give an explanation for harbouring pornography, she said in a disappointed voice, "Oh, that's all it is."

I opened my eyes fully to see her holding up a ring off a can. I hoped she didn't notice my sigh of relief.

She casually picked up the magazine. As she looked through it, my face was colouring up fast and my throat was going dry. My mind was searching for an explanation. Blame it on the kids?

While I was trying to clear my throat to speak, Barbara beat me to it.

"Clive gets this one," she said. "It's a bit extreme but it works wonders for our sex life."

"That's good; ours too of course," I lied. The sweat was now evaporating from my face and my voice was a little high, but I managed to keep it steady. "Of course, it's not to everyone's taste."

Barbara was busy flicking through the pages. She paused to look at a pair of lovers erotically entwined. "Have to keep them out of the way when the kids come. They'd be horrified, you know. But I expect it's the same for you. Funny isn't it? Do it when you're young and a man's being masculine. Do it years later and he's a disgusting old man. Women the same. It's a funny old world we live in."

"It certainly is," I said, finding it hard to believe I was having this discussion.

"Well, I must be off. Let me know if you find the earring. Cheerio, Alice," she said merrily as she made her way out.

"Cheers, Barbara," I replied and collapsed on the floor laughing with relief.

I poured myself a small glass of sherry to steady my nerves. Sitting on the living room sofa, I picked up the magazine. If Clive had these books on a regular basis, they surely must do something for him. I was beginning to sweat just looking at the cover.

I put down my glass, took a deep breath and turned over to the first page. Pink bodies were entwined in such a way that I wasn't quite sure which bits were which. I turned the magazine around to get various views. I had never before examined a man's private area in fine detail and my face turned hot as I realised what I was looking at. One might say it was rather an unusual shot of the copulation act, but it was viewed from an angle impossible for lovers to see for themselves, that is, without the aid of a number of strategically placed mirrors. With great difficulty, I tried to picture in my mind Roger and me trying it out. Somehow I don't think it would work; we would get stuck before getting very far. Apart from which, I rather think the kinkiness of the manoeuvre would be more of a turn-off rather than a joyful mutual experience.

A knocking on the window shook me out of my reverie and I was horrified to find another neighbour was paying me a visit. This time it was the nosiest scandalmonger of the neighbourhood. The last thing I wanted was Glenda catching me looking through a pornographic magazine. I put the thing behind my back as I waved to Glenda to go round to the back door, then I pushed it under the sofa again.

As I reached the kitchen, Glenda, fresh from the hairdresser's salon and wearing a smart town suit, was already on her way in — she is quite a pushy person.

"It's nice to see you, Glenda," I lied. "I was just having a sherry, would you like one?" I was willing her to say no and that she couldn't stop.

"Thanks, yes please," she said, sitting down. So much for my psychic powers! She continued in a conspiratorial whisper, "I've just come round to tell you something dreadful, but not a word to anyone else please, I don't want people to think I gossip. I went to Barbara's last night and what do you think I heard?" Being much too eager to get over her juicy news, she didn't wait for a reply. "I'm sure they were at it upstairs."

"You went straight in without knocking?" I asked, hoping to divert her from telling me more, but I wasn't successful.

"I always knock first," she said, as though that made it all right. "Well, if someone leaves a door unlocked it's an open invitation to enter isn't it? Anyway, I called out before I went right in, just like I do when I come here. But they were upstairs, doing disgusting things."

"Isn't it their business what they do in their own home?" I said, repulsed by my Nosy Parker neighbour.

"Of course it is, but really — at their age?" Her face muscles tightened, gathering her wrinkles together and making her look like an old hag.

"Frankly, Glenda, that is surely up to them," I said haughtily. "Why shouldn't they enjoy sex? Good luck to them. But you can't possibly know what they were doing anyway."

"My dear, I heard them. He was sort of shouting and she was kind of groaning — I can't say any more," she said through tight lips. But she couldn't hold back the mighty gusher: "It was too disgusting!" Folding her arms, she gave her shoulders a heaving shrug.

"Really, Glenda, you just imagined it all. They were likely doing exercises."

I watched her lips tighten into a volcano-like wrinkled red pout; making her look even more grotesque. If she could have seen herself in a mirror the ghastly sight would have given her a fatal stroke!

"Alice, my dear, you didn't hear Clive," she answered, as though talking to a difficult child.

"Neither should you have."

"I couldn't help it. If Cyril tried anything like that, I'd chop it off!"

I was now feeling exceedingly angry with Glenda, but growing more and more jealous of Barbara.

"It really is none of our business," I protested. "I don't think you'd better say anything else, Glenda." I was sounding a bit prissy as well as being hypocritical. Most of us neighbours loved a bit of gossip and usually I was no exception.

Ignoring my comment, Glenda went on, "And do you know what? One of those dreadful pornographic magazines was on the kitchen table. The pictures inside were disgusting!"

"You looked inside, knowing what you would find?"

"How can you judge if something is indecent if you don't inspect it first?"

I'd had enough of Glenda. While she went on chatting about her indecent neighbours — people I find lively, friendly and warm-hearted — I tried to think of how to get rid of her.

"Oh, gosh! Is that the time?" I said, looking at the clock. "I'm supposed to be meeting a friend in town. Must rush. Drink up, Glenda, we'll have to chat another day. Sorry to hurry you."

I walked to the kitchen door to make sure she got the message. She reluctantly swallowed up her drink and, still talking, left the house. I practically closed the door in her face; she just wouldn't stop her chatter.

I had to get out before someone else came. I gave Glenda enough time to get back home and then left the house. I headed for town and that nice little lingerie shop. Roger had told me to use our joint account and I intended doing just that. I made sure the chequebook was in my bag. A credit card would make my life much easier but Roger had always discouraged me from having one. It's not difficult to understood why.

I knew I shouldn't be doing it but I felt driven from within. I had seen something the day before and it had taken my fancy but I didn't know I wanted it then. Hearing about Barbara and Clive in the throws of ecstasy had strengthened my yearning for fulfilment.

The assistant smiled sweetly as I went into the shop. "Can I help you?" She gave a little lift to her eyebrows. "Another little gift for your friend maybe?"

"Not today," I said, walking over to the nightdress rail.

I picked up a slinky white satin nightdress trimmed with exquisite lace. I held it up against me in front of a long mirror. Pleased with the effect, I took it over to the till.

"Wrap this up please. My daughter is getting married and I want to treat her."

"Ideal! I'm sure she will be highly delighted. That will be one hundred and twenty-five pounds please, madam."

I had a long soak in the bath that evening. Afterwards, I drank the rest of the sherry while waiting for Roger to come home. I had my new sexy nightdress on and I kept getting up and walking around so as not to get it creased. I just had time to see the beginning of a sexy programme before hearing Roger's car. I slipped on my dressing gown. I was in the mood for love but the moment had to be right.

Roger entered the house with an armful of brochures. He put his freebies on top of a pile of others waiting to be read. He threw his coat over a chair for me to hang up later, and came into the kitchen where I was making his hot chocolate.

He came over to give me a little kiss. "Had a good day?"

"Lovely thanks. Had a few surprises."

He wasn't listening. He walked into the living room. "I think I can just catch the news. You're not watching this are you?"

Without waiting for an answer, ignoring the wriggling bodies moaning and groaning on the screen in front of him, he changed the programme over to the late night news. "More trouble! It's all bombs and mayhem. Is my drink ready, Alice?"

I had been hoping he would see the sexy programme and we could discuss it; maybe practice what we saw. "Dream on Alice!" I said aloud.

I took Roger his drink. "How are you feeling?" When he didn't answer, I raised my voice so he could hear it above the television. "Would you like me to massage your shoulders?"

"What? No, not tonight. Going to bed when I've finished this."

I sat down and listened to him slurping his chocolate drink. I decided to go to bed and leave him to it.

"By the way," he shouted to me, as I was about to go upstairs, "remind me to pay those bills tomorrow. I should have done it today."

I went up to our bedroom, took off my nightie and hung it up carefully in my walk-in closet. Perhaps the few creases might drop out, if not, careful ironing might help. I looked for the discarded tags and labels in the waste bin. I could say the nightdress didn't fit, or my daughter didn't like it. Then I realised that if I took it back, I'd only get an exchange voucher. I put on my old bag of a nightdress and with a deep sigh, crawled into bed. I wondered if I could sell a few of my pictures to pay for my profligate spending. If Roger knew the financial outlay to get him aroused, it would keep him deflated for months.

Chapter three

Of spice and men

With a lot on my mind, I had a very restless night and only managed a few hours sleep so I was feeling tired and irritable in the morning. Roger, as usual, had snored his way through half the night and after drinking the cup of tea I took him up at four in the morning, went back to sleep again like a baby that's had its night feed.

"That was a terrible night," he complained as he sat down to eat his breakfast. "I couldn't get to sleep."

It's a funny thing that whenever he's kept me awake with his imitation of a pig at its trough, he's the one to have suffered insomnia. He wasn't getting any sympathy from me. Anyway, a lot of planning had been going on in my head and I was itching to put some of it into action.

"I met Tony Bradshaw in the Coffeepot," I said casually.

"I thought he was in the Bahamas," Roger said between mouthfuls of bran flakes. I wondered how Roger managed to get so many flakes in his mouth and dispose of them so quickly.

"He's back."

"Obviously. That's a few thousand Edith won't be able to get her hands on."

"You can't blame Edith for them splitting up, and she's entitled to her share after being married for so long."

"Well, I do blame Edith. She might have been great as his dance partner but from what Tony told me that's where the pleasure ended. He might as well have had a housekeeper."

"She was his housekeeper and she deserves back wages. Especially after putting up with his womanising," I told him, sticking up for Edith, although, in my heart, my true sympathies were with Tony.

"She's had her whack over the years," Roger replied, spluttering on his last mouthful of flakes. "If she'd been a proper wife to Tony he would've stayed home nights."

"Are you saying it's all right to play around if you aren't getting satisfaction? It's hard on Edith. Perhaps she just can't accommodate him any more — too old."

"You're not too old and she's much younger than you are." He shook his head. "No, it's been that way for years. She's never given him real satisfaction from the day they married."

"Perhaps he didn't give her any. It works both ways you know."

"Well, we're okay so you needn't think I'm about to go off with some other woman. You're as much as I can handle."

He gave me a big grin and went off to collect the paper that had just come through the letter box. He sat down again and opened it up.

Before he started to read it, I said casually, "Tony said he was going to ask you if you would mind me going to some of those tea dances with him." So as not to sound too eager, I added, "I'm not sure myself though; it's a long time since we went dancing. I doubt I can remember the steps well enough to dance with someone else."

He looked up from the paper's headlines. "Well, as long as I'm not expected to go as well; I've got enough to do."

"You wouldn't mind me dancing with Tony then?" I persisted, speaking to the newsprint in front of me.

Roger looked at me over his paper. "Why should I? You're not exactly another Susan Briggs. I expect he wants an excuse to go there to pick up another middle-aged glamour-puss, or maybe a flighty female young enough to be his granddaughter. From what I've heard, he's got a randy appetite. Whomever he finds will need a lot of energy to keep up with him. Let's face it, a granny your age doesn't exactly come up to Tony Bradshaw's specifications." Realising I might take it as a personal put-down, he added, "Not even a ravishing beauty like my dear wife."

I knew Roger must be right about Tony's taste in women. It was stupid to think he could possibly be interested in someone older than he was, and yet I felt certain he'd been flirting with me. But had my mind been exaggerating what I wanted to see and hear? Was I desperate to believe I was a desirable woman? He probably made eyes at every woman he met. Perhaps he needed to think he was God's gift to women. A good-looking guy must find it hard to be married to an unresponsive wife. But it was ridiculous to speculate. After all, I'd only been asked to go dancing, so why make more out of it? Yes, Roger, as usual, was right.

I left Roger reading his paper and went upstairs to get ready to go out. I felt better for having had that conversation with him. When I had him in the right mood for discussing my orgasm problem he should be able to understand my need for satisfaction. I could see there were going to be difficulties explaining though. I don't have his equipment to prove I'm failing to get what he takes for granted. I didn't realise it before but now I was able to see, metaphorically speaking, that it was as though for years I'd been eating enough to take the edge off hunger without ever being replete. Would Roger understand that he was merely taking the edge off my craving for sexual fulfilment? It has always pleased me to please Roger, but now I had this desperate longing, not just for an orgasm as such, but for us to be together in that kind of orgasmic unity that Barbara and Clive were obviously getting.

But at that moment in time, something else had to take priority — our mutual bank account was about to hover in the red zone. Sorting through my paintings that I'd mounted ready for framing, I picked out watercolours of local beauty spots. Those were the ones most likely to interest the many tourists who visit the area every year. It was lovely to have such a rich and varied landscape to paint: mountains and lakes, forests and meadows, rivers and streams with tumbling waterfalls. Market towns and old picturesque villages, plus the varied coastline, also presented delightful challenges to a dabbler in watercolours like me. Moving to Cumbria a few years after the boys were born may have ended any chance I might have had of picking up my designing career again, but it had inspired me to use my creative abilities in other directions.

I picked up a picture of Coniston Water with Dow Crag and the Old Man rising above woods and fells, reaching upwards into a blue and slate-grey sky — a shaft of sunlight magically illuminating all within its ray. The golden hue had turned dull bracken into fiery oranges and russets, and had brought life and light to Coniston's dark deep water.

For a moment my mind went back to when I was a dreamy child.

My family never went on holidays. Apart from going into hospital, I was seventeen before I slept away from home. By that time, I was working and could save for such luxuries. But that did not stop me from travelling in my mind. Just down the road, a coach company kept a fleet of vehicles in a huge garage, with coaches spilling out into the yard beyond. Each coach was labelled with its destination. Every time I took Flossy for a walk, I would stop and look at the name, Lake District. I imagined a place of story-book grandeur and I was determined that one day I would visit the place, little thinking that within twenty years I would be living within sight of my dream world. I sighed with contentment at my good fortune and added the painting with those for sale.

By the time I arrived downstairs again, Roger was on his way outside to finish something in his workshop. The pots would still be waiting for me when I returned from town but, never mind, my peace of mind took priority. I hurriedly wrapped the pictures into a large plastic bag. I put on my jacket, picked up my handbag, and set off for town.

The local art and gift shop had been open an hour when I arrived at the door and lots of browsers were mingling with the more serious shoppers. I struggled with my pictures towards the counter, endeavouring not to knock the flimsy crystal knick-knacks from obstructive glass shelving. An assistant told me to go to the room at the back. Mr Pickering, the owner, let me into his office where he'd been framing pictures. I'd talked to him on a number of occasions about him selling my work in his shop, so he wasn't exactly surprised to see me.

"Brought them at last?" he asked, taking the plastic-bag parcel from me. "Well, let's see what you've got. I'm glad you haven't framed them; I'd rather do it myself than pay someone else. Some artists haven't a clue about proper framing."

He took the pictures over to a good light and, making appreciative noises, looked at them in turn. He gave a big sniff. "How much are you asking for them?"

"How much will you give me?" I replied, throwing the ball into his court — I hate bargaining.

"Mm, I'll try these four. They'll suit the tourists. If they sell you can bring some more." He looked at me over his half-specs. "I'll give you forty pounds each." He saw my unimpressed reaction. "If they go quick, I'll increase it next time." He sounded like a generous benefactor, although I knew he would frame and sell the pictures at a very good profit.

"Cash?" I wanted to get the money straight into the bank.

"Don't usually but I'll make an exception. Want to buy something nice? We've got lots you can spend it on." Pickering hated to let go of his money.

"I've already got something nice and spicy to use the money on, but thanks for the deal, Mr Pickering. Maybe I'll see you again soon." I left him wondering what I was finding so delectable.

I made my way to the bank, filled in a paying-in slip and deposited one hundred and twenty-five pounds into our joint account. Breathing a sigh of relief, I made my way to the Coffeepot. I needed to relax with a coffee. As I passed the shops, I was trying to think of a little something to buy for Roger with some of the money I had left. I was having a bit of a conscience over my naughty undies.

It was Market Day and a brass band was playing by the war memorial in the cobbled square. Elderly people, sitting on the nearby decorative wrought-iron seats with their bags of shopping on their knees or by their ankles, were listening to the music of bygone years. I enjoy brass bands but refused to let myself join the geriatrics — to me that would be giving in to my age. Just down the cobbled road, Morris Dancers were merrily hopping and skipping to their own type of music with ribbons flying, feathers fluttering, knee bells jingling and sticks clacking. I stopped and tapped my feet, enjoying the silly nonsense of it all. Market shoppers and visitors to the area were milling around, enjoying the late summer sunshine and friendly country town atmosphere. Feeling happier with life, I headed for a tool stall to see if I could find something for Roger.

To my surprise, coming down the road towards me was Tony Bradshaw — turning the heads of the women who passed him by. He was looking incredibly handsome in white ducks, fine white roll-neck jersey, and smart navy blazer bright with polished silver buttons. The blazer's breast pocket was emblazoned with an expensive badge intricately worked in brilliant colours and shiny metal thread. His silver hair, lifted by the breeze, was catching the morning sun and his blue eyes sparkled with good health. Eyes, nose, mouth, cheeks of his handsome sun-tanned face, crinkled into a smile of greeting.

"Good morning, Alice; we meet yet again." In my crazy mind, I wondered how many of those dazzling white teeth were capped or crowned — they were too much part of him to be dentures.

"Hello, Tony. It is a bit of a coincidence, but then, I usually come into town on Market day," I said coolly, but my cheeks were rapidly flushing as my heart reacted to my stirred up emotions.

"How about we have coffee together in the Coffeepot after I've been to the bank? I need a shoulder to cry on — got a spare hanky?" His face, lighting up with merriment, belied his stated distress.

I laughed with him and said cheerfully, "I'd love to have coffee with you, Tony, with or without the tears. I don't have to hurry home, Roger is busy with something or other."

"Splendid. You go along and I'll be with you shortly." With a twinkle in his eye, he added, "Sit up in the garden if it's warm enough for you, it's more private."

I gave little thought to the jobs that needed doing at home: breakfast pots waiting in the sink to be washed, furniture that needed dusting, carpets that needed vacuuming and a pile of washing that was still hanging around waiting to be ironed. It wasn't like me to be so desultory about such matters. I was usually so methodical. I knew Tony had charmed the pants of a number of women and I have to admit, it tickled me pink that he seemed to be interested in me — someone older than he was and not even glamorous. In fifty years of marriage, I had never even considered being unfaithful to Roger — not that I'd had the chance! But it doesn't do any harm to fantasise over a little flirtation, or so I thought at the time. At that exciting moment I refused to consider where it might lead me.

I sat in the cosy café with its dark oak furniture and neat white tablecloths, looking at the framed old photographs of the town hanging from the walls. They were monochrome pictures with monochrome people, each with staring eyes giving blank looks at the camera. I felt like getting out my pen and putting happy smiles on their melancholy faces.

The waitress came and took my order. While I was waiting, I let my eyes wander over the top of the lace curtain screening the lower section of the window, and wondered if the lovers were in town today. I remembered what Tony had said about the possible consequences of we old folks petting in public. I had to smile at the thought of standing there with Tony as he pulled me up to his legendary equipment while we kissed with tongues. I shook my head as if to rid myself of shameful erotic thinking. I was sitting inside the café, rather than up in the romantic sheltered garden retreat, believing myself to be more protected from the spell that Tony had me under, but obviously I was wrong. My emotions were quickly going into overdrive and I was finding it hard to contain my excitement. By the time he entered the café and made his way towards me, my heart was racing.

He smiled engagingly at the waitress as she brought coffee and Danish pastries to our table.

"Those look nice, " he said to her as though she had made the pastries herself. "Thank you, my dear. Would you mind taking my coat and hanging it up for me?" Without waiting for an answer, he held out his blazer while giving the girl an appreciative body scan and a dazzling smile.

"Not at all, sir," she said, and smiling provocatively went off as though she had just received a big tip.

I could see why Tony got on with women so well. What a charmer!

"I hope you like the Danish pecan slices I ordered. I often have a bit when I come in here."

"Do you really?" He gave me a very wicked look and murmured in a rather suggestive manner, "Danish, Swedish, Italian, French or what you will — I'm willing to treat my taste buds to anything a woman has to offer me."

Was he hinting at what I thought he was doing? It was a rather naughty thing to say to a married woman but I couldn't stop the tingle that went up my spine. "Sorry they only do Danish here. Maybe you would rather have a toasted teacake or a scone?" My attempt to feign ignorance of his little innuendo was not entirely convincing.

As I was picking up a pastry, he bent over to touch my hand. The smell of his expensive aftershave was divine. "What I see in front of me is fine," he said. "But perhaps you would let me treat you to something a little more savoury some time?"

Enjoying the feel of his touch far too much, I pulled my hand away. I was unsure what exactly he was offering but I thought it best to keep up the jolly banter. "I should have thought a whole month on sunny girl-clad beaches would have dulled your appetite."

"You can get tired of trifle every day. I like something to chew on."

Did he deliberately glance at my breasts as he looked from his Danish to my eyes? What a ridiculous thought, but there was no doubt that he was flirting with me. It was just a bit of fun. He couldn't possibly be serious.

"Well, better eat your pastry before you starve to death." I couldn't help but laugh at the absurdity of our conversation.

"You know, Alice, your face really lights up when you laugh."

His manner seemed intensely serious and in no way flippant. But it was such a corny thing to say that I had a rapid flashback to when I was sixteen and a working girl. One night, on my way home, I bumped into one of the supervisors, a man in his forties, who'd been trying to get me to go to the pictures with him. He tried to mesmerise me with his intense gaze and husky voice. "Moonlight becomes you, my dear. You look absolutely ravishing." Although flattered by his adoration, I burst out laughing and ran off.

Tony's words may also have been theatrical flattery but he was different. I couldn't help but respond to his voice, his words and his touch — everything about him. In spite of all my misgivings, I adored everything he said to me. I wasn't used to being charmed and I rather enjoyed the feeling it gave me. The years dropped away and I felt young again. But I also felt guilty for enjoying the experience. I dropped my eyes, as I felt my colour rising.

"You are a very beautiful lady," he whispered seductively. "Roger is a lucky man."

"Some might say that you were lucky to have Edith. She's a magnificent dancer," I said, trying to distract him from my embarrassment.

"A man needs a partner for more than dancing, Alice."

"What makes you think Roger is better off in that department? Have you boys been swapping bedroom talk?"

"Don't need to. You can tell when a man is getting his needs met. It shows in his joints and the way he conducts his personal affairs in the men's room," he responded with a twinkle in his eye.

"I don't believe it. You're trying to shock me," I said coyly.

"Am I succeeding?"

"I guess so, but I don't know why you're doing it."

"You know, my dear, I can tell when a woman is satisfied too," he said, giving me a tender smile.

I looked down at my hands as I felt myself blushing. "That's ridiculous," I replied with a little laugh, but I had an idea he knew exactly what he was talking about.

He reached across the table and took my hand, "I think we both have needs," he said very softly.

I was thrilled by the touch of his hand. But I knew that it would be wrong to encourage him. I took my hand away quite deliberately and said demurely, "I think you say that to all the women you meet."

"Some, but most would agree about their needs. How many men of our generation have been schooled in satisfying women? For that matter, how many of you ladies expect to have exciting sex in your later years? Many never had it even when they were young."

I suddenly realised I was rolling my wedding ring around my finger. I quickly let go of it. Ignoring his questions, I reached for my cup and remained silent.

"I think you know what I mean don't you?" He was trying to look me in the eye but I wasn't cooperating. He was too near the truth for comfort.

"I think we should drink this coffee before it gets cold," I said primly.

"Alice, look at me." It was almost a command.

To do so would have revealed the tears forming in my eyes. I changed the subject. "I spoke to Roger about the afternoon dancing."

This time he took both of my hands into his. "What did he say? No let me guess. He's quite happy for you to come with me because he thinks you aren't my type and will be quite safe. He probably said that I just want a dancing partner to hide the fact that I'm looking out for a floozie. Is that what you think too?"

I looked up and saw his eyes appealing for an answer.

"No," I said softly. "I think you really do want to dance with me. As for me, I would love to start dancing again, even if I do worry about remembering the steps." Looking down again, I said rather coyly, "But I'm sure you're a strong enough dancer to guide me, so I'm very happy to go with you."

"And for no other reason? Be honest, Alice."

Before I could reply, a blast of air and shrieking voices came in from outside as a group of loud-mouthed women, wearing clothes far too young for them, entered the café. How I wished I'd taken a table in the garden as Tony had suggested.

"Alice! I haven't seen you for weeks," said their leader. "What are you doing with that roguish old reprobate? He looks wickedly handsome with that tan — he should be locked up in a cell."

"Preferably with me," said a woman, who was so heavily made up she looked as though she'd just come off the stage — having played one of the ugly sisters in Pantomime.

The rest of the gaggle of geese shrieked with laughter.

"Sorry, ladies, I'd love to oblige but I'm still a married man."

"Not for long — so I hear," said the Ugly Sister.

"How's Roger?" The loudest of all the women asked, looking from me to Tony and back again.

"Fine when I left him an hour ago," I said coolly. "If you ladies are short of male company, perhaps Roger would help you out. But you'd better be good at gardening, he couldn't spare the time for anything else."

"But is he handy with his dibber?" came the rejoinder, and the women all started shrieking again.

The waitress came up and asked them if they would like to sit down at a table she'd prepared over by the wall. The women went off still gaggling. Tony looked from them to me. "I guess we know people in common."

"I think you mean, common people, don't you?"

"Very good. You are so right. Imagine spending a night in a cell with that lot!"

"I'd rather not, thank you."

"I wouldn't mind us spending the night together though," he murmured softly

I was stunned. Did I hear him correctly?

"Only joking, don't look so serious. How about the tea dance tomorrow afternoon? Roger will be bowling won't he?"

"Yes and yes. I really do want to dance with you. But you'll have to allow for me to make mistakes until I get into it again."

"We all make mistakes, my dear." He sighed deeply. "My biggest mistake was marrying Edith."

Maybe that was true for both of them but it wasn't for me to say.

Tony frowned, the deep lines adding years to his handsome features. "But we each make our own bed and have to lie on it."

I merely nodded.

He smiled again. "Some beds can be easily remade. I'll enjoy helping you with yours."

The lustiness of his look sent a thrill throughout my body and I had to turn my head away, fearful my feelings were showing. But I still felt the intensity of his eyes piercing my mind, delving into my thoughts and the secrets of my heart.

"Nice to see the Morris Dancers in town today," I said, looking out of the window and trying to divert the conversation away from the way it was heading. "I don't know how they remember the steps. I'd be giving them bruises with those sticks," I joked, laughing nervously.

Tony took my hand again. "It's just a matter of following your partner," he said reassuringly. "Don't you worry about dancing with me, Alice, I give a strong lead and together we'll be in perfect harmony."

I had the feeling he wasn't just talking about dancing. I looked up at him and he caught me with his hypnotic blue eyes. He was working his charm on me and it was hard to pull away.

"I look forward to it," I said demurely.

Apparently satisfied with my answer, he let go of my hand. "Do you want me to pick you up in my Volvo?"

I loved the way words rolled off his tongue. He made the commonest of phrases sound so sexy. The thought of being enclosed in a car next to Tony made me feel warm all over, but it was too dangerous a risk. "Roger will drop me off at the hall, but thanks for offering," I said, glancing up at him but turning my face quickly away from those spellbinding eyes.

The geese over by the wall were gaggling again. Among the loud voices talking at the same time, Tony's name was mentioned a number of times. I looked up at Tony but he didn't even lift an eyebrow or give any indication that he'd heard the rowdy women talking about him.

"It would be no trouble but if you're certain."

I gave him a nervous smile. "Positive," I assured him. I picked up my cup of now cold coffee, tasted it, and put it down. "Now I must be getting back. Things to do."

Tony took a wallet out of his back pocket and went over to the till to pay the bill. The waitress saw him coming and collected his blazer. I saw him give her a good tip and she gave him 'a come up and see me anytime you fancy a bit' sort of look. I thought to myself that a man either has it or hasn't, and a man like Tony has far more than most.

By the time he came back to the table, my nerves were steadying and I was ready to go. We walked out of the café together with many eyes watching us. He suddenly lifted my chin and lightly kissed my lips in a friendly gesture. As I stood a little shocked, he said goodbye and we parted to go our separate ways.

Roger was going out in the afternoon and he would want an early lunch. I decided to make things easy for myself and took home some fish and chips, plus a double helping of mushy peas for Roger — he loved the things. I hoped he wouldn't be spending the afternoon in a confined space, but if he would eat the mush, he must take the consequences.

We always enjoy fish and chips from the shop and we usually eat them while relaxing on cane armchairs in our small lean-to conservatory. It fills the air with the familiar stink of chips and vinegar, but with the windows open the smell doesn't linger for long. With Roger concentrating on food instead of reading the paper, watching television, or thinking of the jobs that need doing, I had the opportunity to speak to him without being interrupted.

"Roger, I saw Tony again today. We had coffee and that dreadful bunch of women from the clubhouse came in. That lot are sex mad. They teased Tony something dreadful. They even made comments about your dibber!"

"Not surprised about that. I see them more often than you do. They're a daft lot, but they don't mean any harm. As you say, they're just sex mad." He forked up the mushy peas with relish. "Actually, they're quite good fun when you get to know them."

I did not particularly want to get to know them. I began steering the conversation in my direction. "Do you think I'm sex mad, Roger?"

"Hardly — just enjoy it, that's all." He was now digging into his fish.

"Do you think we're missing out on anything? I mean, the things you see on TV make you think."

"Well I'm not, and you've always been happy with what you get. What you see on the television is all show. I've never known women behave like that."

Now that was an odd thing for Roger to say. "How many women have you known in that sort of way?" I asked suspiciously, thinking of the condom I'd found down the sofa in the living room.

He swallowed down some chewed chips. Waving his fork abstractedly, he said, "Only you, my love. You know that already. What I mean is — well — I'm not sure what I mean, but I think you know. Most people are normal like us."

I decided to try a different approach. "Have you seen any of Clive's magazines?" I asked casually.

"What? The Gardening World, or whatever it's called?" he asked, shaking more heart-destructive salt onto his food. I decided not to nag him about it; it would only divert the conversation.

"No, they're concerned more with nature — porn magazines."

"A bit spicy for him at his age aren't they?" he asked, forking up a lump of fish.

"Barbara seems to think they're a good idea. She says they've improved their sex life. Don't know how. Have you seen one?"

"Probably some time or other. I'm happy with what we do already. Don't worry, I won't expect you to get down on your knees before me," he said, laughing at the prospect. "But you can make us some coffee, I have to be off soon."

I went to the kitchen annoyed that Roger didn't want to discuss things properly. When I came back with the coffee, I said, "By the way, I start that afternoon dancing with Tony tomorrow. You'll be playing bowls."

"Good idea, you can keep him from going astray." He picked up his cup and tasted the coffee. "A bit sweet."

"Same sugar as usual."

Ignoring what I said, he pulled a face and continued with his thoughts on Tony's precarious condition. "He's rather vulnerable at present and likely to jump into bed with any good-looking woman who glances his way. He's already had his wife take him to the cleaners. What with that big pay-off to Susan, the poor bugger must be broke. All he needs is another woman to take the shirt from off his back."

"From what I've heard about Tony, she's likely to take off more than his shirt. He's a bit of a sexy beast don't you think?" I wanted Roger to realise what he was letting his wife get into, and take some of the responsibility for what might happen.

"Not being a woman I wouldn't know. Anyway, I must be off."

He went off to the kitchen still drinking the last of his coffee and nearly fell over the washing basket. "Isn't it time you shifted that ironing?" he said crossly, looking at the pile of clothes I'd ignored all week. "It's not like you to leave it this long. I could have done with that clean white shirt too."

I felt terribly guilty. "I'll do it today. Apart from that shirt, there's nothing urgent. Anyway, you've got a new one still in its wrapper. I've been rather busy this week," I said, but he wasn't listening.

He quickly dressed ready to go out, with me hanging around wanting to tell him how Tony was affecting me but afraid of losing what I was enjoying. As he was about to leave, I began, "Roger, before you go—"

"Yes?"

I just couldn't make the confession. Instead I said, "I love you."

Showing slight annoyance at being held up, he mumbled, "I know you do. I love you too." Seeing I might hold him up again, he walked away saying, "Must get off, I'm late already. I'll see you later, Alice."

I was pursuing him down the path. "Roger, when you come home, do you think we might spend a bit of time together? You know — finish what we started yesterday morning?"

"What an insatiable appetite you have, woman," he joked. "But I wouldn't have you any other way. We'll see. I do have plans for this evening though." In a hurry, he slipped into his car, closed the door, started the engine and waved to me as he drove off down the drive.

I knew I could never stop loving him but how on earth could I get him on my sexuality wavelength? With a big sigh, I went inside to do the ironing while I sorted out my feelings. I pushed the sofa back to put up the ironing board and saw the naked pair on the front cover of the magazine busy with their act of copulation. Actually, it was more like an orgy of feasting on what they each had to offer. I picked up the magazine and sat back on the sofa. Like a geriatric student of sexual delights, I turned the well-illustrated pages of my new textbook and began a very unusual course of learning.

One of the photo models was very much like Tony and looking at the picture was doing very disturbing things to me. I put the magazine down and deliberately went back fifty years to contemplate the pleasures of my courtship days with Roger.

After the business of dancing with David, Roger stopped going home every weekend and we spent more time together. We would walk by the river and kiss and cuddle.

"I adore you," he said to me one day and I glowed in the warmth of his love.

How different things were in those days. Unknown to us, Roger's parents, realising someone had entered his life, made discreet enquiries through a network of acquaintances. I must have passed inspection. One Saturday evening Roger came back from a brief visit home — his mother had to be given the pleasure of doing his washing sometime — and brought me back a beautiful present. It came as a complete surprise. I was in our rusty old bath singing romantic songs to myself when my mother came upstairs and said she had something for me. I stepped out of the bath and opened the door slightly. She handed me a box. Inside was a lovely bunch of sweet-scented roses. I was highly delighted, and even more so when Roger told me that his mother had picked them especially for me. As far as I was concerned, the gift was signalling her blessing on the rival for her son's affections.

Warmed by the glow of sweet memories, I picked up one of Roger's old working shirts and began ironing. The heat of the iron brought out the scent of Roger's deodorant and a hint of his manly body odour. I held the warm fabric to my nose and cheek, delighting in the scent and sense of his presence with me. Again, I allowed my mind to freely wander over the past.

I recalled staying the weekend at Roger's home. I had to sleep three in a bed along with his sisters. They were out ballroom dancing in their 'sugar-plum fairy' dresses when I went up to bed. Roger came up after me and I heard him hesitate outside my door. I wondered if he would come in and kiss me goodnight, but it would have been a very daring thing to do with his parents in the house. I knew he was there and telepathy told me what he was longing to do. As I clutched a hard stone water bottle in that cold firm bed, I longed for the warmth, the scent and comfortable feel of his body next to mine. When the landing light went off, no light came into the room. The curtained small window faced a bleak dark hillside and all was quiet and blackness. Only the presence of Roger in the house took away all fear and dulled the sense of loneliness. How I loved him and wanted him with me.

Most weekends, Roger took me out on the back of his Norton. With no springing it was a hard ride but I enjoyed the close proximity of holding on to his broad back. The pleasure of being with him outweighed any discomfort. We drove around the countryside near our Midland homes and visited places where I had never been before. We parked the bike and walked beside the rippling rivers in Derbyshire's deep and hidden dales. What joy it gave me to be alone with Roger, experiencing simple pleasures.

As the evenings were getting darker, we stayed home on Sunday evenings. My parents would let me have a fire in the front room so as to be alone with Roger for an hour or two. We would turn out the light and sit on the old mock-leather sofa in the firelight glow. Flames would cast shadows up the walls and cause my mother's polished brasses to glint and gleam with a flickering radiance. We would kiss and cuddle and then I would make Roger a cup of cocoa and he would sip it while we listened to Albert Sadler and the Palm Court Orchestra playing soft and sentimental music. The fire would be dying down but the room would stay warm and cosy. How easy it was to get drowsy and drop off to sleep. We were already acting like an old married couple.

Although he hadn't actually proposed, by taking me home, Roger had put his cards on the table. The fact that he'd made his intentions clear meant it being acceptable to my parents for us to go away together for a whole week. Apart from which, they trusted him to behave the perfect gentleman. Even now, I can experience the happiness of that week on holiday with Roger. I knew that if it led to marriage I was likely to end up being his doormat but I didn't care — I was a woman in love.

It was towards the end of September and the holiday camp where we stayed was very sparsely populated. There was no queuing for anything. We played tennis just when we wanted to. Not that there was any possibility of getting a good game. Roger always hit the ball so hard I had to dodge out of the way. He was about as good at playing tennis as he was at dancing with me. As already stated, he has no finesse.

But we did go dancing every night and jog around in dances he was uncertain about, which meant all of them except for the odd waltz. Eventually, he would pull me up against him tight and we would smooch around the floor — me with my head on his shoulder. Being held close to Roger made everything else all right.

We would walk on the beach and look for pretty shells brought in by the tide, and seek out little crabs among the rocks. Like kids, we would toss a beach ball to each other. Of course, Roger would throw too hard. I would have to chase the ball across the beach with him laughing as the wind carried it out of my reach. We would paddle in the water and yell at the splashing waves, giggling like little kids when my knickers got wet. Roger would swim a little and I would sigh at the sight of his beautiful hairy body, his broad shoulders and muscular arms and legs. By then I knew better than to think he always carried his big Swiss penknife in his pocket, and the sight of his bulge and the feel of it hard up against me when we kissed was quite exciting. Not that I had conscious thoughts about what he could do with it. I suppose I saw it as a power issue — it was one thing Roger had no control over!

The sun really shone for us that week and it was warm for late September. We walked up the local hill hand in hand and he would put his arm around me and kiss me at regular intervals. Desire for intimacy was growing within us and an urging from deep within seemed to draw me closer to him in a way beyond my understanding. Natural instincts were driving my emotions even if I did not experience dynamic sensations when he pulled me close. I knew that if Roger failed to resist an urge to go further in his love play, I would not be able to deny him anything he wanted.

Towards the end of the week, it was Roger's birthday. We walked into town and bought a bottle of wine to drink that night. After the evening meal, Roger rather naughtily helped himself to what remained on the cheese dish, plus a handful of crackers, and we went to my chalet for a little birthday celebration. We soon started on the wine, drinking it as we kissed and cuddled. I can't say that it was a memorable location for a celebration. It was hardly a love nest. The small white-walled room had an iron-framed single bed, a chest of drawers and wardrobe in cheap painted wood, a washbasin and floral cotton curtains at the metal-framed window. The walls were so thin that you could hear the person in the adjoining chalet snoring. Of course, in those days there were no televisions, and radios were not provided in the chalets or anywhere else. The camp did have a bar, a dining room and a place for entertainment. The unheated swimming pool was out of doors. We shunned the public places that night; we wanted to be alone.

Before long he had his hand inside my blouse and I felt all right about it. My loving desire to please him, reinforced by natural instincts, was melting my frozen sexual feelings and overpowering moral inhibitions. We drank the rest of the wine and ate some of the cheese. I was feeling very warm inside and a little light-headed. By this time I was half undressed and Roger was kissing me more passionately. In spite of nagging guilt, I was rather enjoying it — in a gentle sort of way. My enjoyment was enhanced by Roger's obvious delight. His urgent grunts rose in intensity as my own pleasure swelled in tune with his.

After a while, he said he ought to get back to his chalet. I knew restraint was getting difficult for him but I didn't want him to leave me alone. "Don't go," I pleaded.

It wasn't that I was enjoying electrifying sensations — I certainly was not. I wanted the warmth of his company; it was enough to have him near me. He didn't take any urging to stay with me. He took off his shirt and I kissed his shoulders and snuggled up to him. We cuddled for a while and it was bliss. He looked incredibly handsome with his eyes shining and his face glowing with love for me.

I sighed and whispered sincerely, "I love you."

"And I love you, so very much."

"Will you always love me, Roger?'

"Always and always."

But our romancing didn't last long. Soon he murmured, "I have to go now," and I knew why.

As my mind went over that precious occasion, my whole body longed for Roger's presence in the here and now. I wanted to recapture the whole thing over again. But this time go beyond the simple caressing — on and on until I was yelling in ecstasy. With a little imagination it could happen; I was convinced of it.

I hurriedly finished the ironing and started to prepare for the evening. Somehow we would relive the magic of young love. But this time we would make it rapturous and complete. It would be a new beginning.

Chapter four

I could have danced all night but we only had the afternoon

Roger came home but was soon getting ready to go out again, saying he'd been invited to dine with the committee chairman of one of his more prestigious societies. He only had time for a quick wash and to change into a clean shirt and his dinner jacket. He always likes to make a good impression on formal occasions and he was looking very smart. A summer tan from working in the garden was emphasised by the whiteness of his shirt. His receding grey hair was brushed and shining healthily and his brown eyes behind his glasses were bright with the anticipation of a good night out. Being formally dressed and with his spine straightened up and his shoulders pulled well back, made him seem taller than his average height. I looked at him with admiration. "You look very handsome, Roger; I'm so proud of you," I told him, fighting back my tears of disappointment.

I stood watching him go and then, picking off a dead flower from a rose bush, returned indoors feeling sad and frustrated that my hopes and expectations were now as dead as the blossom in my hand. I sat and looked at the candles romantically placed on the table, and sniffed the meal I had prepared especially for him. It was his favourite dish but one I really hated — tripe and onions complete with a pan of mushy peas. In spite of his previous plans, I had been hoping all day that he would be staying in for a night with me. Clearly, he'd happily broken his arrangements when Mr Snooty Big invited him to replace someone who'd been unable to get to the dinner. I had no doubts concerning Roger's priorities.

I cleared away all that I'd prepared and made myself a cheese sandwich. I sat nibbling it while thinking about going dancing again. It brought back memories of my first proper dance, the Nottingham Arts Ball, and of a young man that I met there. He became my first serious boyfriend.

It happened at the end of the year I began training to be a designer. I had saved enough money to buy a length of blue shot-silk taffeta for an evening dress, which I designed and made at college. It was strapless with a tight-fitting bodice decorated with diamanté motifs. The long swirling skirt measured twenty yards around the hem. After years of make-do-and-mend, wearing that dress made me feel really good about myself.

It had not been easy coming from a poor home background, especially with having a friend like Carol who was never short of anything she needed. Her dad was manager of a local firm, which entitled him to a small Ford car — most people were lucky to have a bike in those days. They lived in a newish semi with a grand piano taking up most of the front room. His wife didn't have to work and could afford to have her hair done every week, employ a cleaner and buy cream cakes for tea. Since they sent their girls to a posh convent school, they expected them to be very good and ladylike. They certainly did not know about Eric, or the way Carol wheedled half a crown out of her granddad every week. She would sit on the arm of his chair smiling at him beguilingly, all the time flashing her big brown eyes provocatively from under her thick curly lashes. A little kissing and her granddad soon had his hand in his pocket. Carol's dad was a strict disciplinarian and would slap his daughters for even minor offences. Carol had no friends in the neighbourhood and so was allowed to go out with me. I wasn't posh but, at least, I was clean and polite. I served as someone he could look down on, or maybe ridicule, to boost his own sense of importance.

I was invited to go with Carol and her parents for a trip into the country in their Ford. I suspect it was to keep their daughter company while they talked to the friends they were visiting without Miss Big Ears around to hear their gossip. Carol used to pick up odd bits of information through listening at doors. She told me that her parents had been talking with friends about how not to get pregnant. Among all the laughter going on she had heard her mother say, "I wear pyjamas." I didn't get it but it seemed to mean something to Carol.

Having accepted the invitation, I borrowed a dress from my sister, mended the frayed bits and wore it for this very special occasion — trips in motor cars were exceedingly rare events for me. Carol was quite excited; she knew we would be going for a walk with her cousin, a young man called Peter. As usual I played gooseberry. Since Peter was a bit of a bore, I didn't mind. We stopped on the way back for a picnic and I was given a honey-spread sandwich, which was quite nice as we only had jam at home.

The whole outing was ruined when we arrived back. I thanked her father for taking me along and he asked me if I had enjoyed it.

"Yes, thank you," I said politely.

"You damn well should have done. If you'd gone on a coach it would have cost you fifteen shillings."

I was mortified — utterly humiliated. I told my dad and he was furious. As a disabled breadwinner unable to work, he only received ten shillings weekly allowance for me. If he'd been able to give the rotter the money he would have done. His pride was badly hurt. Thinking back to those days, I can see the reason why I don't care much for Roger's Mr Snooty Big — he reminds me of Carol's dad. He's very patronising to Roger but my dear husband refuses to see it.

So that blue evening dress I made the following year for the Arts Ball, when I was just turned seventeen, was more than just a pretty gown; it was symbolic of my coming out of poverty and entering a different world where I had more control over my circumstances. No one would ever talk to me again like Carol's father always did. I was determined to get somewhere in life, to make the most of what I had and, of course, never to be someone's doormat like my mother and her mother before her. With a beautiful dress, shapely figure, pleasant looks enhanced by make-up, and my hair bouncing healthily on my shoulders, I climbed into a taxi and set off into the night.

I had a fantastic evening. I was certainly no wallflower. At the end of the ball, a young man asked me to go out with him. He wasn't exactly handsome — his face was too round, his eyes too small and he had a rosebud mouth not good for kissing. He was also a lousy dancer. With him just making syncopated trotting steps not quite in time with the music, I nearly tripped over his feet several times. But he seemed a nice polite person and I was willing to get to know him better.

The first time we went out, his friends came too. We just did a pub crawl with me drinking lemonade and the rest boozing on beer. They also smoked heavily and told a succession of dirty jokes. I was not impressed.

Having caught the last bus that went directly to its garage, it was well after midnight when Alec got me home. He kissed me a few times, saying very little. I can't say his kissing thrilled me but he seemed contented enough. Then he set off home, hoping to thumb a lift but prepared to walk the seven miles — that did impress me. A few more times out and he wanted to go a bit further than kissing. He led me to our side entrance and while he had his lips on mine, his hand started wandering. I stopped him. After one or two more dates, his hand wandered down over my coat towards my groin area. That was the end of our relationship. Was that all boys wanted from girls? I did not like his lifestyle anyway.

Coming back to the present, I took out the porn magazine from its hiding place and thumbed through its pages again, avoiding the Tony-looking model. Ignoring what a couple were doing with their lower parts, I mused on their kissing with tongues — French kissing we used to call it. My mind again travelled to the past, to six months after going out with Alec.

A penfriend, Jean Pierre, with whom I had been corresponding for three years, paid me a visit while he was on holiday in England. He was a few years older than I was and, as it turned out, very sexually experienced. He was quite a handsome young man of medium height and with a build that was both slim and athletic. He had deep dimples, a thickset jaw and soft full lips. We exchanged photographs and I was very impressed when his picture arrived; he looked like a film star. I sent him a studio photograph of me of when I was about sixteen. With my hair plaited and coiled around my head I appeared to be a mature good-looker. Our letters had only been factual so I wasn't expecting an amorous encounter, but when he arrived, I fell for his good looks and adorable accent.

The first time we went out together was for a walk by a wide, tree-banked river, and we sat on a bench to watch the swans gliding serenely on the water. He put his arm around me and I was absolutely thrilled. I felt as if butterflies were going wild inside of me. Sensing my response, he looked at me and smiled and said something in French, which made me feel quite giddy. Things were moving along perfectly, that is, until he ruined my image of him by wanting to demonstrate how much his lungs were tainted by the cigarette smoke he constantly inhaled. He coughed into a handkerchief and showed me the smelly brown stains. I was utterly disgusted but he obviously enjoyed shocking me.

It wasn't long before he kissed me. No one had ever warned me about French kissing. His lips came down to meet mine. I was relaxed, expecting a pleasant sensation, but I soon found a foul-tasting rough tongue being thrust into my mouth. It was totally revolting and I hated it. He began holding me tighter as he thrust his nauseating tongue deeper and harder. I tried to push him away but he was too strong for me. When I was able to turn my head away, he made no apology — he probably thought that I was just being coy!

I should have told him not to do it again but apart from the fact that I didn't think he would take any notice, I was very shy and it didn't seem polite to make a fuss over what to him was normal practice. Avoidance seemed the best policy. Sucking in stale smoky breath from his lungs convinced me I would catch terrible diseases and I wanted to keep his mouth at a distance.

I took him a long walk where I thought I would be safe with other people around. But on the hillside, under a tree in the full view of a family walking fifty yards away, he got me again. We were sitting enjoying the view when he pushed me over and started kissing me. His tongue pegged my mouth while he tried to get his leg over to trap me under him. The more I struggled, the more my skirt came up. It was both embarrassing and frightening, especially when he was trying to get his hand up my leg while holding me down. When walkers started approaching just yards away he was forced to calm the situation. I was so upset, to the point of tears, that he eventually took the hint that he wasn't going to get whatever it was he had been planning. But he was very angry and told me that all the English girls he'd met had let him go all the way. After that, I made certain we went for walks in crowded public places.

He behaved very well for the next few days and so I suggested we go dancing on the night before his departure. He was very agreeable. I wore my evening dress, which I had now shortened. His eyes lit up when he saw me in my finery complete with make-up. I have to admit, I was feeling flattered by his reaction; it was nice to be appreciated. Jean was no dancer but we had a nice time at the Palais and we caught the last bus home. I made him a cup of cocoa while he tried to teach me a few words of French as we sat in the kitchen. The evening had been a pleasant way to end his holiday. Since the flare-up he had been treating me with respect and I was feeling happy and quite warm towards him. But when I stood up to go to bed, he showed his true colours — his intentions were far from honourable. He switched off the light and pulled me to the floor.

I didn't want to make a fuss and wake up my parents or there would have been considerable unpleasantness, which was bad for my father's heart. So I gathered my wits together and prepared for a fight.

While his left hand was gripping my right arm, his right hand was already going up my leg with me grasping at his wrist, trying to stop him. I pleaded quietly, "No, don't. I don't want you to," but he shut me up with his filthy tongue reaching to my throat.

The hand snatching at my knickers had pulled my skirt high up and he was trying to get on top of me. But then he moved his hand away from my knickers with my hand still gripping at his wrist. I hoped he had given up, but to my horror I realised he was opening up his trousers. I renewed my efforts to get away from him. I let go of his wrist and went for his face but he had anticipated the move. He grabbed my hand and pinned me down again.

I could not scream or shout. If my parents caught me now I would die of shame. If I kept my legs together, he wouldn't be able to do much surely? But with his knee, he began forcing my legs apart. He soon had me completely trapped underneath him with my legs wide open.

"Get off or I'll scream," I whispered urgently. "I really mean it," I said, my voice getting louder.

He found my mouth with his and forced his tongue down my throat again. I felt sick, humiliated and utterly terrified. Tears were running down my face. Jean must have felt them but he was ignoring my distress. No girl had ever refused him before and, being arrogant and full of himself, without doubt he must have thought I truly wanted it and that I was just playing hard to get. I was now finding it difficult to breathe and before long I was sucking in his breath to add to my distress. But I didn't feel the bruising I was getting — I was too busy keeping alert for his next move. Without a hand free, surely there was little more he could do? I prepared myself to stick it out until he gave up.

His hands tightened on my wrists and with a swift movement, he pulled them above my head and held both of them down with just his left hand. I pulled away my right hand, and he took his opportunity to grab it and, while I was struggling to get up, move my arm quickly under my body and then pin me down again. My skirt was up to my waist and my knickers pulled loose ready for his pleasure.

"Now, my fine actress, time for the finale," he whispered in his soft French accent.

I felt him pulling at my knickers as he wriggled his body between my legs. But, as his face come close to mine, I snapped my teeth and caught him on his nose. He yelled!

My mother's voice brought sanity into the situation. "What's happening down there?"

I quickly found the light switch and then opened the door. My mother was coming down the stairs.

"Nothing, Mum. Jean tripped and bumped his nose," I said as calmly as I could. "I'm coming up. Jean doesn't need me to help him. He can wash the blood off at the kitchen sink."

But my mother was full of concern and insisted of giving the guest some first-aid. If she noticed the teeth marks she didn't say.

My thoughts turned from Jean Pierre in the past and settled on meeting with Tony Bradshaw. I knew his reputation and yet I was going to go dancing with him — to be held in his arms. I couldn't believe he would force himself on to me in any circumstances, but what if he tried to seduce me? I had to admit that such a thought tended to excite, rather than frighten me. Now that did give me serious cause for concern. Was I being wicked? Surely having one's imagination titillated was no sin — or was it? Consumed with guilt, even though I knew I could never be an unfaithful wife, I was torn between love for Roger and my stirred up carnal desires.

With all my unfortunate experiences of males in the past, hardly surprising I was having problems with my sex life. I sighed and rose from my comfy soft leather armchair to do a bit of housework. Just before nine, I collected my mending and put the TV on. It wasn't long before a handsome doctor had his colleague on the storeroom table, shunting away to shouts of ecstasy. It made me feel so very inexperienced in such matters. I picked up my magazine and continued my education.

When I reached the back page, I saw some things that made my eyes bulge. Surely people didn't buy stuff like that? There were apparently all different kinds of vibrators — even some to stick up your bottom. Ugh! It was bad enough having a doctor stick a finger up — no thanks! I had a look at the horrid-looking pink rubber things. They were being used in some of the pictures of the magazine, and were certainly putting a smile on Miss Prim and Miss Pretty. I saw several varieties that claimed to give a bit of an internal massage at the same time as the vibrating movement — golly! I wondered if they could turn dead meat into sexually sensitive flesh. There were order forms inviting readers to purchase at reasonable prices. I felt very tempted.

The phone rang. I quickly put the magazine back in its hiding place as though the person on the other end of the line would be able to see it. It was going to take some time before I could look at such things without a deep sense of shame. I picked up the phone. Keith, one of our sons, was on the line. Five minutes later, I found myself planning what we were going to eat that weekend. Some of the family were going to be with us for two days so I could forget about sex with Roger for a while.

On Friday morning, I deliberately asked Roger to help choose a dress for me to wear for the tea dance. I wanted him to be part of what I was doing. He decided on an old one that had always been his favourite. Made in a lovely red poppy-print silky fabric, the colours went so well with my hair. I wore a little make-up and Roger was very pleased with my appearance.

He insisted on driving me down to the Victoria Hall and I felt a little guilty as though I had a secret lover and my husband was being cuckolded. When he dropped me off, Roger told me to have a good time. Then just as he was about to drive away, he called me back.

"Bring Tony back with you," he said cheerfully. "We can go to tonight's meeting together — stop him moping about his coming divorce. I'll get the meal ready for this evening. I'll heat up that tripe and onions for when you get back — do 'im good."

I nearly threw up at the thought of the coming meal but then I saw Tony coming up the road and I forgot about distasteful things. My partner for the afternoon was looking very smart and handsome in his formal suit and I felt a girlish delight exciting my body. Since Tony had a reputation for being a good dancer, I knew that, for a while at least, I was going to be in another world where I could be the young and vibrant person that lived within my memories.

"Hello, Alice, good to see you again. Ready to put on an exhibition?" he asked, his well-preserved teeth flashing white as he gave me a broad smile.

"Of me playing the fool?" I said a little nervously. Was he really expecting me to take off on the dance floor like it was yesteryear?

He grinned. "Don't worry, I'll be gentle with you."

Now I should have been annoyed at this obvious innuendo but I was rather chuffed by it. I said to him, "Good, and don't forget I have a bit of angina."

"Heart problems are my speciality too," he said, looking at me tenderly. "I think I can help you there, Alice, if you let me."

My heart definitely reacted. My breathing suddenly increased and I felt colour rising to my cheeks.

He smiled most charmingly. "I think the cure is already taking place."

Knowing I was blushing like a kid, I looked down and made my way inside. I went to the cloakroom, hung up my coat and tidied my hair. I looked in the mirror and saw my eyes shining and my face sort of glowing. I had never felt so fit and well for many a year. I went to the hall to find my partner.

The band was already playing and I could see Clive up on the platform playing the piano. I knew he could play a number of instruments and hoped to hear him give a solo later on. He once sang with a band too and evidently he could still give a husky rendering of the old favourites. According to Glenda, who'd heard him practising with Barbara up in their bedroom, he must have other specialities that could thrill a woman's breast — and other parts of her body. That thought set me off on a sex trip that I found hard to resist. What was happening to me? Whatever it was, I didn't want to stop it, even if common sense told me to desist from such imaginative sprees.

Tony was sitting at a table talking to a couple I didn't know. He stood up and came over as soon as he saw me. After complementing me on my appearance, he guided me over to meet his acquaintances. As we passed by the band, Clive gave me a wink and I wondered if Barbara had told him about my porn mag.

Tony introduced me to the couple at the table: Madge, a good-looking woman of indeterminate age, and her husband Frank, a rather grey sort of person from the colour of his hair and eyes and dull tinge on his skin, to the shade of his baggy suit. He was obviously much older than Madge. We started a pleasant conversation about the old days before drugs came on the scene, and women were more restrained about revealing their assets. Then Madge picked up her favourite theme.

"Nowadays girls have no subtlety and boys have no restraint. Goods are displayed for all to see and nothing is left under the counter for later on. Everything is experienced too soon with little left to look forward to. No wonder they want to try more and more drugs, they are destabilised and nothing satisfies for long. They are forever on a quest for more and bigger thrills."

"Maybe, but our upbringing went too far the other way don't you think?" I suggested, by way of conversation than to be argumentative. "Being a teenager in the late forties had considerable sexuality problems. We were so very ignorant."

I was expecting some sort of agreement but Madge and Frank looked at me in shocked surprise and I wondered if I had made a faux pas. Then Madge put on a haughty mask and gave me a condescending smile.

"You may be right, Alice. I really wouldn't know; I didn't reach my teens until the late sixties."

I felt utterly wretched at my blunder but Tony came to my rescue.

"Well, I can vouch for what Alice says. It was hell being a teenager at the turn of the fifties — the girls always said, 'No!'"

Everyone laughed and I felt easier. Tony took me by the hand and said it was time to foxtrot. I was pleased to get away from the table but nervous of taking my first steps on the dance-floor. I needn't have worried; with Tony holding me close, and with my natural sense of rhythm, he was able to lead me without any faltering on my part. Once I relaxed, Tony began to say what he had obviously been waiting to tell me.

"You know, Alice, you shouldn't give your age away like that. You look younger than Madge and I know she is fifty-seven — she was fibbing a bit."

Now was the chance to satisfy my curiosity about Tony's age. "Were you fibbing about yours too?"

"No, I'm nearly sixty-five. There's very little difference in our ages."

It seemed a lot to a mature, if not overripe, woman like me. "I wouldn't say that. Five and a half years."

"What does age matter when we're young at heart?"

"Well, you look as young as you obviously feel."

"Thanks. I try to think young and see where it leads me."

I thought it best to move away from Tony 's virile manhood. "Thanks for helping me out. I guess I've upset Madge but I really did think she was my age."

"She'll get over it. Madge is a good sport when you get to know her. She's a bit sensitive about her looks though. You see, she was seriously ill not so long ago and it aged her quite a bit. You were not to know."

I was mortified. "Oh, dear, how dreadful of me. I must apologise."

"No, don't do that. She will know I told you. Just make allowances if she seems touchy about her looks and age, that's all."

I noticed Madge was now dancing. "Well, whatever her problem was, and I guess it must have been pretty serious to have aged her, she knows how to enjoy herself."

"As I said, she's a sporty lass and intends to make the most of life. Don't be surprised if she invites you and Roger to one of her fancy dress parties."

I'm not much of a party animal, especially if I don't know most of the people there but Roger always enjoys social events. I used to go with him to office parties, but he would leave me at a table while he mixed with his underlings, joking and laughing to jolly them up. I usually ended up sitting in a quiet corner listening to the woes of one of his office staff. But on one occasion a young enthusiastic trainee manager asked me to dance. It was music from the fifties and it was great to do a bit of rocking and rolling. He told me I had a good sense of rhythm. It did a lot for my ego and it didn't harm his career advancement — I told Roger what a lively keen worker he had in his department.

Did I really want to go to Madge's get-togethers?

"I'm not much of a party-goer, Tony, in fact I'm more of a party-pooper. I don't smoke, I drink mostly orange juice and I avoid party snacks. Apart from which, I'm rather a shy person with people I don't know."

"Well, you know me, Alice. I would look after you."

Now that was a lovely thought. My mind swiftly went over the more recent social occasions I had been to with Roger. I could see myself sitting at a table with two or three other couples, all of them chatting away to each other. Roger highly animated with his arms flying and nearly knocking the dishes out of the hands of the waitresses. And me, only able to hear odd bits of conversation because of the background noise, just nodding and hoping that I was doing so in the right places. There was only one time when I managed to get a word in. The dining room was nearly empty so I was able to hear better. The other couples at our table were discussing how their wives coped when they were away at sea in the Merchant Navy. After singing their praises about the excellent job they made out of rearing their children almost single-handed, I piped up, "Well, I think I did even better. I brought up our four in spite of Roger being at home."

Of course my little joke caused much laughter but in my mind there was an element of truth. When Roger was not at work, he was always busy with something or other. Except on one anxious occasion, even when the kids were born, he was either asleep in bed or busy at work. But then men were not part of the birth process in those days. It was enough to have done the seed planting. The harvesting was the wife's job. He was there for them when needed, especially where discipline was concerned, but I was their nurse, cook, cleaner, nose wiper, listener, playmate and storyteller. He provided the financial security and stability needed for a secure family environment but always based on a rather unemotional masculine type of love. I have enough emotion for both of us but I longed for Roger to be more open about his feelings. The only time I have known him shed tears was when our adorable dog was run over ten years ago. Podge's slipper-retrieving days were over. After giving a little whimper, he died in Roger's arms with both of us sobbing over his poor old broken body.

Tony broke into my thoughts. "You seem far away. Did you hear what I said, Alice?"

"Oh, sorry, Tony. You mean about Madge having parties?"

"No. I asked you if you were happy now that you're on the dance floor — coping exceedingly well, I might add."

I didn't want him to know my mind was elsewhere. "I have difficulty hearing when there's a lot of background noise. Yes, indeed, I'm very comfortable dancing with you."

Meanwhile the dance had come to an end and the bandleader was asking the dancers to stay on the floor for a tango.

"I can't do this, Tony; it's been too long," I told him, in spite of wanting very much to try.

"You most certainly can, Alice. Have faith in me."

With Tony taking me in a firm hold, we struck out across the floor in perfect rhythm. He was right, I had no problem following his lead; my nervousness disappeared and I found the dance very exhilarating. By the time the tango was coming to an end, I was on a high. Tony gave me a jerk, swiftly swung me around, and with great dexterity bent me backwards. My head reached half way to the floor but, with Tony supporting my back, I was not in any way distressed. I was completely intoxicated and knew that from then on, I would always be malleable putty in my partner's hands.

"Thank you, Alice; I really enjoy dancing with you," he said. His face may have been flushed from the exercise but, unlike me, he was breathing quite normally. "I think perhaps you'd better have a little rest, my dear; I don't want complaints from Roger that I've worn you out."

I didn't like the unpleasant reminder that, compared with him, I was a geriatric. But I knew there was something much deeper getting at me. It was the reference to Roger. I knew he ruled my life and had done since the day I married him — no, even before then. This was something I had always accepted, after all, Roger does care about me in his own way. But it was beginning to rankle that others noticed. Even my daughter-in-law, Helen, had once remarked, "Why do you let Dad walk all over you? If Keith treated me like that, he'd soon get notice to quit!"

We drifted to our table and sat down just as the band struck up again for the next dance. This time, Tony asked Madge to partner him. I actually felt jealous and was ashamed of myself. Frank, who was sitting next to me, said that he would like to dance but his arthritic legs were playing him up a bit.

"Nice of Tony to ask Madge, she loves dancing," he said, looking at his smiling wife as she passed us by. "I hope you don't mind though," he added, looking me straight in the eye.

"Of course not," I lied. "Anyway, I really need a rest after that tango."

"I enjoyed watching you," he said, still eyeing me closely. "You're quite a mover."

"Thank you. It's a long time since I danced a tango."

"Not much of a dancer myself, but I can perform in bed without difficulty."

"Oh, really?" I remarked, taken aback.

He winked. "Should you wish to tango between the sheets, I'd be very happy to oblige."

The only other time I had been so propositioned was by an eighty-nine year old when I was a hospital visitor. I had to tell the old lecher that his bed wasn't big enough for both of us — the drip and his heart monitor would get in the way. Clearly, Frank also was not fully in charge of himself — poor man. And poor Madge, how awkward for her. But it was a very embarrassing situation for me too. Rather than slap his face, I decided to let Frank down lightly.

"Sorry, Frank. I've only ever had one bed-mate and I don't think he would be very pleased with your invitation."

Frank didn't press his offer of a good lay. He asked me about my hobbies, and when I mentioned painting he gave me a lecture on his thoughts about modern art. Before long, he was telling me about meeting Picasso in Spain and buying one of his pictures.

By the time Tony and Madge came back to the table, the waitress had brought our teas. After chatting about various subjects, Madge turned the conversation to social events on the calendar. I noticed she was concentrating her gaze on Tony.

"I'm not committing myself to anything at present, at least, as far as parties go — not having a wife or a replacement, so to speak," he told Madge.

She gave him a sweet smile. "You know, Tony, you're always welcome to come to our little get-togethers any time. You don't need to have a partner."

Madge was giving Tony a message that was far from being coded. I guess with a husband like Frank she needed something to balance the act.

Tony could see I was feeling out of things and asked me if I had any late holidays planned. And so, with just a break to go to the toilet, I talked about unusual places we'd visited and about things in general, until it was time to dance again. I didn't spend any more time seated at the table; Tony kept me on the floor and it was absolute magic.

As we were dancing the last waltz, he said, "I'm so sorry, Alice, I shouldn't have introduced you to Frank and Madge — not your sort. I have to admit they're a sexy pair. You have no idea what can happen at their fancy dress parties, especially when the theme is Rome or Pompeii."

"I can imagine."

"You've had some very embarrassing moments. While you were at the ladies, Frank told me about your conversation with him. Now you must hate me for asking you here."

"Oh, no, it's been wonderful," I answered quickly. "You're a fantastic dancer and I've loved every minute of it. As for Madge and Frank and their little foibles, we never know what may become of us, or how we will react to life's problems."

"That is very generous of you, Alice. Actually, Frank is impotent. I reckon he likes to talk to women, the way he did to you, to give himself a buzz. Of course, as you must have realised, he is getting senile in his old age. He was a young war hero when I was just a runny-nosed nipper. He sometimes gets very confused and thinks Churchill still runs the country. Did he tell you about his original Picasso? It's a portrait of him Madge painted while she was ill — she used a lot of anger mixed in with the paint! But please, let's forget all that, I don't want to put you off coming with me again."

"I'd love to come again, I really would," I said with feeling. "I haven't had so much fun for years. But you know, Tony, from now on I'll be wondering if golden oldies might be outdoing some of today's rave teenagers. I wonder if any of them have piercing in their withering body parts — it makes you think."

Tony laughed and said that he hadn't seen any, neither would he want to spoil his own mature manhood with a teenager's craze for adornment. "I can assure you, Alice, my body part doesn't need embellishment — it can stand up for itself."

I laughed with him, but tried to block out my naughty imaginative thoughts.

At the end of the dance, I told Tony that Roger had invited him to have a meal with us and that he hoped they would go to the evening's meeting together. I warned him about the meal that Roger had planned for us to eat. Tony laughed and said that he had to see Edith about something or other, otherwise he would have accepted, even if it was to consume a load of old tripe.

By the time I arrived home with Tony, Roger had the meal already prepared. He was disappointed that Tony was not staying; he wanted to discuss the agenda for that evening but he understood his reason for his not accepting.

"It wouldn't do to cross Edith at this stage of the proceedings, she'd make him pay one way or another," he said, with strong feeling for his fellow male.

While we were eating, I told Roger about meeting Madge and Frank and what an odd couple they seemed to be.

"Actually, I've already met them," he told me, much to my surprise. "You're right, they're a very curious pair. She invited us to one of their parties, would you believe?" He shovelled in another mouthful of tripe. "Mm, delicious, just the right amount of onions," he mumbled, scooping up the sauce with a piece of bread.

"You didn't tell me about it and they didn't mention they'd met you."

"It was a while ago and you can't expect people to remember every person they meet."

"You obviously remembered them. But you didn't mention the invite to me."

"And for good reason. Would you really want to go to a wife-swapping party? Personally I'm happy with what I've got."

"Wife-swapping party? I don't believe it!"

"Well, that's what I heard. Might not be true; maybe a couple had too much to drink and stayed the night in the wrong beds."

"Huh, just gossip. Probably those gaggling geese at the club."

"Actually, you're right there. Sex mad that lot. Any tripe left?"

I handed him the casserole dish to help himself.

"Perhaps they don't get what they need, so they live in a world of make-believe. Roger, suppose one of us didn't get what we needed?"

"The question doesn't arise, so why speculate? Anyway, I must go," he said, rising to his feet. "I've more important matters to think about."

Another unsuccessful attempt to get him thinking my way, but then, I knew things would not be easy. While Roger was at his meeting, I took the porn magazine from its hiding place and looked at the advertisements for vibrators. Now would one of those help me in my quest? Perhaps I could get my act together in such a way as to combine the vibrator experience with what I did with Roger. It might be a way of finding the fulfilment I so much desired in our marital union. It seemed a bit mechanical, but maybe it would work. Not like gaining full experience without aids, but it could be a start. I made my choice and, while Roger was out, posted off my order.

Chapter five

I seduce my husband while being seduced by another man

After a hectic weekend with Keith, Helen and their family staying with us, Monday was also tiring but without having the pleasure of the children around. By the end of the day, what with joints still aching from dancing and the extra boring household duties, I decided a good soak in the bath would be very beneficial. Such relaxation gave me an opportunity to turn my thoughts once more to the pleasures of the flesh.

I expected my little package to arrive at any time and I didn't want Roger opening it up for me. What on earth would he say if he saw what was inside? More to the point what explanation would I give to him?

I had others things on my mind too. Helen had told me that she had taken to massaging Keith's back and feet to help him relax. I asked her to show me how to do it. I thought sensory touch might inspire Roger to want to reciprocate. It might lead to all sorts of erotic experiences.

I lay back in the bath with my imagination working full speed. I could see the sweet-smelling candles lighting the bedroom, a few of his favourite chocolates to act as an aphrodisiac, and my hands moving over his body to encourage relaxation. But before long, my fingers would stimulate his thoughts and desires in the right direction. Then I began forming plans in my mind to help Roger focus on getting me similarly aroused. Then we would experience ecstatic coitus — both of us raising the roof in rapturous delight. Oh, yes! Yes!

I planned to remove all trace of hair that might tickle his nose. I would titillatingly hide the focus of his sexual desires within my new white slinky nightdress. He would slip his hand inside the deep slit and be surprised and delighted by what he would find. In a torrid mood he would pull the garment from my shoulders. Unable to control his passion, he would bring his lips to bear on all my erotic zones. I wondered what it would be like. Fantastic! That is, if the many sexy films on TV were correct and the expressions on the faces of my porn mag girls were genuine.

Now would it be a good thing if I showed him the pictures to give hints towards experimentation? That would be ideal but I was going to have to get him in the right mood first. What a pity I couldn't ask Clive to have a little chat with him but it wouldn't do for me to make such a suggestion. What about enlisting Barbara's help? No, I couldn't expose Roger to the idea that he might be deficient as a lover.

I would soon have my vibrator. I wondered what it did exactly. If it gave the desired sensations then my state of sexual excitation might have all sorts of magical effects on Roger. I was full of hope for the future. Help was on its way and I still had my hidden resources — the nightdress and red undies. Tomorrow, I would get a bottle of massage oil and some means of painlessly removing hair — I didn't fancy using eye-watering depilatory wax. Soon, very soon, the stage could be set for an awakening to erotic sexual satisfaction. Roger would become a rejuvenated man; I would be a new woman. After fifty years, our marriage was destined to enter a new realm of marital unity.

But even as I was thinking of all these things, Tony's bewitching smile kept coming into my mind and a naughty little voice kept telling me that with him, no enticing would be necessary. What is more, he would know exactly how to please a girl and find great satisfaction from doing so. I pushed the thoughts away, I knew what I wanted and who should give it to me.

While I'd been musing in the bath, Roger had finished his crossword puzzle and gone out to post it, ever hopeful of that illusive prize. His chocolate was waiting for him when he returned. The grandchildren had worn him out and he was looking very weary. Once in bed, he soon dropped off to sleep. Not even his loud snoring or early morning trips to the bathroom woke me up during the night; I slept through and woke at six-thirty. I went downstairs to get us both a cup of tea.

While Roger was sipping his drink and nibbling his digestive biscuit, I casually asked, "How about I give your back a nice massage tonight? We can both have a relaxing soak in the bath first, it'll put you in the mood."

"I've still got the minutes to write for the last Institution meeting."

"That won't take all night. Anyway, can't you do it this morning?"

He drank his tea, muttering between slurps, "Bowls practice. We've got a match Friday."

"This afternoon then?"

"Weather forecast says it's going to be fine this afternoon. Must get the grass cut, and rebuild that bit of wall. Why don't you drink your tea, Alice? It's getting cold as usual; you talk too much."

"The minutes won't take long," I argued, ignoring the tea.

"Long enough, and then I'll want you to type them for me. We'll need twelve running off this time — Cyril's joining the committee." He announced in his lordly manner.

I knew I'd been defeated, Roger's jobs had to come first. I was now feeling rather tetchy.

"Oh, really? I'm surprised Glenda will let him out."

"He is a bit hen-pecked. Probably wants to get out of his chicken-coop for a while. He's coming round this morning to get the last minutes to read. I'll leave them on the hall table for him to pick up," my cock-of-the-roost informed me while eating my ginger biscuit with crumbs scattering over the bedclothes.

"Some other time then?"

"For what?" he demanded, speaking with his mouth full of crumbs.

"The massage."

But he didn't hear me, he was too busy choking.

I left him swallowing my tea and clearing his throat; it would go on for the next half-hour. It wouldn't be just the crumbs in need of clearing, overnight build up of mucus needed shifting from his throat as well. Not a romantic way to start the day but I was used to it.

After breakfast, just as Roger was about to go out, I saw the postman coming up the drive. I walked quickly to the door but Roger arrived there first. He opened the door just as the postman was about to ring the bell. Roger was handed letters and a small parcel.

'This is for you," he said, handing me the parcel. "The letters are for me — all junk. Throw these in the bin," he ordered; "Must run, want to get an early start."

It was as easy as that. I took my package into the kitchen; handling it as though it had a bomb inside. I poured myself a cup of tepid tea and sat looking at the bulky padded envelope. I went to the cupboard and got myself a chocolate biscuit to help me think. I broke open the package and took out its plastic-wrapped contents. I was rather appalled at the sight of the sausage-pink vibrating dildo. Of course, I had seen a picture of it, but to actually see and handle it was something else.

Just as I picked up the revolting pink object, there was a knock on the kitchen window. I looked up startled to see Glenda's Cyril grinning at me through the glass.

I quickly pushed my new toy back into its padded envelope. Feeling dreadfully flustered, I walked shakily to the kitchen door. Needing time to compose myself, I deliberately took a long time to turn the key and move back the security bolts.

Cyril was standing there looking a bit concerned. "I'm so sorry. I gave you a shock didn't I? I was hoping to see Roger. I came for some papers."

My heart was still thumping in my chest but I managed to say calmly, "I'm surprised you didn't see him drive off. I'll get you the papers. Roger left them for you on the hall table."

Cyril followed me, mumbling, "I really am sorry I startled you, Alice. I guess you were concentrating on opening your packet."

"Never mind, I'll get over it." I was trying to sound casual but not succeeding.

I gave him the minutes and was moving him towards the door when he suddenly came out with, "I hope you don't mind me asking — are they any good?"

"The minutes? I have no idea, I just type them," I said puzzled.

Looking a bit uncomfortable, he said in a conspiratorial whisper, "The thing in your packet — you know — the pink thingy." Seeing the shocked look on my face, he touched my shoulder and said softly, "I'm so sorry, I've embarrassed you." Looking sheepish, he added, "You see I've often thought of getting one and I wondered if they were any good. I mean, if they work. No, of course they work, you put batteries in. What I mean is — er — do they give satisfaction?"

Cyril now seemed more embarrassed than me. He suddenly dropped his hand from my shoulder as though it had gone red hot and began clearing his throat. It sounded very rough.

"Would you like a tea or coffee, Cyril?" I was genuinely concerned.

"Thanks, Alice; I'd love a coffee, Glenda only has tea in the house," he said, a glum look distorting his already haggard countenance.

"Glenda won't mind if you stay a minute or two, will she?" My motherly concern was beginning to show.

"She's out. An early hair appointment. Don't know why she bothers, she's just as ugly when she gets back. She makes out it's for my benefit — rubbish! She just wants an opportunity to gossip with the other old hags." He sounded very downcast and bitter.

As I was making his drink I could see him looking at my newly arrived package. I was very curious. Was he thinking of getting one for Glenda? Having heard her views on certain matters, and as to what she would do to a randy husband, I almost burst out laughing. I felt sorry for the poor sod — what on earth was going on in his mind?

"I'm sorry, Alice, I'm really sorry," he said, shaking his head. "It's just that Clive told me that you had the same magazines as him. You know what I mean don't you? And I thought that since you have — well — an open mind like, you wouldn't mind me asking," he explained bashfully, unable to look me in the eye.

"It's all right, Cyril, I'm not offended really, I was just surprised," I explained. "But I can't answer your question because I have no idea. I've never used one — never even seen one before this arrived. But, if you want my opinion, I don't think Glenda would appreciate you getting one for her."

"Oh, I wasn't thinking of getting one for Glenda — she'd probably shove it down my throat!" Cyril said with a choking laugh. I'm not sure if it was at the thought of Glenda using a dildo on herself, or the way she would use it on him. "But there's the equivalent for men — or so Clive tells me," he added conspiratorially.

While Cyril was speaking, I had horrific pictures in my mind of Glenda gagging him with the pink thingy and tying him, spreadeagled, to the bedposts while she made an orphan out of Wee Willy. Not a pleasant thought! I had no idea about the other thing that Cyril seemed keen to know about. I didn't think I'd seen one in the magazine, but then I wasn't looking for one.

"This is all new to me, Cyril, but I can understand how you feel."

His eyes lit up. "Can you really, Alice? I see all this sex stuff on television — when Glenda is out of course, she would go berserk if she knew — and I realise what I'm missing." He sighed. "I really envy Clive and your Roger."

I didn't know what to say to him but I was prepared to listen. Unfortunately, he took my silence the wrong way.

"Sorry, it's very rude of me to talk to you about such things — Glenda would kill me if she found out. I'd better go," he said despondently.

I watched Cyril walking back to his house; his shoulders bent as though bearing the pain of Glenda's lash. He might be five years younger than I am, but that day he was walking like a withered old geriatric.

I retrieved my magazine and looked at the back pages. Yes, he was right about such sex aids — or toys. But what on earth could it do for him that his own hand couldn't? But then, perhaps the same thing applied to me. It was something I had never thought of doing. Masturbation was something very much discouraged when I was young. Boys were told they would go blind or something far worse. We girls assumed we had nothing to play with.

I took the pink thingy out of its packaging and removed its plastic covering. The latex smell was horrible — like that rubber glue used for carpets. Would I really want to put that disgusting object inside me? I cringed at the thought of it. I took some batteries out of a torch to see what exactly it was supposed to do. I held it in my hand and felt a sort of tremor but it was of no use, it couldn't excite me because the smell was putting me off.

The telephone suddenly started to ring. I quickly put the thingy in the oven to hide it. I didn't want anyone else coming by the window and seeing my shameful object.

I picked up the phone in the hall. "Hi, Alice," said Roger. "We've decided to go on practising this afternoon. I'm going to grab a sandwich with the boys. I'll be back about half-past five."

"I thought you were doing the lawn and the wall?" I said aggrieved.

"Those can wait — this is important. I'll do the lawn before I do the minutes tonight." He sounded a little cross for having his arrangements questioned.

He didn't hang around on the phone, just long enough to say how well he was scoring. After I put down the receiver, I went to get my coat. If Roger could stay out most of the day, so could I. I wanted a few things from the shops anyway, including massage oil and hair remover. I was determined to keep the home fires burning brightly — my marriage was not going to end in dead ashes and frustrated dreams. Roger had made his priorities clear but I was determined to get him to change them.

The massage oil wasn't as easy to find as I'd expected but then perhaps I'd been looking in the wrong places. Baby oil would have been no problem but I wanted something much more exotic — I wanted to turn Roger on, not put him to sleep. I'd just about given up when I saw some in a chemist's window. It was amongst a pile of old stock that was being disposed of at half-price so I bought four bottles — different scents for different moods. I was taking this massage business seriously.

I bought the hair remover at the same time but since I was afraid to ask the assistant if it was suitable for my requirements, I made a poor choice. Well, if I couldn't use it near my delicate membranes, I would have to carefully shave in that particular area — I only hoped my arthritis wouldn't cause a slip-up.

Although I could have done with a new suspender belt, I didn't go near the lingerie shop again. I knew that in my present mood there was no telling how reckless I might get with the housekeeping money. I bought some extravagant chocolates instead, at least I could share them with Roger. That reminded me that it would soon be his birthday so I bought a whole pound of expensive rum truffles and then went to the wine shop for a bottle of his favourite liqueur.

I decided to visit the Coffeepot and relax with a cup of coffee. Since I was on my own, I examined one of my oil purchases and sat thinking about how I would use it. I was beginning to get little thrills of expectation when a familiar voice broke into my thoughts.

"Hello, Alice, I thought I might find you here." Tony, handsome as ever in pale blue jersey, light beige trousers and navy blazer, was looking down at me with a big smile on his face. "Do you mind if I join you?" he asked politely, pulling out a chair in readiness.

"Not at all, it's nice to see you again." I hoped I wasn't sounding a bit too eager.

Tony ordered his coffee, and then started telling me about the problems he'd suffered parking his car since traffic wardens had been patrolling the town centre. But I was only half listening. I was thinking about how he would react to the things I was planning for Roger. Before long, it was Tony, with his unadorned monument to virile manhood, I was seeing on the bed with me, not my husband.

"Alice, am I boring you?" Tony's voice cut across my dreaming.

"Of course not, I was just thinking about what you were saying," I lied. I could hardly tell him that I had him in bed with me. "I really do enjoy being with you, Tony," I told him truthfully. "Roger is out for the day and I thought I was going to be on my own, but here you are, stimulating my thoughts and keeping me company for a little while."

He held me with his sparkling sky-blue eyes. I found their colour quite fascinating. The irises were actually many shades of blue but at that moment his jersey was influencing my view of them. Emphasised by his laughter lines, he seemed to have a permanent twinkle in his eyes. Giving me a beaming smile, he asked, "How about I take you for lunch? I know a super country inn, you'd just love it. Good food, pleasant ambience, quiet — all that sort of thing. No strings attached. Please say yes, it would make me very happy."

"I like making people happy and I enjoy eating," I answered like a silly kid. "Thank you, I would love to come with you."

It was what I wanted but I wondered at the wisdom of accepting his offer. The excitement of being with Tony was leading me astray.

While we were drinking our coffee, Tony said, "You know, Alice, you dance very well. Since Roger is no dancer, I guess you started early?"

"We were taught to dance at school," I told him with a smile, for my thoughts were travelling back to those halcyon days of when I was fourteen.

"You're smiling; I wonder what you're thinking; obviously something very pleasant."

"Of the times the boys came across the town to join us for ballroom dancing classes," I said, seeing again the school hall where we had our sessions. "It certainly brought them down to size. Just imagine, stumbling around on a dance floor in front of a whole class — and with a teacher ready to criticise. It was a hellish torment for the boys."

Tony laughed. "It must have been. Go on, tell me more."

"Some of us girls may have been a bit shy but we were ready to have a go, after all, most of us could already dance a few steps. The profusely sweating boys would huddle into a corner refusing to cooperate. The teacher would winkle one out and treat him mercilessly. She would drag the victim across the floor and slap him up to an embarrassed girl. The rest of the boys would race to grab a girl before the teacher could do it again. Nearly every lesson started the same. You'd think the boys would have got the message after the first time but I guess it was just the herd instinct huddling them together."

"Well, at least, it's one way to get acquainted," said Tony, who seemed to be looking far away and grinning at his own thoughts of teenage youth.

"Yes. Actually, it was at one of those lessons I met a boy called Daniel. I remember him so very well. He was quite good-looking: farm-fresh face, dark curly hair and athletic build. I can just see him at our first dance session — mopping his face with his snowy-white handkerchief every time he had to press up to me."

"Very embarrassing no doubt, but I'm sure it had its compensations," Tony remarked, glancing at my rather full breasts.

I coloured a little and went on talking to cover up the sensual feelings rising within me. I casually crossed my arms to hide the revealing evidence. I saw him smiling at my manoeuvre. Blushing, I chatted even more.

"I was surprised when he asked me to go out with him. We went walking by the river and he showed me how to fish. But I hated to use hooks and would only use nets. He laughed and said I would never catch anything. But he was wrong. I floated a chunk of bread on the water and a large trout took it. That was a laugh. I think the poor fish was tired of being caught and just gave himself up!

"After a few weeks, Dan started to get amorous. He was taking every opportunity to kiss me. But it didn't stop there. Eventually he had a go at fondling. That did it. Bad enough what he did, but he'd just been handling worms, for goodness sake! Anyway, it brought our relationship to an end. I couldn't understand the obsession boys have with breasts. I just hated being fondled."

Tony was watching me very carefully. He took hold of my hands and said, "Hated? That means you don't hate it any longer. That is, when it's done lovingly and the time is right."

By taking my hands, Tony had exposed my raised peaks, which were showing through my clothing. The exposure and Tony's glancing in that direction only increased the erotic sensations I was getting from his presence. I pulled my hands away. Blushing, I said a little nervously, "I think perhaps that is only too obvious."

"Maybe we should be going from here," he said softly, now trying to fix his gaze deep into my eyes. "I think we are both a little worked up; a nice relaxing drive is what we need right now. How about it?"

"It seems like a good idea," I answered, but I had a suspicion that he had other plans for us too and my excitement was hard to keep under control. I kept telling myself that I must resist any advances.

Once outside, we made our way through the streets now busy with shoppers and tourists enjoying the late summer sunshine. Tony gave me a hand into his comfortable Volvo estate and we were off.

In spite of occasional coach traffic jamming the narrow roads in places, it was very pleasant driving up among the mountains and looking down over the picturesque valleys and lakes. But I wasn't concentrating on the scenery; I was finding Tony's company very stimulating — he'd visited so many places and done so many things. I asked him how he managed to keep so very fit and he told me that he worked out at the local gymnasium several times a week, and did a lot of swimming, sailing and walking. "I've walked most of Cumbria's footpaths and bridleways — comes in handy when I want to find somewhere secluded, as I'm sure you will soon appreciate."

What had he in mind? My excitement was rising. I tried to stay cool. "Sounds interesting. I must remember how we get there so I can come again with Roger."

"Good idea. I think you will find the spot quite romantic."

"Now I am intrigued."

"It seems to me, Roger needs his imagination stirring. Perhaps I can help you, help him."

My excitement increased. There was nothing wrong with my imagination even if Roger's was a bit deficient.

Eventually, he stopped the car well off the tourist routes for us to gaze at the view. We were silent so as to appreciate the peace and tranquillity. Sheep quietly grazing on the fells, wispy clouds drifting over the mountain peaks, a few birds flying over woodland, and little white yachts caught by a gentle breeze on the lake below us, were the only movements we could see. I couldn't help but mentally paint the view: rugged mountain peaks, grey and forbidding, standing up from the mottled greens of woods and fields, with the brilliant blue of the water reflecting an azure sky.

By the time we were ordering our meals at a lovely old-world pub, it was after one o'clock. We had decided to eat outside in the garden so as to breathe in the fresh air. It was quite magical and I was feeling so very light-hearted. I sat back in the warm sunshine and drank in the sweetness of the late summer flowers around us.

"Oh, Tony, this is fantastic; thank you so much for bringing me here," I said, sighing with the pleasure of it.

"They have lovely cosy bedrooms too." Seeing my startled look, he quickly added, "Don't be concerned, Alice, I was thinking of you bringing Roger here." His voice softened to a gentle murmur. "But I want you to know, my dear, if Roger can't give you what you need, it would give me real pleasure to satisfy your hunger."

I looked out at the garden, trying to avoid his eyes; my emotions torn between desire and loyalty.

"You do have a yearning to be a complete woman don't you?" he persisted. "Roger's a great guy but he's never struck me as being the tender lover. Perhaps at one time, when you were young and everything was new, but now? He probably treats you like one of his bits of wood — give it a quick planing, speedily bore it, and complete a dowel joint to his satisfaction. Am I right?"

I kept my face turned away — he was far too intuitive for comfort.

"You don't have to say anything, your silence answers my question," he said tenderly. "I don't want to split up a marriage — not my style. But I do enjoy helping women realise their full sexuality. No strings. If anything, I've helped marriages survive. You'd be surprised how many. Once a woman knows what she wants, she can show her husband the right way — to their mutual advantage. How can you know what you're missing, if you've never had it?"

His words were so apt, so knowing. I felt like asking him to take me, show me, thrill me — give me an orgasm! But my reasoning self held my lips sealed.

The waitress, bringing our food, broke the silence. "This looks delicious," I said and I glanced up to see Tony looking at me; his smile was saying that he understood.

"Thanks, I think we have everything we need," he said to the girl, and she left us to get on with our meal. Turning to me, he said quietly, "Are you sure you have everything you want, Alice?"

I looked straight into his eyes, "Yes, of course," I said defiantly, but then seeing his disbelieving smile, I confessed, "No, but I could never contemplate adultery."

"Let's eat up, we can talk about it later, that is, if you want to. This really is a magnificent Cumberland sausage. How's your poached salmon?"

I guess the topics of conversation were connected but everything seemed quite unreal. My nerve endings were becoming exceedingly alive to the closeness of Tony. He was so much in tune with my thoughts and feelings, it was uncanny.

The delicious meal took my attention for a while and I would have lingered in that delightful place but Tony had other plans. The waitress came to ask us if we wanted a sweet but he declined for both of us and said that we had to be leaving. "Are you happy to go now?" he asked me and I nodded rather demurely guessing as to what he had in mind.

The waitress handed Tony the bill. "You pay at the bar, sir," she said sweetly.

I reached for the slip of paper. Tony simply put up a hand and, slipping his wallet from his trouser pocket, walked inside to pay the bill. I took the opportunity to visit the toilet. I saw myself in the mirror. Hair a little untidy maybe, but my face was pleasantly flushed, my unremarkable blue-grey and hazel eyes were shining brightly, and my lips seemed to be a little fuller with a youthful curl at the corners. There was no doubt about it, just being with Tony did something for me and whatever it was I could take home to Roger. Surely any man would prefer a brighter, livelier wife? I had no reason to feel guilty; after all, I was merely enjoying Tony's company, not looking for extramarital sex.

Tony drove his Volvo carefully down the narrow lanes, until stopping near a stream that came tumbling down a hillside. Being the perfect gentleman, he assisted me out of the car. We walked alongside the gurgling rushing water for a while and then turned away to climb up amongst the trees. The woods thickened and the main path disappeared, branching into a number of small tracks. But we went on walking, enjoying the exercise and each other's company. The ground was getting rather rough but the trees eventually thinned out again and I heard a bubbling stream running close by. A few more steps and a small tarn, glinting in the afternoon sunshine, appeared through the trees in front us. Everywhere was so very peaceful with only wildlife breaking the silence.

"It really is lovely here," I whispered, afraid to break the sanctity of the place. "I think we should be getting back though, time's getting on," I said, but more concerned that I was alone with Tony in such an isolated spot.

I was sexually alive to his presence, wanting his touch and yet afraid of where it might lead. I felt him come up close behind me and I knew what was going to happen. He turned me to him. Holding my shoulders, he kissed me lightly on the lips. It was just heavenly — so tender and yet gently stimulating. I didn't resist. Somehow it seemed the natural thing for him to do and I loved every moment of it. He put me against a tree and kissed me again, this time a little more firmly. I sighed deeply with pleasure and then pleaded, "No more, Tony, we've gone too far already."

"Are you sure, Alice?" he asked. Responding to my silence, he whispered, "Just relax — let go. Let me spend a few moments feeding your needs. Nothing else." He gently stroked my hair. "I'll do nothing you're not ready for, it's not my style."

Taking off his blazer, he threw it on the ground. He pushed up the sleeves of his blue cashmere jersey, exposing his darkly tanned forearms covered with golden hair bleached by the sun. I was enthralled and tremulous as he unbuttoned my jacket and allowed his hands to wander to the small of my back. Pulling me close to him, he kissed me once again.

"All right, Alice?" he almost sighed in my ear.

"Yes, but enough, Tony. Please, let me go now."

Of course, he knew I wanted more but he respected my plea. No doubt it was as hard for him to pull away as it was for me. I could tell that he was aroused — men can't hide that sort of thing. His sexuality drew me like a magnet but I loved Roger and would not be unfaithful to him. Many women had kissed Roger, and many men had kissed me over the years, some putting more effort into it than others. But kissing at parties and under the mistletoe was a different ball game to being alone with a man in an isolated spot. It had been a beautiful experience and as much as my body cried out for satisfaction, I had to be satisfied with a sensuous kiss and return home to my husband for the full treatment.

As he drove me home, I sat thinking things through. Somehow, I had to get through to Roger, he was the one who should be bringing my sexuality to life. Oh, why couldn't he see it for himself? Perhaps it was because neither of us had known anything different. We had lost nothing since our marriage, it wasn't completely there to begin with.

Occasionally, Tony looked at me and smiled. "Feeling all right?"

I smiled back at him. "Fine. But it can't go on, Tony, it isn't fair to Roger."

"We'll see. I won't push you into a relationship you don't want. Think of today as education. Get Roger to take you to places like we've been today. After lunching in a country pub, go walking off the beaten track where you can make wild exciting love under the open blue sky. There's nothing like untamed nature to bring out a man's primitive urges."

My mind went back to the place we had left. I knew with Tony, making love would indeed be wild and passionate, but with Roger? "Mm, it's a lovely thought," I told him wistfully.

"Are we still dancing this week?" he asked, glancing briefly in my direction to give me an encouraging smile.

"Yes, please," I said eagerly.

He smiled at me again and said that he was looking forward to having me in his arms once more. I caught my breath as my erotic zones began dancing with my pleasurable thoughts.

He stopped his car outside my house and insisted on getting out to open the passenger door. He helped me out and reached inside for my things.

He turned to go. "Thanks, Alice, I have really enjoyed our time together, we must do it again sometime."

I simply smiled and changed the subject. "Would you like to come in and have a word with Roger? His car's in the drive, so he must be home."

We had both agreed not to hide the fact that we had been out together. I didn't want the deceit and he preferred as much openness as possible. We walked up to the house with Tony admiring the shrubs and neatly trimmed grass. I could hear the mower in the back garden and knew that it would be Roger cutting the lawn into perfectly measured stripes. Tony came into the house with me, carrying my bags from the morning's shopping.

As soon as we approached the kitchen door, a dreadful smell met our noses.

"Roger isn't heating up that tripe and onions again is he?" Tony quipped.

"Oh, no!" I shrieked, suddenly remembering where I'd hidden my pink thingy.

When I opened the door into the kitchen the smell of burning rubber was horrific. Standing back, I carefully opened the oven door and black smoke came billowing out, reaching into the hall where it set off the smoke alarm. I closed the oven door quickly, switched off the oven and turned on the extractor fan. I closed the door into the hall and opened the one leading outside.

Tony was very concerned. "Can I help?"

"Thanks, but I know what it is," I said, trying hard not to giggle.

Tony was clearly puzzled but waited patiently for me to explain.

"Hold on and I'll show you," I said, running water into the sink.

I put on my oven mitts and carefully opened the oven door again. Not so much smoke this time, which was just as well as we were beginning to choke on it. I produced a blackened shrivelled rubber object from the oven.

"Well, that's one way to sterilise it!" I said laughing.

Before long, I was choking and giggling at the same time. Tony looked closer at the thing floating in the sink. When he realised what it was, he shook with laughter.

"But how?" He started to ask.

"It's a long story," I interrupted. "Roger is on his way in — I'll tell you later," and I grabbed hold of my burnt sacrifice and wrapped it in a plastic bag ready for the dustbin.

"What the hell is going on?" demanded Roger. Then he saw Tony through the disgusting smoke. "Started the fire or come to put it out?"

They both laughed and started choking. Roger led Tony to the door for some fresh air.

"Did you put the oven on, Roger?" I asked, feeling a little apprehensive.

"Yes, who else?" he responded rather impatiently. "I was going to put in the beef casserole I should have had at lunchtime. But I started on this job and forgot about it." He sniffed the lingering acrid smoke. "What was in the oven? It smells like burning rubber."

"I left some rubber gloves inside the oven when I was cleaning it this morning and forgot to finish the job," I lied. I planned to tell Roger the truth at a more suitable time. "I went out shopping and met Tony in the Coffeepot. He took me a little drive and we had lunch together in a grand little pub. You don't mind do you?"

"Of course not, Tony needs a bit of company." Smiling, he turned to Tony. "Pity Alice hasn't got a younger sister. Just as well she's an old wrinkly — well, too old for someone who likes a bit of skirt. I could get jealous."

"I think you should get jealous," said Tony gallantly. "Alice might have reached her three score years and ten but she's quite a handsome woman."

"She's not bad — she suits me," Roger answered, putting an arm around me and giving me a hug. "Are you eating with us tonight, Tony?"

"Thanks, but I think Alice has seen enough of me today."

"We're going to have tripe soup for starters. Can't I tempt you?" Roger pleaded.

"Almost, but I'll do my best to resist. Thanks for asking but some other time. I really must be getting back."

"What a pity, it's my own recipe," Roger said, walking with him to the door.

"Why don't you come to a tea dance?" Tony asked Roger, as he was about to leave. "I thought I would take Alice again on Friday — if that's all right with you. It would be great if you joined us."

"I did something like that many years ago and ruined her happy time. No thanks, not my thing," said Roger shaking his head. "Anyway, I'm behind with the garden. Must get the shrubs done this week — if the old joints let me."

"Let me massage them for you," I put in quickly. "I bought some oil today; just for you, Roger darling."

"Now there's an offer," observed Tony. "I'll leave you lovebirds to get on with it." Giving me a farewell smile, he left by the front door.

Roger saw him to his Volvo, chatting about all the things he had to get done before the end of the summer. He came back nodding his head. "He's a good guy but don't presume on his friendship with me too much. I wouldn't want him to clear off and leave the Committee — we need him."

Later on, I persuaded Roger to leave the minutes he'd been working on. I said I would use his rough notes and do him a first draft in the morning. I managed to get him to have a relaxing soak in the bath after a quick dip myself. It didn't take much doing for him to allow me to wash his back in a gentle caressing manner. It was just one step away from the full body massage.

Having let go of planning the multiplicity of tasks he had in mind for the near future, the reality of which would require him to be mentally and physically agile past the age of ninety-nine, he obliged my latest whim. He stretched out on the bed in all his manhood glory — bottom side up.

The appreciative moans and groans were reward enough for the stress I was putting on my back and joints. While I was on my knees, following the path of his muscles with my oiled hands, I mused what it might be like if we were having sex with me on top. After a good massage, I could ride him like I'd seen the lovers on television — bobbing up and down like a jockey in the Grand National.

It was a very interesting prospect but my knees were already objecting to their present stressful situation. Even so, I was prepared for a little discomfort in the cause of true love.

"Mmm, that was great," Roger said appreciatively when I finally had to stop.

"Do you like the aroma of the oil? Don't you think it's rather sexy?"

"You're sex-mad, woman," he joked. "Can't you use liniment? Better for my aches and pains." This time he was serious.

"Turn over, I want to look at you," I said lovingly.

"What on earth for? I look like a beached whale," he chuckled, but he turned over to oblige me.

"No, you don't, Roger. On your back you look great. Your belly is quite flat. Your face is smooth too — no wrinkles. And the rest of you hasn't changed since the day we were married."

"How long is it since your eyes were tested?"

"You'll never be any different to me, Roger."

I was running my fingers over his body and kissing him gently — his lips, his chest, his belly, his....

"What are you up to?" he asked suspiciously, just as I was tickling my nose on his wiry hair, but he wasn't resisting my kisses, in fact, as he lay back relaxed, he was getting very aroused.

"Don't you think it's time we tried something new?" I whispered, trying to be seductive.

"Take that bag off for starters then," he responded in his playful gruff manner.

He was, of course, referring to my cotton housecoat. This was going better than I had imagined and I hadn't even used the other weapons in my arsenal — the slinky nightdress and the red undies.

I took off the offending garment and stood before him, wishing I had made the effort to get rid of my pubic hair — it looked like a jumble of fuse wire. The rice-pudding-skin apron was just above his eye level and I wished I had something to drape over it. I put my hands to the loose flap and pulled it in. "I wish I could get rid of this," I said apologetically.

"Come here," he said, stretching out his arms. "You'll always be beautiful as the day we met."

With great expectations, I moved close to his body and prepared myself for that oral communication we had not yet tasted. His hands ran over my breasts and then his mouth followed the path of his fingers — how I wished his dentist would file that chipped front tooth! When I flinched he murmured an apology and then returned to his comforter. His fingers began moving further south. On arriving at his destination, he immediately started up his planing wood action, quickly followed by rapid filing of metal. It was too soon and too quick. Feeling the volcano within him about to erupt, he turned me on my back and kept his pile driver on full throttle for the whole of twenty seconds before collapsing.

'You wicked woman," he sighed, "you'll wear me out."

Disappointed, I slipped on my housecoat and went downstairs to make his hot chocolate, wondering if we would ever get our act together.

Chapter six

A man's best friend

I deliberately kept out of the Coffeepot for the rest of that week, seeing Tony would only increase my growing desire to experience what I knew he could, and would, be pleased to give me. I had things to do, including making a special iced cake for Roger's birthday and organising a surprise party for later on in the month. I'd also promised an old friend, Betty Mayfield, to meet up with her for coffee on the Thursday.

I rang Betty and asked her if we could meet at the café opposite the local supermarket. We both had shopping to do and it was very convenient. They also served good coffee and the most delicious cream cakes. I could do without the latter but I needed to do a bit of anxiety eating. Evidently, Betty was feeling the same. Two cream horns for a short size-eighteen woman, who's trying to slim because her favourite clothes are refusing to span her girth, are unlikely to solve her clothing difficulties. I concluded she must have a very real problem. It didn't take her long to spill it out.

"Albert has found himself a floozie half his age," she complained, and rightly so. "Well, not exactly half his age but she can only be in her forties."

"How awful for you. Is he serious about her?" I sympathised.

"Don't know — not enough to want a divorce. I think he wants a last fling before he's past it," she said, eyeing the tempting cakes turning on the lit-up carousel.

"Are men ever past it?" I asked. "With these new drugs, they can be with it until they're measured for their wooden suits."

She gave a little snort in reply. I appreciated how Albert must be feeling. He'd had thirty-five years of marriage to a woman who'd always been diffident about sex — she complained about him often enough. I was dreading being asked for advice.

"Do you think I should throw him out?"

I inwardly groaned. "Sounds a bit drastic."

"If he wants her, she can have him," she said vehemently, between mouthfuls of cream. "He's useless anyway."

"Oh, I wouldn't say that, Betty. Albert has his good points."

"He's not a bit like your Roger. Albert wouldn't know a nail from a screw. The shelves he put up, fell down. Did I tell you about it?"

She told me every time we met for a chat. To her, Albert was useless and my Roger was a shining example of manhood: he fixed things, built things, knew things. If Betty had a problem, Roger would know what to do, what's more he had the energy to lift, shift, throw and mow, saw, hammer and screw. Roger was a human dynamo and the object of Betty's complete adoration. Albert, being useless, paid someone to do jobs around the house. It gave him time to do the things he wanted to do but to which she objected. She said Albert wasted money on buying her flowers and fattening chocolates — her favourites so she couldn't resist them. She complained about the cruises they went on, the exotic places they visited and the surprise visits to theatres.

I felt like asking her if Albert ever craved for tripe and onions and insisted on dragging her on industrial archaeology trails. And if she never had the opportunity to type boring minutes for him, or live in a tip while he spent months and years on home improvements. Poor Betty, life was clearly tough with Albert for a husband.

"Sometimes Albert behaves as though we were just married; he's always after sex. I get weary of it. I mean, at our age, it's ridiculous don't you think?" She gave me no time to answer. "Once a month should be enough for any man — too generous really for respectable people like us," she said with a sniff.

"Perhaps he needs to change his technique. You know, do something different," I suggested, trying to be helpful.

She leaned over to whisper, "My dear, I wouldn't like to tell you what Albert's wanted to try — it just isn't decent. There's only one civilised way, the rest isn't natural." She gave another sniff and stuffed her mouth with cream horn, which made me think that she was suppressing desires impossible for her to admit to.

So now Albert had found himself another woman who was both willing and happy to satisfy his needs. I felt like saying, "Good luck to him!" Albert had always been so very attentive to Betty. Every time we'd been out in a foursome, he'd waited on her hand and foot, supplying her wants before she even asked — and her wants were very many. Trying to be sympathetic while feeling like giving her a good shake, I gave her the benefit of my wisdom.

"It seems to me, Betty, that you have a good husband in Albert — one worth hanging on to. You'd really miss him if you sent him packing. Then if it came to a divorce, everything would be split; you'd both lose half of what you now share."

"Yes, I know. Don't think I haven't thought about the disadvantages," she said, scooping up a dollop of cream with a last bit of pastry. "But things can't go on as they are; people talk — it's so embarrassing." She sounded exceedingly agitated and was eyeing the carousel of cakes again.

"Has Albert changed towards you?" I asked, trying to get an overall view of the situation. "I mean, is he nasty and horrid? No more flowers and chocolates? No more outings and taking care of you? No running you around in the car. You know, that sort of thing?"

"Oh, no. He's got a guilty conscience and spends more money than ever. He's even getting the patio done with decking just like on television. I've always wanted something doing with that bit at the back," she said, shrugging her shoulders and smirking as though getting what she wanted was absolute proof of Albert's adultery.

"I thought you had that nice paving done just a few years ago." I replied, trying to keep envy out of my voice — I'm still waiting for Roger to do ours.

"Yes, but things have improved since then," she said impatiently, as if I'd asked a silly question.

I sipped my coffee, giving myself time to think. In many ways, Betty was a kind and generous person. She would visit the sick and take them flowers, host coffee mornings for the starving poor and shop for a housebound neighbour — or, at least, send Albert out on the goodwill missions. She was also kind to animals and wrote frequently to her MP about the cruelty of transporting live animals. But Albert was a lovely man and had put a great deal into his marriage. Surely he must have good reasons to go astray? I put down my cup and faced Betty, trying to ignore the blob of cream at the end of her nose.

"It seems to me, Betty, many things have improved for you since Albert got his girlfriend," I told her, my irritation beginning to show. "If you don't want what he wants, can't you put up with the gossip? It does make you into a bit of a celebrity — the wronged wife deserving of support and sympathy."

Betty folded her arms and gave a little snort. "It's all right for you — you have that lovely Roger," she said heatedly. "My Albert's turning out to be just like that Tony Bradshaw. I don't want people thinking I'm like Edith, she's a cold unfeeling person, but I'm not, I just like things in moderation," she said with a sniff. She lowered her voice to pass on a bit of juicy gossip. "Tony's absolutely sex mad from what I hear."

"Oh, really? I wouldn't know."

I pointed out the blob of offending cream on her nose. It had to go. With her last remark, I was finding it difficult enough keeping my face straight. Unperturbed, she wiped it away with her napkin and continued in full flood.

"I don't want my husband bracketed with a man like Tony. Apart from which, why should he have the privileges of marriage and act like he's single? You can't have your cake and eat it," she declared pompously, moving her eyes from the crumbs on her plate towards the turning carousel.

I was getting cross at Betty's one-sided approach to her problem. "From what you say, he isn't getting any cake."

"I didn't say that. He watches television and it gives him ideas — disgusting ideas — if you know what I mean," she said, leaning over and giving a little nod and showing me the whites of her eyes. "As long as he's normal I don't object to him doing it occasionally. I'm not heartless like Edith; a man has his needs. He's got nothing to complain of. That is what makes me so angry!"

Betty's grumbling was making me feel uncomfortable about my own desires and I'd had enough of it. "Since he's so unreasonable, I guess you'll just have to dump him then," I advised her, but hoping she wouldn't take me seriously. "He can have his Miss Free and Easy and you can find someone like Roger who might enjoy your offering of rock buns when he needs a nibble!"

Betty was speechless — which makes a change. So I took the opportunity to give her a few words of wisdom. "You have a treasure in Albert. Why don't you try to be a little more accommodating? Either give way a bit, or let him have his fling? Life's too short to quarrel. We're too soon over the hill — enjoy what you've got before the sun goes down and you with it."

She was utterly shocked. She raised her eyebrows, turning her forehead into a ploughed field. "Really, Alice, I am surprised at you. I had no idea you were so liberal. I thought you would understand, but you're on Albert's side." She sounded terribly hurt.

"I'm not on anybody's side. I do understand — better than you think," I told her with feeling. "I'm at least ten years older than you are, Betty, and that hilltop draws closer every day." I stood up. "I have to go now, Roger wants his lunch early. Unlike Albert, he expects his meals ready spot on time and served with a dash of humble adoration. I'll see you again sometime."

When I arrived home, I found an e-mail waiting for me on the computer. It was from my old friend, Rosie. We write a long letter to each other once or twice a year but we haven't met for some time. She and her family moved abroad about the time we moved out of the area of my youth. I printed the message for easy reading. While Roger's gammon was grilling, I sat down in the kitchen to read Rosie's news.

Towards the end of the letter, she mentioned that her brother, Alfred, had died just after Christmas. She said that he had been quite deaf and almost blind for some time, and had been in a nursing home for six months. He had become dreadfully confused and was not safe to be living alone. Evidently he'd lost half his weight and was almost unrecognisable. It came as quite a blow to me, far more than Rosie would have realised.

Turning down the grill so as not to singe Roger's gammon while I was preparing the rest of the meal, I let my mind wander back to the days of my youth and when I first met Alfred. It must have been soon after the war when I was a young teenager. I liked him at first sight. He was tall with curly blond hair, and had beautiful blue eyes. With a powerful physique similar to Johnny Weissmuller of Tarzan fame, he stood out in a crowd. How sad that old age had brought him so low.

Unknown to anyone, we once had a little innocent affair going. One day he caught me alone in my friend's house. He took me in his arms and kissed me.

I was stunned. My heart sprinted for several minutes trying to keep up with my emotions. Finally, he released me and said he was sorry.

"Don't be," I said. "I quite enjoyed it."

Holding me even closer, he kissed me again and I was feeling a little dizzy with the passion of it. He said softly, "I've wanted to kiss you ever since I got home."

I was amazed by the admission but too stunned by the kissing to say anything.

"Please don't say anything," he whispered, when we heard someone coming. "I'm much too old to be kissing a youngster like you. Put it down to just getting back from the war. You're like a fresh mountain stream to a thirsty man."

Yes, he was a bit of a poet too. I didn't tell a soul. I was very flattered that a very much older man should find me attractive and enjoy kissing me. Apart from being taken by surprise, I can't say that the heavens opened and I heard angelic music, or that the earth shifted under my feet but it was quite an experience and the secrecy made it even more exciting.

The secret relationship went on for a few weeks but I knew it wouldn't last. I was growing quite fond of him but the age difference was too great. He was old enough to be my father. Eventually he told me that he needed more from a woman and I was too young for that sort of thing. At least, having tried for a bit extra and been refused, he was honest enough to make a clean break.

Coming back to Rosie's letter, I suddenly realised that if the relationship had progressed — became open and led to marriage — I would have had many years of caring for an elderly husband and would now be a grieving widow. I looked out of the window and saw Roger putting away his gardening tools. I sighed deeply. "Don't ever leave me, Roger, I couldn't bear it." A tear trickled down my cheek.

Heat and smoke set off the fire alarm — I had forgotten Roger's gammon! Roger came in as I was moving it from under the heat.

"What's burning now? A pair of socks this time?" He saw his smoking gammon as I was forking it on to a plate. "You really must keep your mind on the job — always going off on flights of fancy." There was a hiss from the hob. "The peas are boiling over now." He picked the pan up as I reached for a cloth to mop up the water. He saw my tears. "It's not that bad, Alice. I can have a poached egg like you. Look, there's a bit of the steak that's not quite black."

My tears flowed even more.

"Come on, Alice." He wrapped his dirty hands and arms around me. "It's only a bit of meat."

"I love you, Roger," I said between sobs.

He sighed. "But why are you crying?"

"Oh, it's nothing. An old friend has died. It just makes you think — that's all."

He gave me a bit of a cuddle. "Go and get your hair done, it will make you feel better."

He hadn't even noticed. "Roger, I had it done this morning before I met Betty Mayfield for coffee."

"Oh, now I understand, she told you about Albert. Don't worry, Alice, I've told you before, I don't need another woman, you're as much as I can handle."

Roger intended being out for the whole of Friday with his bowls match business, so during the morning, I decided to do my hair-removal thing. Throughout the week, I had finished two lots of minutes for him and written his letters, done his washing, cooked his food, baked him his cakes and pastries. I had been acting the good little wife he'd always known me to be, now I was going to let my hair down, or in this case, get rid of it.

It wasn't as if I intended exposing the area to anyone other than Roger, or that I expected to get it touched, fondled or handled in any way whatsoever — by any person known or unknown — until Roger had recovered from his exertions earlier in the week. Apart from which, I wanted to do it for my own satisfaction of knowing what it would feel like after a proper job had been done on the area. The shaves I received in hospital were grim affairs, leaving the skin prickly with stubbled hair.

Having completed the task, not an easy one with my back and knees still creaking from massaging Roger, I looked at myself in the mirror. I burst out laughing. Being used to certain things, it comes as a great surprise when a sudden change takes place. Smooth skin instead of greying wiry hair is one thing but the shape of the area also appeared to have undergone change. My triangle of old fuse wire had become a duck's bill sideways on. As I opened my legs the split parted making the appearance even more hilarious. I opened and closed my legs going "quack-quack" and howled in amusement.

The doorbell ringing quickly sobered me up.

I slipped on a dressing gown and went to the window. Of all people, it was Clive waiting on the doorstep. Calling to him through the open window, I said I'd be down in just a couple of minutes. I slipped on a lightweight jumper and a pair of trousers to make myself decent and ran downstairs, wondering why he'd come when he must have known Roger would be out.

I took Clive into the kitchen and made him a cup of coffee. He sat down and helped himself to a home-made biscuit from a batch I'd baked earlier on. "These are nice," he said. "Make them yourself?"

"I bake most of our cakes and goodies, but you haven't come here to taste my culinary delights have you?"

"It's worth doing just for that — these are very good," he said, helping himself to another biscuit from the cooling tray. "I was wondering if you were dancing this afternoon, if you would like to request something. I thought I might sing today. Anything you fancy?"

"That's kind of you, Clive. Can't think of anything offhand though."

I was wondering if I was going to have to do some more baking — Clive had surreptitiously slipped a couple of biscuits into his pocket. I didn't mind really. Barbara was always helping me out with something or other, and Clive gave Roger a hand when needed, especially with ladder jobs.

"How about 'My Way'?" he suggested, spraying a few crumbs at the same time.

"Mmm, sounds good to me."

"I thought so. I've been watching you, Alice; you've really come alive lately. Something's making you brighter and, if I might be allowed to say so, younger and even more beautiful." He gave me a wink. "Could it be Roger's magazines I ask myself?"

I was shocked. "Good heavens, Clive, I hope you haven't mentioned that magazine to Roger, he knows nothing about it."

"Actually, no. No reason to really. But I thought it was his." He seemed puzzled.

"I suppose Barbara told you about seeing it. I only bought it for a laugh. I had no idea what was in it," I lied, rather unconvincingly.

He looked at me with a whimsical smile on his face. "It's all right, Alice, no need to be coy; I've got a pile of them in the wardrobe. You can borrow some if you like. They've pepped up our marriage routine quite a bit; but perhaps Roger doesn't need ideas, eh?"

He gave me a saucy wink and I felt a bit flustered. All this sex business was moving too fast.

"Good heavens, Roger would be devastated if he heard this conversation. He's not like that. Neither am I, for that matter. I told you, I only bought the magazine for a laugh."

I turned to the sink and began washing a few dishes to hide my blushes and sense of confusion. I didn't hear Clive come up behind me. He started speaking in a gentle, friendly manner.

"You've changed lately, Alice. Babs told me about the magazine but I've seen you with Tony. That man brings out the real you."

"Just a different side of me, that's all. We are all complex personalities."

"I agree. But most of us want to experience what life has to offer before that heart attack, stroke or whatever the grim reaper has in mind for each of us. Modern youth has it all — we oldies have a lot of catching up to do."

I was leaning over the sink with tears in my eyes, thinking of poor Alfred. Clive had summed things up very nicely. He could tell I was upset and he put his hand on my shoulder. "I'm sorry if I've offended you," he said gently, sounding both contrite and anxious.

"No, you haven't," I replied with my voice a little shaky. "I'm just not used to all this sort of thing. I guess I'm going through an old-age crisis or something. I don't think Roger understands — he's all right you see. He doesn't need any more than he's got already. Oh, my goodness, he'd be horrified if he knew I was talking like this. Please, let it drop, Clive."

He patted my shoulder. "I'll see you at the tea dance and I'll be singing your song. Enjoy Tony's dancing — he's a good guy. And whatever you do in life, Alice, do it your way."

Clive left me standing at the sink in a state of bemusement. I eventually came to and realised I had been washing the same dish for the last few minutes. I made myself a coffee and sat down to think about Roger and me.

To have sex twice in a fortnight is remarkable enough but to expect him to perform at the drop of a hat, or knickers in my case, would force him to rearrange his priorities and he'd never allow that. "Oh, Roger! Why can't you want it like I do?" I yelled at the ceiling. "Why won't you thrill me, fill me, wear me out with ecstasy?"

I gave a very heavy sigh. I picked up another dish before realising the phone was ringing. Could this be Roger saying he was coming home, that he'd had a sudden revelation and wanted to spend the afternoon with me to perfect our relationship? I went into the hall and picked up the receiver. "Hello?"

"Hello, Granny, it's me," said my teenage granddaughter, Jenny. "We're going to talk about life in the forties and fifties at school this afternoon. We've got as far as relationships. Did you have many boyfriends, Granny? Would you mind telling me what you did together? I mean dancing, and that sort of thing. I know about the other — everybody does that."

Jenny's assumption, that everybody engaged in sex then as they do now, made me think very hard about what is normal in life. It came out in our little talk that I'd only had one bed-partner during the whole of my lifetime. Jenny found that quite amazing and totally impractical. But I wondered if casual sex was a good thing. Surely sexual experience should be in the context of a stable relationship? But I was no longer certain about anything where sex was involved. It was all most disconcerting.

After Jenny had finished her investigation of my past lovers, or rather lack of them, I noticed time was slipping by and I hurried to get dressed. Leaving thoughts of my past aside, I put my stockings on, carefully rolling them down to the toe before slipping them over my feet. But Tony was now looming in my mind and butterflies were playing havoc with my guts. While putting on the second stocking, I caught a nail on the fine threads and saw the resulting ladder zip down the leg. "Damn!" I exclaimed aloud and reached for another pair. Even as I did so, I could see Tony's fingers tracing the ladder and telling me that I worried too much.

I sat for a few moments and tried to calm down. I told myself that I was acting like a lovesick teenager. Unbidden, my first love came into my mind. Eric, the rotter, cad, bounder, the breaker of hearts — wanting my knickers to win a bet and boast to his pals! Would he have wanted them if he knew they were navy-blue gym knickers? Probably, boys were more interested in what they covered.

I was on my way downstairs when I stopped and went back up again. I stripped off my white cotton panties to replace them with my black lacy knickers. I seemed to feel the need for more exotic underwear. I went downstairs just as the phone was ringing again — another delay.

"Hello?" I said, picking up the receiver. I've stopped giving our number or our name to callers — can't remember why. Probably Roger told me not to and that was reason enough.

A familiar soft cultured voice sounded on the line. "Alice?"

"Tony?"

"Yes. I'm so sorry, Alice, I can't make it this afternoon. Something's come up."

"Oh, I see. That's all right, Tony," I said cheerfully, but I didn't mean it.

"It won't stop you going to the dance will it?" He sounded anxious.

I was shattered but perhaps it was for the best. The mood I was in, Tony could have taken me off and done anything with me.

"I don't think I can go on my own but it doesn't matter, I'm not that bothered about going."

"I think you are actually; you were looking forward to it as much as me. Look, I've got an idea. I know your neighbour Cyril wants to go. Has been for a while but Glenda refuses to go with him. He was thinking of going this afternoon. I'm about to ring him. Suppose I pick you up at the same time and drop you both off at the Victoria Hall?"

I cringed at the prospect of dancing with Cyril but I wanted to see Tony. Was being with Cyril worth a few minutes with Tony? I didn't think so. I was just about to give a polite refusal when Tony made a further proposition.

"Actually, Alice, I was hoping you would say yes. I thought I could pick you up from the dance hall about half-three, after I've seen my solicitor. We could take a little drive somewhere. Afterwards, I could take you home and sample Roger's tripe and onions. He invited me when I saw him the other day — didn't he mention it?"

"No, but then he's always asking people to sample his favourite Friday special but they never turn up. No prizes for guessing why."

"Well, after two of us eating onions, I guess everyone at the committee meeting will know he had a guest tonight." I could hear him laughing.

I had to laugh with him — he was so right.

"Will you go with Cyril then, and let me pick you up later at the hall?"

I felt ridiculously excited. My nerves were making me shaky and I couldn't think straight. I knew I must not accept; being alone with Tony was dangerous. But adrenaline was pumping through my veins and my whole being was on fire to be with him and suffer, or rather, delight in the consequences.

"But what about Cyril?" I asked, my sensible-self looking for excuses not to be alone with Tony. "How will he get home?"

"Anyone will drop him off. It's less than a mile to walk anyway. He just needs encouragement to go — not to come home."

"Oh, I suppose so."

"I'll see you in about ten minutes then."

"Yes, I look forward to it," I said, hardly able to keep the excitement out of my voice.

"And, Alice, if I get the opportunity and the time seems right, I'll try to get Roger to talk about his love life tonight. Perhaps work him round to thinking more deeply about your relationship and how he can improve things. You understand me, don't you?" He sounded so very gentle and encouraging, how could I help but warm to him?

"Yes, Tony, I do, and thank-you, I'd like that," I said, but it was the afternoon events that were of more concern to me, the rest I could think about later.

Just as he said he would, Tony picked me up ten minutes later. Cyril was already in the car and smiling cheerfully.

"Hello, nice to see you again, Alice," he said, giving me a big smile.

He looked a different man. Was it getting out of Glenda's clutches or had he been taking some rejuvenating tonic?

"You look very smart, Cyril."

"I like to dress up occasionally. I used to do a lot of it you know — dancing I mean. Years ago I won a few cups for ballroom dancing," he said, beaming with pride. "Can't get Glenda to go though — she thinks we're both past it." His voice actually changed at the mention of his wife's name. I thought I heard him softly mutter, "Silly bitch," but couldn't swear to it.

I couldn't get over Cyril's transformation. With him looking so young and sprightly, I was actually looking forward to dancing with him.

"I'm afraid you outclass me, Cyril," I told him in all honesty. "I have no medals or cups for dancing."

"We could change all that," he replied with a twinkle in his eye.

Was this really the man who'd talked so woefully to me about his little problem with Glenda? I wondered if he had managed to get himself that sex toy he wanted and if the thing really did work wonders.

"I hope you got what you were looking for, Cyril," I said, just loud enough for him alone to hear. "You remember mentioning it when you came for the minutes?" I wondered if I was being too bold with such a personal question.

His eyes were really sparkling now. "How could I forget? I rang Tony before Glenda got home and he gave me a bit of help in the right direction. Going to this tea dance is another of his ideas. Yes, Tony's a real friend in times of need."

I wondered if Cyril had told Tony what he'd seen me with. I looked at Tony; he'd been silent since picking me up. Of course, he had to concentrate on driving but I had an idea he was giving Cyril a chance to talk to me, especially since he'd sat us both in the back seats. From where I was sitting, I could see Tony had a contented look on his face. Perhaps things were working out well for him too. He saw me in his mirror looking at him and he gave me a broad smile. My heart seemed to give a little flutter and I looked away, afraid of showing my feelings.

We arrived at the Victoria Hall and Tony stepped out to open the passenger doors and to give me a hand. He was always the perfect gentleman in respect of old-fashioned courtesies. I like that sort of thing. No way would I ever join the bra-burning brigade! As soon as Cyril removed himself, Tony said his farewells and drove off leaving the two of us to join the dancing.

There were more people in the hall than the previous week and the atmosphere was quite lively. As soon as I returned from the cloakroom, Cyril walked towards me to ask for a dance. Here was a dapper, straight-backed dance enthusiast; amazingly, the same man that just a few days ago looked bent, old and decrepit. Soon he was sweeping me across the floor with a lively body rhythm. He was confidently holding me close with one hand lightly, but firmly, pressed against my back and the other one holding my hand in exactly the correct position; his whole body language ensuring I followed his lead with utmost ease.

What a dancer! No wonder he'd won competitions in his younger days. I was feeling full of youthful vigour again and so happy I wanted to shout for joy. As we passed the platform I could see Clive looking at me while blowing a trombone. He gave me another of his winks and I couldn't hold in a little laugh.

"You sound happy," remarked Cyril. "I hope it's with pleasure and not because of my dancing."

"Oh, but it is because of your dancing; you're fantastic and you make me feel so light-hearted."

At that moment, the dance came to an end and we were about to move to a table when Clive spoke over the microphone. He told us he was going to sing, "I did it my way" for a very special lady, and that he was going to accompany himself on the piano.

I felt quite excited, Clive was singing especially for me, even if a little voice within told me that he said the same thing to all the ladies. I sat back soaking in the mood, rather than the words of the song. Clive's deep husky voice sounded quite sexy and it suited my frame of mind.

The two hours before Tony was due to collect me just flew past. I had a word with Madge and Frank and one or two others, but most of the time I was dancing with Cyril. After we had been on the floor for a little while, he began to talk more. He shocked me out of my complacency by saying, "How did you find your pink thingy? Any satisfaction?"

"Not really, I found it too hot to handle," I told him, smiling to myself.

"Really? Too effective eh?" He sounded impressed.

I told him what had happened to it, and we had to sit out for the rest of the dance. We were laughing so much that Cyril needed to make a quick visit to the toilet — a man's problem evidently. If I hadn't had my bladder difficulty fixed some years before, I would never have made it to the toilets. I would have provided the Victoria Hall with a water-feature. Old age does have its little challenges.

So it was with a light and merry heart that I left Cyril chatting up one or two ladies who were itching to dance with him. Tony was waiting just outside the hall with his car engine running. He was in a no parking area. I quickly moved in beside him — like a young lover relishing the time ahead. He threw the car into gear and was off.

Chatting merrily, I told Tony about my afternoon with Cyril. He was very pleased for me. I then said that I hoped he wasn't having problems with Edith.

"I've always had problems with Edith," he said with a sigh. "Ever since our wedding night. Would you believe I honoured her virginity right up to the time of wedlock, and where did it get me?"

"Not far, I take it." I really sympathised. For a sexy guy like Tony, it must have been very taxing.

"Too right. I was gentle and considerate on our wedding night but she wasn't having any. So I gave her time and then more time. We had fun together just as we did when we were courting but somehow I couldn't get past the barrier she'd built up." He paused, concentrating on turning a bend. "I eventually had a word with her mother. It turned out Edith was frightened of getting pregnant. I managed to reassure her and eventually she let me into her inner sanctum, but it was clearly out of duty."

He paused once more, concentrating on overtaking cyclists. When he spoke again it was with a mixture of anger and sorrow.

"Before we were married I thought it was just a moral thing. She was happy enough to be kissed but didn't want to be touched. But it's something very much deeper. After our marriage, I felt wretched using her body without any emotional response, but she would have been hurt if I'd gone elsewhere. I put up with it for years hoping she would change."

"Sounds as though she needed professional help," I said, feeling sympathy for his very delicate situation.

"She's always refused help — says it's me, not her, who has the problem. Eventually, I found satisfaction elsewhere. I didn't do it lightly. Believe me, Alice; I did want my marriage to work. I had known girls before Edith came on the scene and I knew what good sex was like — for both partners."

"I'm surprised you were attracted to Edith in the first place," I said, wondering what could have drawn such a debonair character to someone sexually cold.

"She was a lovely young woman and in many ways, warm-hearted. I had no idea how things would turn out. I loved my wife and in her own way Edith loved me. But it's hard making love to a woman who regards sexual activity as some sort of sacrificial offering on the altar of duty. Anyway, forget about Edith. Whatever money and goods she takes away, I still have something precious to offer a woman — that is, a real woman."

Tony seemed to know all the lanes within a fifty-mile radius; probably much further but there was no time for deeper penetration into the wilds of Cumbria. He suddenly turned into a lane, little more than a track, and after about a mile brought the car to a halt in an old quarry. With a sigh of satisfaction, his eyes did a sweep of the view around us.

He turned to me. "Stay in the car, or walk to get a better view of the lake?"

"I think I would like some fresh air."

Staying in his Volvo Estate could mean only one thing and I didn't want Tony to think I was expecting, or desiring, his advances.

We walked over an area of rough slate waste, and then on to where silver birch trees were pushing their way up through the finer debris. From this position we could see the breeze-rippled lake below and the rugged peaks of mountains going off into the distance. With the sun shining through the trees and making dappled patterns on the carpet of flaked slate and moss, it was a truly magical spot.

"Oh, Tony, what a beautiful place. The view is fantastic. Thank you for bringing me here," I said in awed delight.

"I thought you would like it."

I turned to speak to him and saw that he was looking very intently at me. I moved my eyes away — little thrills were setting my nerves alight. My heart was going into overdrive. I was afraid that passion would overtake moral judgement and common sense, and yet knowing what to expect, I had allowed myself to be alone with him again.

He took off his blazer and spread it on the soft ground. "Sit a while, Alice. Close your eyes a moment and think about bringing Roger here.

But I could not see Roger wanting to make love under the open sky. Maybe when we were courting he might have thought of such things, at least for kissing and cuddling. But now, being a practical person, I felt sure Roger would prefer his own bed. But it was not difficult to imagine Tony bringing me into a state of ecstasy on that couch of crumbling flaked slate. Naughty Alice! I opened my eyes to clear my vision. Tony was gazing at me and smiling.

"Now, wouldn't this be the perfect spot?"

"Yes, but somehow I can't see Roger as the outdoor lover."

"People can change, Alice. Give him chance to learn. Maybe it will take a little while but after all these years, a few weeks is no time at all."

The warm scent of Tony's body so close to mine, the sunlight filtering through the trees above me, the babbling of a brook not far away played gently on my senses. I caught Tony's eyes and they drew me like a magnet. He brought his mouth down on my slightly parted lips.

Before long, I was experiencing considerable pleasure as he tenderly stroked and caressed my face. I knew what he wanted to do next with his hands but I also knew that he wouldn't touch me unless I showed willing. My body was crying out for it but I was resisting the urge to give way — I was so afraid of where it might lead.

Putting his arms around me, he gently let us fall to our backs and then locked us in an erotic embrace. He kissed me again and, this time, with him pressing his body to mine I could feel the full force of his desire. Delicious sensations brought to life all my erotic zones. I felt my cheeks flush as my heart started pumping faster and my breathing became more rapid.

"All right, Alice?" he asked. He seemed genuinely concerned that his torrid embrace might have offended me. "There's nothing wrong with you, my dear — it's Roger who needs educating."

I gave him a little nod and an uncertain smile.

"I must leave you alone now. This can only lead to something you might regret later." He rose to his feet and offered me a hand.

I allowed him to pull me up. "You're right, Tony, I would be left with a guilty conscience. Kissing is one thing but—"

"I know. I'm sorry." He held my shoulders to steady me. "I should not even be kissing you."

"Maybe, but no harm's been done." I gazed into his kindly blue eyes, wondering if I was falling in love with him. "It's been a wonderful afternoon. You're a very special person, Tony. What a pity Edith isn't able to appreciate your lovemaking."

"What a pity Roger is only sensitive to his own pleasure. You must talk to him, Alice. Let him know how you feel."

"I have tried but it isn't easy after all these years. Until I saw it all on TV, I didn't know myself about — well — you know what I mean."

"Yes, I do know. Somehow I'll bring the subject up tonight. Keeping you out of it, of course."

Roger was already home when Tony pulled up outside our house. As soon as I opened the door I could smell the tripe and onions I'd prepared that morning. Roger may know nothing about cooking but he was capable of putting a casserole into the oven — if he didn't forget it. Years ago, when I was ill, he had a go at cooking some liver and making a rice pudding. The liver turned out like black leather and the pudding had to be hacked out of the dish with a sharp knife. Since he can't cope with failure, he abandoned all attempts to cook anything other than soup and various things on toast.

Roger was euphoric because Tony was dining with us. He seems to have a mission in life to convert everyone he meets into being a tripe and onions addict. It was embarrassing the way he told friends how he'd converted me from disliking into enjoying his favourite food. I still hate the stuff, but being his willing doormat, I go along with his fantasy.

As to whether Tony enjoyed his meal it would be hard to tell. I knew he wanted to keep Roger in a good frame of mind so he could bring up certain aspects of human relationships, and if that meant lying through his teeth, he would do so.

Roger insisted on Tony sharing a bottle of beer with him. "Just the thing to wash it down with," he insisted as he went off for the glasses.

Tony looked at me and grimaced. "We're in for foul weather at the meeting tonight. Stand by for gusts of eighty miles an hour blowing from the south. Take cover and hold on to your hat!"

We were still laughing when Roger came back. He poured the frothing beer into glasses. "It's good to see you two getting on so well together. How was the dancing today?"

"Tony had to see his solicitor, but he picked me and Cyril up and dropped us off at the hall," I told him truthfully. "You wouldn't believe the change in Cyril; he's looking younger and so very dapper in his light suit. He's a fantastic dancer — has medals and cups would you believe?"

Tony gave me a brief knowing look. "It does a body good to get a little of what they need in life, Alice."

"I'm sure you're right. I certainly feel better for enjoying myself and exercising my joints."

Tony smiled. "We may not be able to get all we want in life, but the important thing is to know what we actually need and go for it."

"Well, Tony, dancing seems to work a treat for both Alice and Cyril. It's very good of you taking the trouble to drive the pair of them to the Vic and bring them home again."

"I picked Alice up from the dance early, Cyril stayed until the end. I needed someone to tell my troubles to. Your wife is a wonderful listener."

"So I've heard. Did she tell you that she's had training in counselling?" Roger boasted on my behalf.

"That was a long time ago, Roger. Tony doesn't want to hear about that," I cut in, now feeling embarrassed that my husband was actually bolstering my pretext for being alone with his friend.

"She does a damn good massage as well," Roger said, looking at me and smiling with pride as though showing off his prize cow.

"But that's reserved for me. She can use her ears on you anytime though," he added, giving a little chuckle.

"I'll remember that," Tony responded. He gave me one of his bewitching smiles.

When Roger came home that evening — he had gone to the meeting in Tony's Volvo — he seemed quieter than usual and I asked him if he had a problem.

"I've just been talking to Tony," he answered thoughtfully. "Edith wasn't much of a wife to him — made me feel lucky to have you."

My guilty conscience led me to say something positive about the woman. "Well, it's nice to know that, Roger, but I think perhaps Edith has problems; probably to do with her upbringing."

"You'd think Tony could melt her a bit though. After all, he seems to have winning ways with most women." His forehead wrinkled into a frown. "He's told me a lot; well, not all that much because we weren't in the car for long, but it was all very interesting — very interesting indeed."

At last it looked like I had a genuine opening for discussing my little problem. "Tell me what he said, Roger. Was it about his methods — that sort of thing?"

"Can't see it making any difference to oldies like us. We're too set in our ways," he said, shaking his head dismissively. "Anyway, we're all right as we are. I told him so. But he said that wives should be consulted and to ask you. Huh! I should know my own wife after fifty years."

"Perhaps you should but—" I began, but Roger didn't let me finish.

"I've got what it takes. You've had no cause to complain have you?" he asked, looking at me directly. "It's quite something that we still do it at our age. You know, I've been thinking; perhaps it's Tony's technique that's at fault with Edith. Too much of all this modern stuff might be upsetting to a quiet woman." He was now wagging his head in his usual all-knowing manner.

"I'm not sure how anything to do with sex can be thought of as modern," I said with irritation, but there was no response. Having given his verdict of his talk with Tony, he'd switched off from the subject. I thought it was time for me to get his attention.

"Roger?"

"Yes?" he answered, without looking up from the paper he was now reading.

Trying to sound mysterious, I asked him, "Would you come upstairs please? I want to show you something."

He glanced over his paper. "Hello — been buying more new clothes? Won't it do when we go to bed?"

"It's very important to me; please come up now."

I ran up first, quickly stripped down to my black lacy knickers and waited for Roger to arrive in the bedroom.

He stood by the door looking puzzled. "I've already seen those — or are they a different pair?"

I pulled them off and threw them aside — like I'd seen TV strippers doing.

His eyes boggled at my neatly shaved V. "Good heavens!" he exclaimed loudly. "What have you done?"

"Don't you like it?" I asked him, fearful of a disappointing answer.

"It's rather kinky. But what made you do it?"

"I thought you'd like it. You do like it, don't you, Roger?"

"I'll think I'm in bed with the wrong woman," he joked.

I took his hand and pulled him towards the bed.

"Feel how silky it is."

"Not now, Alice."

"Please, Roger."

"Oh, all right...Mm, yes, very nice."

"Lie down with me," I whispered seductively.

With my arms curled above my head, I lay stretched out on the bed while he stood over me looking very puzzled.

"I can't make you out lately, Alice," he said, scratching his head. "First the undies and now this. I must say I find the smoothness very fetching — quite alluring really. But, let's face it — it just isn't you! Why have you done it? Don't be afraid I'll go off with another woman, I'm satisfied with the one I've got."

"Take your clothes off and come by me," I begged, patting the bed.

He gave a little shake of his head. "It's late, Alice, we'll save it for another night. I must go and check through the minutes. I don't think I made a note of the absentees."

He went downstairs. I put on my dressing gown and followed him, thinking to myself that Tony may well become a serious contender for my affections at the rate things were going. I felt so angry and frustrated, I made his hot chocolate and slapped it down in front of him without speaking. He was too busy to notice. I went to bed, hoping I'd get to sleep before my dear thoughtful husband got the chance to keep me awake with his snoring.

But I didn't sleep. My mind drifted to my afternoon outing. What if? In my imagination, I could hear Tony whispering, "Oh, my dear, it's as smooth as silk; how lovely. May I?"

A voice broke into my erotic musing. "Alice, I need a few e-mails typing first thing in the morning; unless you can do them now. There's an angling contest tomorrow. Fred and Tom will be off early. They weren't at the meeting tonight and they don't know we're having a bowls practice on Sunday."

Chapter seven

That's what friends are for

By the time the following Tuesday dawned, I was feeling quite weary. It had been a happy weekend with some of the family popping in, but it always leaves me feeling low when they all clear off again. Monday had been a busy day too — what with washing and ironing, and fitting in Roger's minutes because he wanted them doing early. During the evening, I'd made the Christmas puddings to give them plenty of time to mature.

But I still had a pile of letters to write for my dear husband. How I wished he would use the computer and type them himself. It wasn't so much the job of doing them that irritated me but his constant complaining about the slightest imperfections. It wasn't enough to use the spellchecker; I also had to refer to the standard dictionary because of his distrust of computer software. As always, Roger has to be right, and his letters beyond criticism. It's odd how some people take such delight in proving others to be wrong and themselves to be perfect. Roger's letters have always been examples of his nit-picking perfectionism and I have come to the conclusion that many are written not out of necessity but to bolster his own ego.

Tuesday morning, Roger told me he was meeting one of his committee buddies for lunch. He said it would give me a bit of a break. So I decided to get his letters done and then go out myself. Managing to get them finished before he went off, I got him to sign them, that is, the revised copies, and went off to town to get them posted. I must admit, it was for my benefit too; I wanted to go to the Coffeepot for morning coffee in the hope of seeing Tony.

Tony was as good as a workout for raising my heartbeat rate, and he made me feel young and vibrant with life. He brought excitement into my otherwise rather humdrum existence, apart from which, I felt the need for a little gratuitous appreciation. Making a woman feel good just for being herself, was Tony's forte.

I had just ordered my coffee when Betty walked in. I groaned inside and hoped she wouldn't see me. But, of course, she did and headed straight for my table.

"Hello, Alice, I'm glad I've caught you; I need a friend to talk to."

"Hi, Betty. I should have thought after the last time we met, I would be the last person you'd want to talk to."

Betty was making herself comfortable in the chair opposite me while trying to catch the eye of the waitress. After putting in her order, she gave me her full attention. Speaking very quietly for her, she said, "You know, Alice, you're the only one that's been of help to me."

"Really? I thought I'd offended you," I said, surprise showing in my voice.

"You did," she replied in a hurt tone. "But I got to thinking. I really do love Albert you know, and I'd miss him dreadfully if we split up." She gave a big sigh that heaved up her ample bosom.

Perhaps Betty was at last realising just how much Albert did for her and that life without him would be pretty bleak.

"Well, Betty, what are you going to do — let him have his fling or accommodate his desires?" I was being very brutal, but then, Betty was gumming up things for me just by sitting there.

"Evidently, Tony had a word with him. Now we've reached a sort of compromise," she said. And then looking a bit demure, she added, "It's not so bad really, I—" Suddenly clamming up, she changed the subject. "How's the dancing going? Glenda told me Cyril's going now."

We talked for a while about the change in Cyril. Of course, I said nothing about pink thingies or the problems he was having in his love life — or lack of it. Betty was doing most of the talking and before long Cyril was left behind and most of our mutual friends were being criticised for one thing or another.

I was drinking my coffee and only half listening to Betty's character assassinations. I kept looking past her to the window hoping to see Tony. But would he come in if he saw Betty with me? I suddenly realised I was being asked a question.

"I'm sorry," I said, "I didn't quite catch it; I'm a bit deaf you know."

"No, I didn't know," she said with a look of surprise. "I suppose it's to be expected at your age though. I'm so sorry." She gave me a sympathetic look and a very patronising pat on my hand. Raising her voice to make sure I heard her, she asked, "Has Roger finished the bathroom yet?"

"No, it's a big job and he's got other things to do while the weather's fine," I answered in my normal voice, annoyed that Betty was now speaking far too loud. Some of the big-eared customers were listening in.

She gave a deep sigh that lifted her buxom bosom and let it drop again, coming to rest unceremoniously on her folded arms. I wondered why she wore those tight-fitting jumpers and skirts. I had to stop myself from giggling — she reminded me of the Christmas puddings I'd made the night before.

"Roger's good-looking for his age, very clever and so energetic. You really are lucky to have such a perfect husband."

Now she was beginning to irritate me. "I don't think even Roger would say he's perfect."

Betty's coffee and Danish slice arrived. She picked up the Danish straight away and gave a satisfying smile as she swallowed her first mouthful.

"How's Tony Bradshaw?" she asked, suddenly changing the subject and looking me straight in the eye to see my reaction.

But Betty wasn't the only one gazing at me. Tony's name had caused even more stares in my direction.

"You have been seeing him haven't you?" Betty persisted in a rather suggestive manner, her voice getting louder as she remembered my hearing affliction. "I mean for dancing," she continued, clearly speaking to her audience as well as to me.

I wondered whom Betty had been gossiping to. I told her, "We've been dancing together once and I might be seeing him at this Friday's tea dance. Roger thinks it's a good idea. He doesn't dance himself and he's too busy to go anyway. He likes Tony and he knows I enjoy dancing. So why not?"

"Roger is so broad-minded. A lot of husbands wouldn't like it," she added, more for the benefit of her audience. She let out another of her bosom-heaving envy sighs. "He's very good to you."

That did it. Betty was getting me really cheesed off. "I should hope we are good to each other." I stood up ready to leave. "I'm sorry, Betty, but I have to go now, I've lots to do. I'm glad things have worked out for you and Albert. You should both come to the tea dance, it knocks the years off and keeps you active."

"With my arthritis? I don't think so," she replied with a pained expression on her face.

"Well, it doesn't do mine any harm. See you, Betty. Must dash," I said, hurrying out before she went into details about her many 'impossible to find relief' sufferings.

I was feeling disappointed as I walked home. But perhaps it was good that Tony hadn't come to the Coffeepot, I would have felt awkward with Betty there as well. As discrete as he would have been, Betty would have found something to gossip about and what she couldn't discover, she would make up as she went along.

As I expected, Roger was out when I arrived home but I was surprised to find he'd left me a note. I picked it up wondering if it was a reminder to make sure I'd posted his letters and also to check his e-mails. But it wasn't and I was lifted out of my melancholy mood as soon as I began to read. Tony had rung to ask Roger if it would be all right for him to take me out to lunch. He said he needed to bend my ear again as he was having trouble with Edith. Roger told me to meet Tony at the Black Cat Inn if I wanted to hear his woes. Since I'd got his letters written and posted, he said it was up to me as it was fine by him.

"Big of you, Roger darling," I said aloud, but the sarcasm wasn't really anger directed at Roger, but merely a statement recognising my own ineptitude of allowing my husband to dominate my life in an age of female liberation.

Actually, I was elated beyond belief. Not even deep-seated guilt dispelled the euphoria I was feeling at seeing Tony again. I ran upstairs to get changed into my white cotton blouse, red-flowered skirt, red jacket and knee-length stockings. But first, I did a quick shave down-under and patted on fine silky-smooth talc. Feeling terribly wicked I put on my red undies. Then I began to hesitate — what on earth was I was doing it all for? I glanced at the clock — no time to stop for an internal debate on motivation. I had no intention of doing anything naughty with Tony; I just wanted to feel good about myself and there was nothing unusual in a woman wanting to do that.

It was almost one o'clock when I arrived at the inn. Tony met me at the door and took me to a room at the back where I followed him to a table in a shady corner by the fireplace. There was a nip in the air and a small but bright fire had been lit, its flames reflected in the many polished brasses hanging from nearly every available spot. With only one smallish window and a low beamed ceiling, it was a very cosy and intimate room. Most of the customers were either in the bar or the smoking lounge and we had this small snug to ourselves.

"Tony, this is lovely!" I exclaimed. "I've never been in here before."

"I rather like it myself. I knew you would, most women do," he told me, giving me one of his bewitching smiles.

I wondered how many women Tony had brought there to dine with him, and if they had stayed the night afterwards in one of the few bedrooms. I must admit I was feeling jealous. It was the sort of thing I would like to do with Roger, or so I lied to myself, knowing full well that it was Tony who was driving my emotions and occupying my hidden thoughts.

"Thanks for inviting me," I said as we made ourselves comfortable. "I was ready for an outing."

"Good. I'm pleased you were able to come."

I remembered why I was there. "Roger left a note saying you wanted to talk about Edith."

"First, tell me what you would like to eat and I'll order at the bar," he said, handing me the menu. "While you're choosing, let me get you a drink. What would you like?"

"I'd love a ginger beer thanks, but any fizzy drink will do."

For a brief moment, he stood gazing at me sitting in the firelight glow. "You look really beautiful today. Thanks again for coming," he said softly.

Oh, what it was to be appreciated! I was like a child full of excitement and expectation and I guess it was showing. "I'm pleased to be here," I said.

He snapped his fingers. "Right, ginger beer it is."

He left the room and I had a few moments to calm myself in the balmy mellow atmosphere before he returned with the drinks. We spent a few minutes discussing the menu. Once that was out of the way, we relaxed back in our plush-upholstered armchairs and gazed dreamily into the fire.

"Makes you feel carefree and sleepy," I said in almost a whisper.

"I thought it was just me feeling like bed," he answered, but I wasn't sure what was behind the remark. He was looking at me closely as though carefully judging my reaction.

"It would be a shame to leave this lovely fire for such an indulgence," I said, returning his gaze.

Tony lifted an eyebrow but smiled and said nothing. We sat for a few moments sipping our drinks and then, remembering why I was supposed to be there, I said, "What did you want to talk to me about, Tony?"

"Actually, it's nothing to do with Edith. I only wish I could help her like I've done other women."

"Some people might think your help is just a euphemism for sexual therapy, and being of greater benefit to you than to your client."

He wasn't offended. He smiled at me. "Well, I have to admit, I do enjoy my helping role."

"Are we talking about the sort of thing that happened last week?" I asked him although I was afraid to know the answer.

"A passionate kiss? It can be much more than that."

I turned my eyes away and gazed into the fire. My nerve endings were becoming excited as my imagination refused to play dead. Was there something about red undies that caused the parts they covered to ignite?"

"I can trust you, Alice, so I'll tell you. No doubt you've heard plenty of rumours about me; you might as well know the facts."

I wasn't sure if I wanted to hear about all the women he'd taken to bed, apart from it putting me in a minor league, I knew it would cause me to be jealous. But clearly, he wanted me to know so I just smiled and prepared myself to listen. I forced myself to remember basic counselling techniques. That is, putting aside your own baggage, respecting the client, empathising — oh, no! Go no further, Alice. Empathising with Tony could lead to only one thing — 'the gruesome twosome'!

Tony relaxed back in his chair and fixed his eyes on mine. "Leaving aside a few little romances that come my way, I do have a friend who, for medical reasons, can't do it any more. Wives as well as husbands suffer when men become impotent. So I've been helping them out, after all, what are friends for?"

I wondered how someone I thought so much of could be so cruel. "That's like rubbing salt into a wound but knowing it will never get better. Oh, Tony how could you?"

"You don't understand, Alice," he answered calmly. "The man loves his wife and wants her to be happy. The husband also enjoys a bit of voyeurism — it's not all altruism on his part."

I had already broken the cardinal rules, now my counselling training went to pot completely. "You mean he watches you at it? I don't believe it!"

"It isn't as if I'm the first to come between them — so to speak. Only now it's a shared experience for them. The husband doesn't need to pay for his voyeuristic sexual activity, and the wife doesn't need to stray. What's more, with careful timing on my part — not easy, takes skill and practice — they can reach their orgasms together. I assure you, Alice, there is no jealousy, only mutual understanding."

I turned my eyes away from him, staggered by what I had been hearing. Again I was feeling a stab of jealousy because of other couples getting orgasmic pleasure, and that rather frightened me. He could see I was looking a little uncomfortable and so he switched the conversation to Roger and me.

"Roger might have told you that I had a word with him."

Surely he wasn't going to suggest that he oblige Roger and me? I sat in awed silence, waiting for him to continue.

"By talking about the problems of married couples generally, I was getting him to think about a woman's sexual needs in particular," he said quite casually. "He seemed rather interested."

I told him what had happened after Roger came home from the meeting and, as I came to the disappointing end, Tony took hold of my hand and squeezed it. Before he could comment, the food arrived and another couple came into the room for a meal. We ate mostly in silence, only remarking on the quality of the food, which was excellent. We didn't stay for a sweet or a coffee.

While we were slowly driving through pleasant countryside, Tony told me that it was vital I talked to Roger about our problem. "You must let him know how you feel about your sexual relationship. It's for his benefit as well as yours, Alice."

"I don't want to hurt him or diminish him in any way," I confessed. "He's happy with the way things are. Surely he won't want to change? After all, he obviously gets his orgasms, what more is there for him?"

"As far as orgasms go, there's sex, good sex and superior sex. It seems to me, Alice, Roger is only on the first rung of the ladder and he's got you just hanging on with one foot.

"You think Roger could have better sex — even at his age?" I asked him, somewhat surprised at Tony's grading of sexual satisfaction.

"With knowledge and practice, he might even get to the top rung. Believe me, Alice, he doesn't know what he's missing out on." He gave a slight shake of his head. "And it's so unfair on you — but you know that already."

"It isn't just Roger, Tony. You see, I've never expected anything different myself — well, not until recently. Perhaps if I'd been a better wife in the past and encouraged him to experiment, then maybe he would be different with me now."

"I think you're a wonderful wife. Never think anything different. You're very warm-hearted and responsive to touch." He gave me a little smile. "You certainly do things to me, but I don't have to tell you that — it becomes only too obvious. Shall I stop the car soon to refresh your memory?"

I knew he wasn't being flippant, and even just listening to him I felt myself getting moist beneath my red undies. He would never force himself onto me but I could see he was waiting for my acceptance. I wanted his touch desperately but I was so afraid I wouldn't be able to control the situation.

He seemed to sense my dilemma. "Can I take your silence to mean yes?" he said softly.

I gave a little moan of anguish. "I don't know. I should be romancing with Roger, not another man."

"I agree, but you must tell him what you want. Don't expect the poor man to guess. After all, you haven't complained all these years — how is he to know?"

"I've been giving him hints — well, sort of," I said with a sigh. "I'm afraid he will be disgusted if I tell him straight out. And, as I said, I don't want to diminish him either."

"I doubt if either of those things will happen. But if his pride gets wounded, it's for his own good." He gave a slight shake of his head. "You can't treat him like a delicate child for all of his life."

He came to a narrow lane and slowly drove down it, careful not to catch the Volvo's exhaust on the ruts. After a short distance, he stopped the car just inside a field. "We'll be more comfortable in the back," he said looking into my eyes for a response. "Don't worry, I'll not push you into anything; please trust me, Alice."

My body was aching for his touch. I tried hard to resist but a little voice was asking me why I'd shaved and put on the red undies if they were not for Tony. I got out of the car while Tony cleared the back seat. He hung his jacket on a hook by a window partly covering the glass, and did the same with mine the other side. He pulled down a net sunshade he had fixed to the back window and then invited me to step inside. My heart was beating too fast for comfort. I was getting far too worked-up. I took deep breaths and tried to calm myself.

He looked at me very tenderly. "You do want to do this, don't you?"

I wasn't sure what "this" was but I nodded shyly. He knew what I wanted all right.

"You must tell me when to stop. I'm putting you in the driver's seat today, but I'll have my engine running," he assured me. "It's up to you how far we go."

I looked into his smiling eyes as he started to unbutton my blouse. I began to quiver in expectation but, when it came down to it, I just couldn't let him go on. I put a hand on his and he immediately stopped what he was doing. He nuzzled up to my ear, murmuring softly his words of encouragement. "Let go, my love. Relax, soak up the delicious feelings."

He kissed me with those soft full lips of his, touching me with the tip of his tongue and sending quivering waves of delight throughout my body. He then began a gentle stroking and caressing routine around my face, neck and arms. I willingly responded by rubbing my cheek next to his smoothly shaved face.

"Mmm, you're so soft and yielding; beautiful, beautiful, my love," he whispered softly in my ear.

I wished that Roger would adopt such an empathic, unhurried but thrilling way with me. "Oh, Tony, you do such wonderful things to me," I moaned.

"Then may I go on from here?" he asked gently.

"No — yes — no. Please, Tony, not today."

"Very well."

He kissed me again — all soft and tender without being wet and sloppy. I was so very tempted. My flesh was alive — I had butterflies in my undies going wild to be released. If only Roger was there beside me — no on top of me, sending me into paroxysms of delight! I knew it would happen if only...

Tony wrapped me in his arms and pulled me close. He murmured, "Let go, Alice. Relax, bathe in the pleasant feelings."

Oh, yes, he certainly was stirring me sexually and it was divine. Simply being there, close to a man who desired to please me — a man who knew how to be gentle and yielding to my desires rather than merely satisfying his own urges — was enough to turn me on. He could have a string of women only too willing to give him anything he desired, but Tony had chosen to be there with me, accepting the little I felt able to give. I could hear myself moaning as he kissed and caressed me, and before long Tony was groaning with his own pleasure.

He suddenly stopped kissing and, releasing his hold of me, slipped out of the door. I didn't watch him. I waited a moment and slipped out of the car myself, tidied my hair and clothes, and took deep breaths of the lovely fresh air.

Tony appeared in front of me. "Ready to go?"

We were quiet for the first miles home and then Tony told me his thoughts.

"Talk to him. Get him to try different things. Get him to experiment. But above all, let go and enjoy it — all of it. Let him see and hear you enjoying sex, it's the greatest aphrodisiac there is. You see what you do to me and we hardly did anything!"

I thought about what he said and sat back in the car quietly content. Life seemed so much brighter — rosier. I was full of hope for Roger and me.

"Thank you, Tony, you're a real friend," I told him, my voice full of emotion. "Thanks for everything — the meal, your company and what you've done for me. No — for us.'"

"That's what friends are for," he replied with a smile.

I had a sudden fear that Tony might now drop me and leave everything to Roger. "We will be going on as friends won't we?" I asked him as he was stopping the car close to a village tea shop.

"In a personal way? As long as you need me," he assured me. "Now we had better get a quick cuppa before I take you home. And Alice," he said, looking straight into my eyes; "the pleasure of our friendship is two-way you know — you do a great deal for me."

It was with a warm glow that I entered the tea shop. Tony inevitably had that effect on me. It wasn't so in the past. I saw him sometimes when I was with Roger at social events to do with their mutual activities. We would have a little flirtatious banter; everyone expected it, especially Roger. But the sort of thing we now engaged in had gone beyond that light-hearted teasing, and our relationship was much deeper at all levels. Tony was now just as much my friend as he was Roger's, and I didn't want to lose him.

"Alice! Fancy meeting you here."

It was Doreen, a friend from my school days. She was sitting drinking tea and eating sandwiches with her husband Bill — Roger's old school pal. The couple had first met at our wedding and had been our joint friends ever since, although, after we had moved from their area, we seldom met up with one another. They both stood up and we embraced, Bill giving me a kiss on the cheek. I introduced them to Tony and they shook hands, muttering polite greetings. We joined them at their table. A waitress appeared from the back and took our order for a pot of tea.

Doreen and Bill were wearing walking gear and we soon found out they had been up to Scotland. They had stopped off overnight to break their long journey back south, and to do a little walking to exercise their joints.

"We intended popping in to see you and Roger, but when we rang this afternoon there was no answer. I guess you were both out," said Doreen, looking first at me and then at Tony.

I could see written on her face, "Does Roger know where you are, and whom you are with?" I answered her unspoken questions.

"Pity Roger isn't with us. He's tied up all day and sent me packing with Tony. After an excellent lunch we've been driving around the lakes. Rather lazy compared with your activities. We just stopped for a cuppa on our way back. Roger will be sorry to have missed you."

Tony joined in. "So, you are both old friends of Alice and Roger? Going back to schooldays is quite a long friendship, outdoing a Golden Wedding!"

"Actually, our united friendship is just as long as Roger and Alice have been married," explained Doreen. "I had been living away from home and I only met Roger at the wedding. Bill had been working away and hadn't met Alice until the wedding. So if they had not married, I guess we wouldn't have either. That makes our friendship rather special."

"It certainly does," said Tony. "I met Roger soon after they moved up here but it's only recently that I've got to know Alice really well." He glanced at me and gave me a coded smile.

"You should have known Alice when she was a young teenager. You wouldn't believe the things we got up to." Doreen turned to me and grinned. "Do you remember, Alice, when we went looking for mushrooms and ignored the bull in the field?"

I laughed. "It didn't ignore us though! What a run we had. Only just scrambled over the gate in time! What about when we climbed that tree to get plums off the top branches? I held onto your dress while you wriggled along a branch. Golly, Doreen, you sure did have faith in me!"

"Seems to me, we both had too much faith in that dress. If you remember, the stitching burst at the waist and you were left holding my skirt while I fell halfway down the tree!"

"Ah, yes, you climbed down the rest of the way, but I fell through the branches and landed on top of a pile of grass cuttings."

"What luck! We used to do all sorts of daft things and never came to harm. What about the time we went rowing on the boating lake with that posh friend of yours — was her name Carol? You know, Alice, the girl with the flashing eyes and come and get me smile? I reckon it was her that drew those lads to us. Do you remember? There must have been four or five of them in their double-oared family boat. They tried to get hold of our boat and pull us over to that little island in the middle of the lake. You slapped their hands with your oar — ouch! They soon let go. They must have thought you a right Boadicea. A pity really, I actually fancied one of them!"

We all laughed. But I was remembering a lot about Doreen that I had no intention of repeating. She was very like Carol, both in looks and in being boy mad. We both had boy friends when we were at the local school. Mine, Phil, hardly spoke and it took him a whole year before he had the courage to give me a single kiss, but Doreen's Barry was quite forward and not at all shy. Apart from being known for his dirty jokes, he had quite a reputation with the girls. One damp day, while I was walking with Phil in the local park, we saw Barry and Doreen under a tree with his hand inside her blazer — and it wasn't to keep his hand warm. I wasn't surprised at Barry but Doreen, how could she be so brazen? They were not at all embarrassed, just gave us a wave and got on with it. It made me wonder what they did in private. I don't expect Doreen ever has a problem getting an orgasm!

"Now don't you go thinking Alice was boy-shy, Tony, she went out with quite a few. Beats me why she married Roger. As much as I love him, he's a right chauvinist. To think Alice was set to be a highly successful designer. Huh! Would you believe it? She only had a few years getting somewhere before Roger messed up her career. He soon had her tied to house and home."

I rather think Doreen is envious of our children. They don't have any. She chose a career and left it too late. I thought it best not to mention the joys of family life.

"Roger didn't drag me to the altar with a club in his hand," I said defensively.

"Maybe not. Actually, we all thought he must have got you pregnant or something, but no, you became his doormat with your eyes wide open."

"And it was our choice to have a family, Doreen, not just Roger's."

"Knowing Roger, it's more likely your choice just happened to fit his plans. I'm sure he loves you, always has, but he takes you for granted, Alice. He can't help it, he believes woman was made for man — full stop."

"Now come on, Doreen," Bill chimed in, "Roger isn't that bad. I've known him since we were at the Grammar together. Apart from taking sneaky looks at the girls playing netball in their gym knickers — like the rest of us — he was always respectful to girls, and to the women teachers."

"He had no choice with his teachers and you didn't have mixed lessons. I expect you were too busy fondling the girls behind the bike sheds to know what Roger was up to after school."

We all laughed again.

"Talking of navy bloomers," continued Doreen, "do you remember how the lads used to hang around the bottom of the stairs hoping to get a view? God knows why! I guess there must be something very sexy about being so well covered. Skirts below the knee, socks nearly to our knees, shirts worn buttoned to the neck and a school tie; there were only flashing eyes and blushing faces to observe in all their nakedness."

"Ah, yes," said Tony, warming to the theme, "that is the whole point; what you can't see is what entices a male."

"Well, I didn't entice anyone," I told them.

"Come off it, Alice, don't you remember when those lads were caned for whistling at us in the school yard? And what about that lad called Phil?"

"What? It took him a year to kiss me. Although I must admit he did get your Barry in a rugby tackle when he tripped me up. I didn't like Barry; I thought him a proper rotter."

I had the feeling that Doreen preferred to forget about Barry. I suspect they went further than any of us realised, especially when they were alone in the park after dusk.

"Anyway, Alice, I guess Roger suits you and he's a great guy," Doreen said, smiling at me. "Even if he is a know-it-all, I love him dearly and would do a swap with Bill anytime. You have a lovely house and that garden of yours is fantastic. Bill can't put up a shelf or even plant out a window box."

"Don't need to. I keep a woman to do that sort of thing!"

More laughter. But there was an element of irony in his remark. Doreen tended to wear the trousers in his house.

Bill looked at Tony. "Are you married, Tony?"

"About to be divorced. But then my wife isn't the little slave that these two ladies seem to be."

Doreen pulled a face and the rest of us laughed. The banter and pleasant chatter went on for a little while but I knew that Tony needed to get back for a late afternoon appointment. I swallowed down the rest of my tea and looked at him with a barely whispered, "Ready to go?"

Having said prolonged farewells, within five minutes Tony was opening the passenger door to his Volvo for me to slip inside. From the café doorway, I heard Doreen's voice, "Now that's what I call a real gentleman!" As she passed the open car window on the way to their Land Rover, she put her head down and whispered, "He's a bit of all right, Alice. Go for it!"

On the way home I thought about Doreen's advice. She probably fancied him herself. Apart from which, I strongly suspect she had seen Tony's coded message to me. I knew both she and Bill had had their little flings during their long marriage. They were quite open about it. Doreen had said that the occasional change kept their marriage alive and kicking. She claimed it wasn't adultery because they were in agreement, and the sex with others meant nothing to either of them. Roger had joked about it at the time.

"Well, I'd be all right, a sexy devil like me, but who on earth would want to have a fling with Alice?"

Having heard Doreen's disparaging remarks about Roger, I was in an unsettled mood that evening. After all, he was my husband and my choice. No one had the right to say that I was his doormat — that was my privilege alone. I told Roger about meeting Doreen and Bill, but I said nothing about what was said about him. Anyway, he already knew Doreen's views about him and men in general.

After enjoying a cheese and ham omelette with peas and corn, Roger settled in his armchair in front of the television to read his newspaper. "I'll have another cup of tea, Alice," he said, looking at his empty cup on the table by the side of him. "And I think I'll have a bit of that cake you made the other day."

"The cake's all gone. The kids ate it."

"Typical!"

"Do you want a buttered scone?"

"Did you bake them today?"

"No, but—"

"No thanks, you know I only like them fresh. I'll have a chocolate biscuit."

I should have said they were fresh. He never knows the difference when I warm them up. I fetched his tea and biscuit.

"Roger, suppose we go out for a drink?"

"What? We never go out for a drink. You don't like going in pubs."

"I thought it might be nice to drive up to the common with a bottle of wine. We could put on Classic FM while we watch the sun go down. Maybe cuddle in the car. Or, when it gets dark, on a rug under the stars."

Roger put his paper down and looked at me in astonishment. "What? Act your age, Alice. It's Doreen isn't it? She put you up to this. That woman's daft in the head."

"That's just it, Roger, I want to act my age, before I'm over the hill. For me, Roger, do it just for me."

He sighed. "I don't know what's the matter with you, Alice. Oh, all right, since there's nothing on TV till nine-thirty. But I'll have to get a few notes written when I get back and you'll have them to type. Mm, I'll take my camera; I need a picture for the photo competition."

It was a glorious sunset with golds and pinks contrasting with patches of turquoise-blue overlaid with brooding layers of indigo. For a few minutes the bay below us shone with a shimmering brilliance. The rock-strewn common, the woods and distant fells, picked up the setting sun's radiance in a fiery glow. We were bathed in the beauty of it all. Like soaking in a soft warm bath after a heavy day, it was relaxing to the soul.

After Roger had taken his photographs, we sat listening to his tape of relaxing classical music. We nibbled chocolate and sipped wine from a couple of plastic cups — Roger refused to take glasses.

Roger let out a deep sigh. "We should do this more often. Good idea of yours, Alice. Very relaxing."

"Would you like to sit outside on the rug?"

"A bit chilly for that."

"We've got two rugs. We could lay back and watch the stars come out."

"We can sit in here and watch the stars."

"Not the same as being on your back and looking at the sky. For me, Roger; do it for me, please?"

"Oh, all right. Don't blame me if you get cold and stiff."

He sat in the car while I went outside and spread out one of the rugs. I put the other ready to cover us up. He turned up the music a little so we could hear it outside and came out to join me. We lay back looking at the bright twinkling stars. The sun had now disappeared and it was a perfect evening.

After a little while, I rolled over and kissed him.

"Now what are you up to? A bit open here for that sort of thing."

"There's only the sheep to see us. It's too early for the lovebirds."

He kissed me back, lingering longer than usual. It was pleasant — delicate, and not at all hurried.

"Mm, something to be said for fresh air," he murmured and began to unbutton my blouse.

I gave him a hand, thrilled that he was turned on. Before long my bra straps had left my shoulders and Roger was making good progress. I was getting quite excited. What with Roger's growing lust and the naughtiness of doing it in the open, my body was reacting in very pleasant ways. Roger's hand was now moving up my skirt.

"You know, I like the smoothness. Mm, very nice."

Perhaps it was the softness that inspired him to be gentle, but he certainly was taking things steady.

"What the—"

We both jumped up. Warm liquid was being sprayed over our heads. We heard someone shout and a dog barked close by — too close by!

Back home we both took a shower. Although quite disgusting, it was hard not to laugh. I offered to massage Roger's back as a sort of recompense for our aborted act of love, hoping that it would turn him on again.

He groaned with pleasure as my fingers worked their magic on his tired muscles.

"How about a nice hot chocolate when you've finished?"

Wrapped in a bathrobe and humming happily to myself, I ran down the stairs to get Roger his drink. I put in a drop of rum, thinking he was going to need a stimulant to see him through the next half-hour. Oh, yes! The stage was set, Roger was in a good mood and we were both ready to finish what had been started — even better, we were bathed and who could tell where it might lead him.

I walked up the stairs in wild anticipation.

Roger was fast asleep!

I sat on the bed and drank his chocolate. Pretty good. I climbed into bed and thought erotic thoughts. With Roger snoring, what else was there for me to do?

Chapter eight

If at first you don't succeed

A golden opportunity arose to talk to Roger about our sexual relationship. I had just come home from the hospital where I did voluntary work when my very angry husband met me at the door.

"I wanted to work under the car but I couldn't because someone's taken the batteries from my torch. Where the hell are they?" he demanded to know.

I opened my mouth to tell him but he went straight on with his usual diatribe about the grandchildren.

"Every time the kids come something goes missing," he shouted. "You'll have to have a word with the lads. Get them to keep their kids in order. You're too lenient with the lot of them; always have been. If they want batteries they should get their own. It's just too bad," he groused, his face twisted with annoyance.

"I took them, Roger; the kids have nothing to do with it," I said calmly. "I'm sorry; I forgot all about it. I intended getting some more but it slipped my mind."

"You took them? What on earth for? They wouldn't fit your shaver," he said with his face wrinkling up in puzzlement.

"Do you remember me leaving my rubber gloves inside the oven?"

"What have your burnt gloves got to do with my torch batteries?"

"There were no gloves in the oven but your batteries were — inside a pink thingy," I told him, expecting him to explode once he twigged what a pink thingy was.

"A pink thingy? What on earth is a pink thingy? Why would you put some sort of toy in the oven? Are you going senile?" He shouted in exasperation.

"It was a vibrator. It needed batteries to work it," I said calmly.

He shook his head in puzzlement. "You're not making sense, woman. What does it vibrate and why does it need warming up?"

"It's to give a woman sexual pleasure and I didn't put it in the oven to warm it up."

"It does what?" he bellowed. "You mean you actually use one of those things? Why? Oh, I get it. One of your sexy friends loaned it you, and you wanted to sterilise it. But what a daft thing to do. I can't understand you, Alice. Why did you want to try it? Did you try it?" He demanded brusquely.

"No, I didn't. It had a horrible smell," I said, unperturbed by his blustering. "But I didn't get the chance to anyway because you put the oven on."

"I can't understand it, I just can't understand it. Why the hell was it in the oven?"

"I was hiding it," I answered in a matter-of-fact way, as though concealing thingies in cookers was quite normal practice. "But that's not important. We have to talk, Roger. We have to talk about our sex life," I said calmly, as though addressing a stroppy teenager about the need to do his homework.

Roger sat down, elbows on the kitchen table and with his head in his hands. "I can't understand you, Alice; all this sex stuff — and at your age!"

"Age has nothing to do with it. Please try to keep an open mind, Roger, we have to discuss things sensibly," I pleaded, putting my hands gently on his shoulders.

"Why on earth did you want to try it?" Before I could explain, he jumped to his own conclusion. "Did that Greta Smithson give it to you? I've heard she's a lesbian — no telling what they get up to."

"Oh, really, Roger, you're so prejudiced. It has nothing to do with Greta or any other woman. It has to do with us — us!"

"What's wrong with us?" he asked bewildered. "Why do you want a replica when you have the real thing? Isn't mine big enough? Not good enough? I can assure you it stands up well next to the rest in the pee line!"

He was obviously hurt as well as angry. I took off my coat and pulled up a chair next to my disconsolate husband. I put an arm around him and took hold of his hand. "It has nothing to do with your manhood, Roger. I can't say how your equipment compares with anyone else's anyway. You don't realise it but I just get frustrated. Not because you haven't got what it takes — you have that all right. Golly, if it got any bigger it would rival the Eiffel

Tower!" It was a stupid, wild exaggeration but he needed his hurt ego bolstering. "It's me that's the problem. I don't get an orgasm."

"That's just a fancy name someone's invented to justify bawdy goings-on," he retorted with a mocking laugh. "We've been all right for fifty years. That television's put fancy ideas into your head. All that yelling, moaning and groaning — just acting, making you think they're getting something you're not. Really, Alice, I should have thought you had more sense than to fall for that," he said bitterly, pulling his hand away from mine.

"You're wrong. I am missing out — have been for fifty years! It's all right for you, you get what you want and when you want it," I barked at him, angry by his refusal to even consider I might have a problem. "Do you ever ask me if I'm satisfied? Do you ever think that I might want to do things differently?"

"You're just going through a crisis because you've reached seventy," he reasoned, refusing to engage in any discussion beyond his understanding.

"How typical! I've been going through a crisis ever since we married but I didn't know it!" I told him, trying to keep calm but failing badly. "I want an orgasm, Roger," I said, refusing to be diverted, "and I want you to give it me — not some rubber toy, not another man—"

"Another man? Fat chance at your age!" he laughed derisively.

"You're not taking me seriously, Roger; I knew you wouldn't," I moaned, feeling hurt by his sarcasm. "You think your manhood is being questioned and your ego's upset. Just for once, put yourself in my shoes. I only want what you get every time we do it. Don't you see? I want us to get our act together and be united in ecstasy. Is that so hard for you to understand?"

"If that's so, why the rubber substitute?" he retorted — smirking, thinking he'd caught me out.

"That was a mistake. I thought it might bring me on — you know, so that we could make it together. But I must have bought the wrong sort. I didn't like the look of it and the smell of latex put me off," I said honestly. "But I didn't get chance to try it anyway —you cooked it! I wanted to see if I'm capable of getting feeling inside me, that's all, because I have to tell you, Roger, when we do it, I'm just dead meat!"

"I find that hard to believe," he said, shaking his head.

"Oh, yes, I know you can get me worked up, but it doesn't get me anywhere. Once you get plugged in, that's it. Full stop for me — full steam ahead for you!"

I burst into tears, sobbing my heart out. Roger was bewildered. He stopped being concerned about his virility and put his arm around me. "Why didn't you tell me? All these years and you've been unhappy. You make me feel like a selfish rotter."

"I don't want to upset you...I just want to feel you...enjoy you...I want things to be different...for us to be closer," I spluttered between my sobs.

Roger leaned on his elbows and put his hands over his face. "All this time and you've said nothing, and now this," he mumbled. "You make me feel really mean — a selfish bastard — useless." He gave a big sigh, got up wearily and informed me that he was going to cut the grass. "I can't sit here all day long doing nothing. I can't work on the car — you've seen to that," he groused in his usual petty manner.

"No, don't leave me, we have to talk," I pleaded, getting up after him. "I'm not trying to make you feel bad, I just want us to get things better for both of us. Only you can give me what I want and need."

"Apparently not," he replied tetchily, his facial expression revealing his wounded pride. He opened the kitchen door. "I'd better go and do something I know I can do."

I rushed over to him and gripped his arm. "No, please don't go outside, Roger. Stay with me, I need you," I urged him. "We need each other. It's not the fault of either of us." I pushed the door closed and put my arms around him. "It's how we were brought up — our lack of education and expectations. Can't you see that?"

"Things were different then," he mumbled irritably, his head bent.

"Of course they were, that's what I'm saying." I put my arms more closely around him. "I'm at fault just as much as you are, in fact, more so. Please don't be unhappy, we can work it out. You're probably missing out on a lot yourself. How will you know what some things are like if we never try them? This could be a new beginning for both of us." I gave him a little kiss on his cheek but he shrugged me off.

"I'll have to think about it. You've dropped a bombshell," he muttered, refusing to be comforted. Shaking his head again, he left me and went out to cut the grass.

Later on we had our meal in near silence, he didn't want to talk. We were both miserable. I knew that's how he'd take it. It was always the same — anything that hinted of criticism and he'd sulk for days. I shouldn't have listened to Tony, it was going to take ages for Roger to get over it. Would he want to have sex again knowing he couldn't satisfy me? It's a bit of a turn-off for any man. Well, if he turned his back on me, too bad! My tutor was waiting in the wings; there would be no hitches performing with him.

But, I must admit, I was beginning to feel angry — with Roger, with Tony with any man that came to mind. Men ruled my life and they always had done. They determined what I could or couldn't do. After many years I was realising that I had to rely on a male for something I wanted and needed — sexual fulfilment. It was utterly galling. Perhaps lesbians had got it right. Maybe I should have been one. Could that be what was wrong with me I wondered.

My childhood friend, Carol, came to mind. I was staying with her while her parents were away for the night. If they had truly known their daughter, they would have locked her up rather than let her loose.

She showed me how to drape her satin bed-quilt into an elegant gown, and between us we had it pinned to her beautiful naked body. Then, at her request, I took her photograph with her Box Brownie. She became much more daring when she threw aside the quilt and insisted I photograph her completely naked. I thought it a very shocking thing to do but I could never refuse her anything.

"What will your parents say when they see the photographs?" I asked her.

"They won't see them. I've got plenty of money to get them printed. Come on, let me take your photo with nothing on,"

"No thanks," I said.

I was really scared her parents would find out. Bad enough, we had been sticking pins in their silk quilt, but a rude photograph of their daughter? Would her dad throw me out and tell my parents?

Would he want payment for the quilt? As it turned out, much to my relief, the light had been too poor to get even a shadow.

But that was not all that happened on that very adventurous evening. The main event was a revelation to me. She had us playing realistic wives and husbands. What an education she must have had at that convent school to make her so open to experimentation. She knew a lot about what boys did to girls. She wanted to show me, and before long she had us both naked and in bed. She fondled my breasts and it had felt quite pleasant. Afterwards, she had me doing the same things to her. It was only adolescent exploration but later on I burned with self-recrimination and I never stopped feeling the shame of what we had done. My getting touched by men had changed things and it all became so very squalid — a breaking of a taboo. But, at the time, my experience with Carol had seemed natural and not at all shocking.

We had pooled our knowledge, mine being confined to the deflowering of Flossy event. But enlightened with such facts of life, for once, I was able to inform Carol of something she didn't know — male and female only come together when the female is on heat. If Carol was right about what husbands and wives did, it seemed to me to be an incredibly disgusting business. But the touching had been all right, as each of us had been blessed by the other's ignorance of sexual taboos and practices. But would I have been happier as a lesbian? Never!

"Oh, to hell with it!" I yelled aloud, now angry with myself. I was just an old geriatric with nothing else to think about.

Roger was still sulking the following morning. The night before, he'd resisted all attempts to let me give him a soothing massage and he didn't want me to wash his back. Now he didn't want a cup of tea in bed. I prepared the breakfast and began to wonder if I should go dancing that afternoon. Perhaps I should be at home in case Roger came back from bowls early.

I was about to call him to let him know his breakfast was ready when I heard him on the telephone. I guessed he was talking to Tony.

"When you bring her back from dancing, will you stay for a meal?" There was a brief silence and then he said, "Good. I really would like to talk to you. You know, about what you were saying last week." His voice dropped to a whisper: "It's Alice, can't talk now but she's got me worried." Another pause with grunting. Finally, "Thanks, Tony, you're a real friend." He put the phone down carefully and came for his breakfast.

I was in a very mixed up mood when Tony came with his car to pick me up for dancing. I couldn't ask him anything because Cyril was already in the car. I was surprised to find Clive and Barbara also going with us, and I was glad to be sitting in the front with Tony where there was more space. As soon as we arrived at Victoria Hall, Clive dived out of the back to get inside and on to the platform. Cyril, the perfect debonair gentleman, assisted Barbara out but I stayed with Tony while he drove off to park his car.

It just gave us a few minutes for me to express my anxieties. I quickly told him of Roger's reaction to my telling him about my problem and of its coming to light through the battery business. Tony couldn't help but smile. He said I was lucky the batteries hadn't exploded. He could see I was not amused. He squeezed my hand and said that it was all for the good.

"He has to face the truth sometime, the sooner, the better," he assured me. "Don't worry, Alice, his misery will turn to joy once he gets used to the idea of trying something new. I'll talk to him, he trusts me."

I thought what an odd situation it was — my would-be lover giving my husband advice! But then, everyone seemed to regard Tony as being a remarkable man.

Just as I entered the hall from the cloakroom, Madge beckoned me to go over to her table. Tony was already there and so were Frank, Cyril, Barbara and a few people I didn't know. I was introduced to the others: Roderick Cross, a retired police sergeant, with his wife, Joyce, and Raymond Pickford, a retired headmaster, with his wife, Joan.

We chatted about the weather, the rise in house prices, the cost of insurance, and other boring subjects. Frank started up about terrorists, saying what he'd like to have done to them. I was trying to give the reasons why people became terrorists but no one wanted to listen. As soon as the band struck up for the next dance, Tony took my hand. "Shall we?" he asked, glancing at the dance floor. I was very pleased to accept.

While we were dancing, Tony explained, "Frank's nephew was killed, and his ageing relatives injured in a terrorist attack. I won't go into details. If he wants to tell you about it, he will. It was a big shock to Madge and Frank just when Madge had been diagnosed with, lets say, her serious illness. So you see why no one replied to what you said? They didn't want to hurt or offend, and I suppose they were embarrassed too. It's a very tricky situation."

"Gosh, how awful for Frank and Madge."

"Yes, but don't dwell on it, Alice. Now, others will want to dance with you this afternoon. It would be a good thing if you accepted. With the present tricky situation regarding Roger it wouldn't do for us to be the subject of tittle-tattle."

"You're right, of course," I agreed, but I didn't really want to dance with anyone else, including the perfect dancer, Cyril. After the unpleasantness with Roger, I had been looking forward to being in Tony's arms.

For the next half an hour several men asked me to dance, including the newcomers, Roderick and Raymond. Roderick was of heavy build, his large brown eyes were emphasised by heavy-framed glasses and his well-greased hair was dyed black. He was dressed very formally in a dark suit and a brilliant white shirt. The simplicity of his clothes served to emphasize his rather jolly red-spotted bow tie below his chubby double chin. I could just see him as the proverbial laughing policeman, which rather belied his name, Cross.

Raymond Pickford was much thinner and a little taller. He had very thin grey hair brushed sideways over his bald patch. His bulging watery grey eyes were framed by thin wire-framed specs. His sharp nose was very shiny and had a leaning towards his rather protruding chin. He was wearing a dark grey suit with blue shirt and silver and blue striped tie. I could imagine him wearing a gown and ready with a cane in his hand to whack the boys, but Tony told me he had been a very popular head of a housing estate junior school and the kids loved him.

Roderick tended to bounce as he danced which was a little disconcerting but, in a way, rather invigorating once I got used to it. He had a habit of laughing at the slightest thing he thought amusing, which was rather good for my self-esteem. I told him that when I was a child I thought sergeants were called bobbies because they were in charge of twelve coppers, and that the police station should have been called the police pound as they took down a lot of notes.

"And what about the criminals?"

"Oh, they were just bad currency."

He laughed. "I like you, Alice. Has your husband got a sense of humour?"

Roger's sense of humour, or lack of it, was something I preferred not to think about at that moment. "Well, he married me!" I quipped and, of course, Rod did his laughing policeman act.

When Raymond was dancing with me, he was practically massaging his aftershave over my hair and face. I wouldn't have minded but it rather clashed with my own delicate perfume. But his conversation was bright and joky. I asked him if teaching had become more difficult over the years.

"I've been out of it a little while — took early retirement. Too much red tape, tests and exams, and not enough of the nitty-gritty teaching. I miss it though. You know, seeing kids grow and develop. They can be so funny too — keep you on your toes. You think you're getting somewhere and they come out with something that really throws you."

"Having four sons and ten grandchildren, I have an idea what you're talking about."

"Well, multiply that by hundreds. They are all interesting individuals but you can get some proper characters."

I was thinking he was a bit of a character himself. He was a reasonable dancer but every so often he would do a little twiddly foot routine on his own and then carry on as normal.

"I well remember a grand little lad that hadn't a clue. I deliberately chose him for a little play for assembly. We were enacting the story of Jesus and his healing of Blind Bartimaeus. You will know the story: Bartimaeus calls out to Jesus, Jesus asks the beggar what he wants and Bartimaeus says he wants to see, and so on."

"Yes, I know it; a very familiar story. I'm not sure about miracles though."

"I know what you mean. Scripture should be geared to how best children can receive it, don't you think? I always liked the kids to act stories in their own words — more natural."

"Sounds good to me," I said, after he had completed one of his twiddly hopping routines.

"Young Jimmy, a sprightly young lad, was the blind beggar and he did his yelling to Jesus bit. A slow boy, Tommy Timms, was playing Jesus. He asked Bartimaeus what he wanted. Jimmy yelled that he wanted his sight back. Poor Tommy was nearly in tears. He looked across at me and spluttered, "I haven't got it, Mr Pickford!""

I had to laugh. "Poor kid. I guess you never know what goes on in children's minds."

"Teachers do their best to find out. One of the hardest things these days, with magician stories being so popular, is getting children to understand the difference between miracle and magic."

"Miracles don't happen very often, that is, ones that are obvious — healing the blind and all that," I told him after another of his Lord Of The Dance foot manoeuvres. "With all the suffering in the world people lose faith."

"I know what you mean, Alice, but you know sometimes you can see little miracles take place under your very eyes. Take young Angela. We were all worried about that kid. She came from a very deprived home — Social Services were involved." He stopped while he was guiding me around a couple that had decided to have an argument in the middle of the dance floor. "Her blond hair was long and untidy as if it was never combed, and she was poorly and unsuitably dressed. She was always thin and pale and had little sores on her arms. Not surprising the child had difficulty reading or doing anything that needed concentration. Being a bit smelly, the kids kept away from her." He stopped talking a moment while we were passing a noisy couple. "So we gave her the leading part in a little play. She was the princess. She didn't have to speak — just look pretty. Mrs Hall, my deputy, made her a fantastic pink dress and she made a special effort with her hair — washed and curled it, and tied it up with flowers and ribbons. That kid was a picture. She smiled when she saw herself in the mirror. Her whole face lit up. No one had ever seen her smile like that before. The other kids looked at her in astonishment. 'Doesn't Angela look pretty' they said. And Angela beamed even more. There had been no jealousy, which was another little miracle. Things began to change for that kid. She's a nurse now. So you see, with a little cooperation, we can bring about small but very real miracles."

Hearing stories like that put my own petty problems into perspective. What I had was more than many people ever hoped for and with patience, maybe I could achieve what I wanted. It didn't have to be done in a rush. I decided I had been too hard on Roger. Maybe some rum truffles would cheer him up.

At the end of the dance we made our way back to the table. I was surprised to see Clive leave the band and come over to join us. He gave a quick greeting to those present and then took my hand and led me to the floor. I looked at Barbara but she just smiled at me and stood up to dance with Tony. I felt a pang of jealousy.

Before we started dancing, Clive nodded towards the platform and someone put on a record and announced that by special request from the livelier senior citizens, we were going to get a bit of rock-n-roll.

"Take your partners and lets rock around the clock!" The announcer boomed into the microphone.

Clive was no slouch when it came to moving around the floor and I must admit it was fun. I was young again, no matter that my joints were telling me otherwise. I saw Tony moving with Barbara and even Cyril was on the floor with Madge. How that man could shake his hips! In spite of myself, I couldn't stop an image coming into my mind of him making mad and passionate love to a velvet and plastic image of his heart's desire.

After the dance, I was about to sit down when Clive insisted I had a waltz with him. "Sorry, I consumed most of your biscuits last week. Babs was very cross. She said I was a greedy boy, which of course, I am — a very greedy boy in every respect! I've been instructed to buy you chocolates. Sorry, I keep forgetting."

I had a picture in my mind of Barbara, dressed in black leather, whipping Clive's naked bottom for being a very naughty greedy boy! I had difficulty stopping myself from laughing.

"Don't bother, Clive, I'm trying to give them up. Thanks just the same. I'm glad you enjoyed the biscuits. Anyway, you sang my song and that was payment enough."

He began leading me towards the tables so he could get back to the band. I was pleased to be able to sit and rest for a while as my body was forcing me to acknowledge my age.

Before long, Tony came and sat next to me and we had a pleasant little chat. Most of the others were on the dance floor. He leaned over and whispered in my ear, "Clive will be picking his car up from the garage later. He's taking the others back. How about we slip out now? We can have a little chat before I take you home."

I looked into his twinkling blue eyes. "I'd like that, Tony." I knew full well that we would be doing more than talking.

As we stood up to go, I saw Madge look in our direction and give a knowing smile. I didn't want others to think what Madge was thinking, so I emphasised a little limp to give the impression that I was ready for home. Supported by my escort, I serenely made my way to the cloakroom.

Forgetting all about shopping for Roger's truffles, it didn't take us long to get to Tony's car. Soon we were off, out of the busy town and heading for the narrow winding lanes used mainly by the farming community.

Tony took us to a quiet spot so that we could talk, or so he said. I must admit, I was hungry for his passionate kisses and his tender caresses. Before we started cuddling, he asked me if I'd ever had oral sex. Somewhat shocked by his question, I said that it was something we'd never done — that I'd never fancied doing. I didn't tell him about my more recent thoughts and fancies.

"You'd enjoy it," he assured me. "It's probably the hygiene aspect you're worried about and rightly so. In days gone by, we were lucky to get a bath once a week and most of the year we had to wash in cold water."

I had to smile at the truth of what he was saying. I remembered lack of coal to heat the water meant many a freezing wash, and our bathroom being so cold in winter that I rarely stripped. Even when coal was in better supply, the water took an hour to make its way through the furred up pipes to fill the rusting bath with the regulation five inches of quickly cooling water. For some stupid reason, my mind settled on the bathroom toilet, and then on the squares of stringed newspaper with which we wiped our bottoms when Izal or Miss Muffet rolls could not be had. That led me to thinking about the toilet seat. My dad painted it dark green. Paints were very different in those days and took ages to dry. More than one family member yelled as the drying paint acted as a hair remover! I was much cleverer. I put newspaper over the painted seat, but I ended up with newsprint stuck on my bottom! With difficulty, I brought my mind back to what Tony was telling me.

"Things have changed. Keeping clean isn't difficult," he said in a casual manner. "You don't have to boil everything for twenty minutes for peace of mind."

He was smiling, but I nearly burst out laughing at the pictures his words inspired in my naughty mind! I made no comment.

"I'm only asking because I intend mentioning it to Roger, along with other things I think he needs to know. If he tries something with you, I don't want him to be rejected."

"I can't see it happening," I answered after a moment or two. "I just can't imagine Roger doing anything like that, especially after what he said about TV sex. I saw it in the magazine I bought but I found it hard to look at. Do people really enjoy it, or is it all pretend?"

"Those that do it are obviously keen. Those that don't usually haven't tried it, or for some reason have been put off."

"I remember over fifty years ago, someone giving me a French kiss and I was nearly sick. His mouth was foul — horrible. I felt somehow violated. What you're talking about, the hygiene bit, is a similar thing isn't it?" I asked, feeling surprisingly comfortable about doing so.

"Yes. I suspect you've had a number of off-putting experiences. Anyway, that's what I wanted to talk about and to give you a mild demonstration."

"You mean you're going to—" I began, as his mouth was about to enclose mine.

"I could hardly do that. Just imagine it," he murmured.

He left me to consider what else he could be doing with his lips and tongue as he kissed me. With my imagination in full flood, I was utterly thrilled and looking forward to the main event with my husband.

Roger had arrived home first. He was busy in the kitchen when we walked through the front door. He was still having a bit of a sulk with me but he was bright and cheerful with Tony. He hadn't cooked the meat pie I'd made; instead he'd brought home some tripe and was busy cooking it with a double dose of onions — especially for Tony. I inwardly groaned and gave Tony a pitying look. He merely smiled and told Roger that he really shouldn't have gone to so much trouble. Knowing Roger's cooking skills, I was genuinely worried that he was going to end up with replacements for the soles of his trainers!

The men were early setting off for the meeting because Roger wanted time to talk with Tony. Knowing Tony would be recommending erotic love-play was making me tingle inside with excitement. I went upstairs to soak in the bath and to wallow in my thoughts of what might happen. I lay in the water thinking about the oral sex Tony was recommending. I was willing Roger to be open enough to listen and then to be eager to try it out. I was feeling very sensuous as I stepped out of the water, and decided to put on my white slinky nightdress to charm Roger out of his sexually despondent mood.

At ten, I heard a car draw up in the road outside the house and Roger's voice asking Tony if he wanted to come in for a hot chocolate. I assumed Tony declined as I heard a car drive away and Roger's footsteps approaching the house. He sounded perky enough. Things must surely have gone well.

I had the milk already warming for the chocolate as Roger walked into the kitchen. He came up behind me and put his arms around me. My heart leapt for joy. I turned to him with tears in my eyes. "Is everything all right, Roger? Are we back to where we were?"

"No! We'll never be back there again," he answered emphatically. He nuzzled the back of my neck murmuring, "From now on things will be different." Then he turned me to face him. His eyes were shining and his face was aglow. "I promise you, my darling, we'll start again together. Tony made me see the light. He's made everything seem so exciting."

"Oh, Roger, I'm so pleased," I said, feeling a mixture of relief and joy.

"My poor darling, I've been so unfair to you, but from now on you'll bless the day I had this chat with Tony," he assured me, giving my bottom a squeeze — too hard of course, but I didn't complain about the pain.

He looked at me soulfully. "I feel real bad talking about you to him, but I couldn't keep you out of it. Forgive me?"

"Oh, Roger, drink your chocolate and let's get to bed. I've got something to show you," I said excitedly, putting my arms around him and giving him a hug.

When I walked in from the bathroom, Roger was waiting semi-naked in bed, his pyjama bottoms neatly folded on a chair, giving away his intentions. I threw off my dressing gown and walked to his side of the bed. I smoothed my hands over the shiny satin and turned around so he could see the full effect of the winter landscape of white hills and valleys.

"You look fantastic," he said, his eyes shining brightly through his dark-rimmed glasses. "Very sexy, but take it off and come into bed," he demanded but in a rather sensuous manner.

I needed no persuading. I cuddled up to him and he started kissing me, and moving his hands over my body. I was utterly enraptured. At last, fulfilment was at hand. Miracle? Magic? Or simple education? No matter, for Roger was switched on after all those years and my happiness was to be his happiness too. He began to follow the downward path of his hands with his lips. My heart was beating fast; I was tremulous with anticipation. But I felt his tongue contact my belly button and irritation rather than pleasure caused me to wriggle. The way he was doing it — like trying to get the last bit of ice cream out of a cornet — was driving me mad. Obviously thinking I was overcome with erotic delight, he worked his tongue with greater fervour.

"Enough, enough," I yelled.

He took this as a sign of peaked ecstatic pleasure. He skipped following the downward path with his lips and turned to more familiar habits. He began his rapid woodworking routine.

"Slow down, darling, you'll tire yourself out," I pleaded tenderly, but thinking more of my own discomfort than of him getting weary.

But Roger was determined to give me an orgasm, and he worked away getting himself up to a proper sweat. But that wasn't all he was getting up. I knew he would soon be out of control.

"Please slow down, Roger, Vesuvius will erupt before you get anywhere," I murmured gently but firmly into his ear.

He groaned and started to roll over on top of me. I wanted to scream, "Not now!" Instead I said, "Let's do it differently. I'll come on top."

I was surprised when Roger rolled over on to his back and let me climb over him. In his usual engineering language, he said, "Can you plug it in all right?"

No problem there but I had no intention of making this the usual quickie. But Roger was too eager to get on and before long, unable to keep in rhythm with him, I was riding a bucking bronco, our flesh slapping noisily together and my knees getting more painful by the second. I didn't know whether to laugh or to cry but at least my mount was enjoying it, I'd never known him so vocal. After about twenty seconds, he yelled out like a champion tennis player achieving the winning point! It was embarrassing loud. With the window slightly open, anyone close to the house would surely have heard. It had been far too hilarious and much too sudden for me to experience sexual enjoyment but at least it had been different!

I rolled off him. Roger remained flopped out with a silly grin on his face. I was more than a little anxious.

"Roger, are you all right?"

He sighed happily, "Wasn't that great? What an old temptress you are."

"You poor darling, you're flaked out. I'll get you a nice cup of tea." I gave him a peck on the cheek. "I'll put a little brandy in."

"Bring a couple of biscuits too," he ordered. I thought it was just like he'd given blood. "Phew! What a woman," he declared happily. "You've knocked the stuffing out of me." There might have been some truth in that remark!

His words echoed happily in my mind as I slipped on my dressing gown and hurried downstairs. I was back in five minutes hoping that he was recovered enough to give me just a little pleasure before dropping off to sleep — just a kiss and a cuddle, nothing that would exhaust him further.

Hobbling along with my painful knees, I made a quick visit to the bathroom while he was nibbling his biscuits. I returned washed nice and fresh, only to find him peacefully snoring. I assumed that would be it for a while, at least as far as Roger was concerned. Such exhilarating, satisfying episodes were likely to last him for ages. But at least, he wasn't sulking any more and we had taken a big step towards change. Of one thing I was very glad; he hadn't tried the kissing of tongues routine. Another dose of onions that night and I would have thrown up.

Chapter nine

Practice makes perfect — or does it?

During the following days I was feeling a rather old and decrepit geriatric. I found myself taking painkillers for my knees so as to get through my regular round of duties, charity work, and social engagements.

On the Saturday morning we went to the wedding of a grandson, dined in the evening with some of Roger's bowling friends and, on the following day, we attended a baptism of a recently arrived granddaughter. All of it was rather splendid but very tiring. On the Monday, apart from the usual household duties, it was my turn as a member of the Parish Pastoral People, or PPP as our trendy vicar liked to call us, to visit some of the bereaved and housebound parishioners.

Visiting can be a very rewarding task, even though one or two of the more senior housebound ladies grumble because the vicar never comes. "Old Canon Blotchly used to visit every week, come rain or shine," was a regular grouse of Mrs Smith. No use telling her that the Canon had two curates to assist him and that things were done differently these days. Mrs Smith would sit me by a large gas fire and then begin her diatribe. Listening carefully is a tiring business and before long I would be resting my elbow on the arm of the chair with a finger surreptitiously holding up an eyelid to keep me from dropping off. But on the whole, the ladies and few gentlemen were very welcoming and insisted on making some tea and serving it in a china cup.

I was asked to visit Mr Southland, a recently bereaved elderly gentleman who, although not a well man, was now living alone.

"Hello, it's you," he said as he opened the door. "I'm glad you've called. I'll get us some tea. Violet always gave her visitors tea."

"Would you like me to get it for us, Mr Southland?"

"No, thank you. Just make yourself at home, it won't take me a minute."

I was taken into the cosy living room of his small cottage. A coal and wood fire was burning in the grate and I wondered at the wisdom of elderly people having open fires. But, I must admit, in similar circumstances I wouldn't like other people telling me what I could or couldn't do. I smiled at my thoughts. Mr Southland was not so very much older than Roger and yet I had put him in the old-and-feeble bracket. Obviously, getting old is something very difficult to adjust to when you still feel young inside. From what I'd heard, Age Concern had been unable to help him. He'd said, "Bugger off," when someone called at the family's request. "Go look after those who want it — I'm not ready for the knacker's yard!"

I sat down in a wooden armchair away from the fire. Apart from not wanting to roast before my date with the crematorium, I didn't fancy sitting in a badly stained cushioned chair, no matter how comfortable it looked. I tried not to look at the dust that had settled on the furniture, or at the dirty stained tea towel hanging from the sink in the adjoining kitchen. But the odour of dirty water and grubby dishcloths floated towards me from the open door in an almost visible trail. I remembered that his wife used to soak her dirty washing in an old white enamel pail. It had the same stench. Clearly, unless the pail had been there since his wife's death, Mr Southland was following the family tradition.

Muttering that he couldn't find the biscuits, Mr Southland emerged from the kitchen carrying a pretty flowered china cup in a saucer with gold rims. He handed me the tea with shaking hands. I quickly took it from him before there was more liquid in the saucer than in the cup.

I tried to hold my breath against the strong odour of sweat from his food-stained jacket, and the acrid smell of urine and body stench issuing from his fraying trousers. "Thank you, Mr Southland, just tea is fine, I'm trying not to eat biscuits at present." Seeing old lipstick stains and dried dribbles on the cup, and knowing what went on in the kitchen, I felt like giving up tea as well.

For the next hour, he talked about his Violet and I sat back and did my best to empathise with his feelings. But with Roger and me heading faster every year in the same direction, part of me is always holding back. I didn't want to feel his pain — it was too close to home. But enough of it came through to bring tears to my eyes.

"She suffered terrible you know, but never complained, no, not my Violet."

"She was a very special person, Mr Southland."

"Special? She was that all right. Did I tell you…"

And so he told me, as he did every time I called, about all of Violet's saintly acts of courage and mercy. Of course, everyone knew that Violet could be a right cantankerous harpy when the mood took her, but who are we to judge? Essentially, she was the person her husband preferred to remember, and that was all right by me.

As I left, he thanked me profusely for coming and said that I had made his day. I felt good about my visit, but Mr Southland's heartfelt eulogy concerning his angelic wife had pricked my conscience about the way I grumble about my dear husband. I called at the butchers on my way home to get some steak and kidney to make Roger's favourite pie. To punish myself for my petty complaints, I fried him plenty of his adored home-grown onions to go with it.

The following day, I was escorting visually impaired outpatients at the local hospital. That was always a very enjoyable task. It was good to meet up with other volunteers for a cuppa and a chat afterwards, as well as helping very appreciative patients. So, in a way, it gave me a bit of a break before Wednesday, when I was helping in a charity shop all day. Meeting customers is quite pleasant, especially when good sales are made or old friends drop in. But, since I only help part-time, I usually spend most of the day sorting and ironing in a back room. Rather boring really.

It was Roger's birthday on Thursday. It so happened to fall on the day the local Society of Retired Professional Engineers held a morning lecture followed by lunch. Since Roger wanted me to go with him, I put off visiting our latest grandchild to another day.

I wore my soft grey trouser suit with a blue top. I always like to dress well on these occasions, more for Roger's benefit than my own. There are usually about ninety people present and nearly half them are women, mostly in the older age bracket. One thing all the women have in common — they are all smartly dressed. No twin sets and pearls with these ladies, but suits, dresses with jackets and the latest in casuals.

Roger likes to meet up with a few ex-colleagues. Their wives, a little younger than the men, are well made up and always immaculately dressed. They know each other and engage in a lively conversation which, when the dining room is full, I have difficulty keeping up with. But, if I can't keep up with sparkling conversation, I can at least look interested and intelligent by trying to give the right reactions. Since the lines in my face are emphasised when I'm bored, I always try to keep my lips curled up at the corners, stay alert and when the others laugh, laugh with them. It is quite a strain but Roger wanted me there and I couldn't let him down. After all, being a fellow of his engineering institution and sitting on various committees, he doesn't want to look as if he has an idiot for a wife.

The lecture took place in a large and rather airless room, made worse by overcrowding. I like to sit at the back so I can move around a bit. The Chairman, Sam Bingham, whom I always regard as Mr Snooty Big, brought his new wife, a woman in her middle fifties, to the back and asked Roger to keep an eye on her while he was at the front. She insisted on sitting so close to Roger that she was almost on his knee and then chatted throughout most of the lecture. We heard all about their latest expensive trips abroad, their villa in Spain, her personal achievements, her distribution of wealth to the needy, her fondness for Roger, but we heard very little of the lecture! She probably thought that being the Chairman's wife entitled her to do just as she wanted. I was very annoyed. If it had been me chatting, Roger would have told me to shut up in no uncertain terms. I guess he was flattered by her attentions or didn't want to offend Snooty Big. That man had too much power over Roger and I resented it. Not wanting to hear more about the Binghams and their luxurious lifestyle, as soon as the lecture was over I beat a hasty retreat to the toilets to prepare myself for my luncheon act.

We joined Roger's dining colleagues for a glass of pale sherry. After a few polite exchanges we found ourselves a table where we could all sit together. It was a large dining room with tall windows looking out over extensive gardens, but we had to sit in a gloomy corner so as to have a big table. I put on my approved smile and, barely able to hear the conversation, I carefully watched lips and body language.

A lot of noise was going on at the next table. The Snooty Bigs were recalling the round-the-world flying tour they recently enjoyed. I glanced in their direction, wishing they would take a rest from bragging. Then out of the cacophony of voices assaulting my brain, I became aware that someone was speaking to me.

"What about you, Alice," said Jim who was sitting next to me, "have you tried using one?"

"Er, sorry, I didn't quite catch it."

"A vibrating tool. Lorna couldn't wait, she sent away for one. She gets no end of pleasure using it."

"I certainly do," Lorna appeared to say. "I really would recommend one, Alice. With Roger busy doing his own thing, you really would enjoy having a go."

I couldn't believe what I was hearing, or thought I was hearing. Well, if that was the way the conversation was going, I might as well join in.

"I did get one but never used it — Roger cooked it in the oven."

I thought my humour would get a little laugh but all I received were blank looks. Roger was glowering at me. I felt a right idiot.

"Er, he accidentally put the oven on. He didn't cook it on purpose," I stammered.

"Why did you put your engraving tool in the oven, Alice?" Lorna asked, looking very puzzled.

I suddenly twigged what they had been talking about. Like me, Lorna was an arty-crafty person and we both liked to try out different crafts.

"Oh, it was a vibrating glass-engraver you were talking about. Yes, I do have one. I'm sorry, I thought you were talking about a vibrating toothbrush," I lied, not entirely convincingly. It raised questions as to why I would enjoy playing with a battery-powered toothbrush while Roger was enjoying his own thing. "I dropped it accidentally in the bath. I tried drying it out while the oven was just slightly warm. Roger put the oven on to cook a casserole and it — well — sort of—"

"Exploded?" suggested Jim.

They all burst out laughing. Roger was doing a trick of laughing with them while frowning at me.

"I have an electric toothbrush. Useful little things," said Lorna, giving Jim a coded smile.

"Yes, indeed," I said, hoping I had heard correctly. "They give a very good massage — gums, that is."

All, but Roger, tittered loudly. I was wondering if they all thought I had been pleasuring myself in the bath while Roger was otherwise occupied. I felt my cheeks getting hot. Paul Pumphrey, Roger's previous deputy manager, came to my rescue.

"Well, Alice, you certainly have very good teeth, so you must have healthy gums. I must get one of those brushes myself."

The food arrived. Much to my relief, the conversation turned to the quality of what we were about to eat, for which, I was truly grateful. I must admit though, Lorna had made me wonder about the possible uses of electric toothbrushes. Maybe something good would come out of my embarrassing situation.

Friday morning, I felt incredibly tired. What with giving Roger a thorough massage the night before to make up for embarrassing him on his birthday, plus all the other week's activities, I could have done with resting rather than dancing that afternoon.

"You'll let Tony down if you don't go," Roger said emphatically. "Anyway, he'll be coming here afterwards for his tripe and onions dinner. He doesn't get it anywhere else. Then we'll be going on to the meeting as usual. We're going to have another little chat," he said, giving me a knowing look. "It's part of Friday now. Buck up, old girl; don't let the side down. He's picking you up at two."

The thought of seeing Tony again thrilled me, but I was afraid that now he had Roger moving in the right direction he would back off. In the small hours of the morning, memories of his gentle romantic love play filled my mind and set me longing for more. My emotions were all churned up. I was afraid he would go on but fearful he wouldn't; worried he'd drop me but troubled we'd already gone too far even though it was only kissing and tender caressing.

I spent Friday morning sewing curtains for one of the kids. I realised my eyes were getting dimmer and that I needed stronger lenses for close work. I was also getting more conscious of the cataracts that were beginning to form. I realised too, if I wanted to avoid tricky situations, I needed one of those micro hearing aids. When I rose from my chair to get Roger a coffee before he went out, my knee gave way. It was all so very depressing.

I was debating whether to ring Tony to tell him not to pick me up when the phone rang. It was Jean Smith — the last person I wanted to talk to.

"Hello, Alice, it must be ages since we had lunch together. Can you make it today?" She sounded very pushy.

"Sorry, Jean, it will have to be some other time, I'm snowed under at present," I said, hoping she wouldn't try to arrange something for later.

"We'll make it next week. I'll phone you, I'm not sure how I'm fixed at present," she replied, bossy as ever. "I just wanted to tell you the news about Pat; she's getting a divorce — at her age! And did you know that Reggie Burrows has dementia? Poor Rachel, it's always hardest on the wife you know."

Once roused, there was no stopping Jean's chatter. She went on and on. Just as I thought she had finished, she started up again. On and on she rattled, like the little steam train that ran along the Esk valley. I waited for her to run out of steam.

"You must have heard about Janet's stroke. I don't know how her husband copes," she declared, enjoying her bits of melancholy news. "Of course, you must know about George. You do, don't you? After all, you are both friends of his. His cousin Lucy is just waiting for him to have another heart attack. I don't think you know Mary Brown — or is it Green? My memory is going, old age gets us all in the end." What Jean couldn't remember, she was bound to make up any way that suited her. "Well, Mary collapsed. Her husband tried to pick her up and he had a heart attack. Poor things — they're both being buried next week!" It was said as a sort of punch line. She paused to give an exaggerated deep sigh. "I suppose it's nice to go together. Don't you think so, Alice?"

I was about to give my opinion when she said, "Sorry, Alice, I'd like to chat a bit longer but I have to be in town for twelve. My back's been killing me and I'm getting a bit of acupuncture. You should try it, my dear. It's better than pills, you know. Nice to have a chat but must go. I'll ring next week. Cheerio!"

"Goodbye, Jean," I said but the phone had already gone dead.

Feeling totally depressed, I made myself a coffee and sat thinking about the vagaries of life. Jean thrived on bad news. Strange how the misfortune of others gave her, and many like her, a buzz. I reached for my painkillers and took a couple, thinking perhaps I should go and have a lie down; after all, it had been a busy week.

While drinking my coffee I picked up the newspaper to read. The headlines told of a politician caught in a public lavatory with his trousers down. "Big news!" I exclaimed. Half the world starving and because someone's sensibilities can't cope, that poor sod is getting blasted. Probably entrapment anyway. "Never mind, mate," I said aloud, "We could all be dead tomorrow!"

I was about to walk upstairs when the phone rang again. I couldn't bear another Jean-like chat and decided to let it ring, but then I remembered Roger saying he might call me if he decided to come home for lunch. Wearily, I picked up the receiver, "Coming home then?" I asked.

"Alice? It's Tony. What's wrong? Are you ill?" He sounded genuinely concerned.

I broke down in tears but managed to mutter, "Oh, Tony, I'm a mess. I feel so old and haggard, I can't go dancing today — I really can't."

"What's the matter, Alice?" he asked as though speaking to a hurt child.

"Nothing really. I'm sorry, but you won't miss me, there's so many spare women just itching to get you on the floor." I nearly laughed hysterically, as my tired mind became aware of what I'd said. I was imagining Tony on the floor with a pile of women on top of him! "But please come for your tripe tonight, Tony, or Roger will be cross with me." Instead of laughing, I was now sobbing like a kid in trouble.

"Alice, listen to me. Put your glad rags on — do it now! I'll be there in fifteen minutes. I'm taking you to lunch — no arguments! Is that clear?" He was sounding very masterful.

"But, Tony, I'm a mess!" I almost wailed.

"You have fifteen minutes to clear the mess away. Get cracking!"

The phone had gone dead. I sat on the stairs wondering what to do. The phone rang again. I picked it up thinking Tony might have changed his mind. It was Jean again.

"Hi, Alice, I'm just waiting here for my appointment and I remembered I forgot to tell you that Ann Granger's funeral is next—"

"Sorry, Jean," I cut in, "I'm just on my way out — must dash!"

I silently cursed mobile phones; they were lethal weapons in the hands of people like Jean. I put the answerphone on and went upstairs to get changed.

I washed my face and quickly put on a trace of make-up, brushed and combed my thinning hair into some sort of order and then tried to decide what to wear. Before long, I had stripped and put on my black lacy undies. I found some black stockings and an old but pretty black suspender belt I'd had in the drawer for about twenty years — the elastic had gone a bit so it fitted all right. I found a black waist-slip to wear with it. From my closet, I retrieved an old but pretty multicoloured flowered button-through dress and tried it on.

"You shall go to the ball!" I shouted. The bell rang to let me know my coach had arrived.

Tony was standing there looking both worried and puzzled. "I thought I heard you shouting. Are you all right, Alice? But, I must admit, you look fantastic. You really do. I'm not just saying it to cheer you up."

"Thank you. I'm okay now," I told him with a big smile. "Come in a minute. I'll get my coat."

I closed the door behind him and threw my arms around his neck. "I'm so pleased to see you, Tony. Please hold me and make me feel a woman — not a decaying carcass."

He instantly obliged and it did the trick all right. Soon he was helping me on with my coat. "There's nothing decaying about you, Alice," he murmured as my arms slid into the sleeves. "However you may feel, you look great — you're still a youngster at heart."

It was what I wanted to hear, and the way I wanted to hear it — with tenderness.

A little later, we were driving to a county inn and I was giving Tony a brief account of my problems and fears about old age. He drove slowly so as to give me some attention. He stopped the car in a gateway. "I can understand all that you're saying," he said. "I guess all of us oldies get those feelings from time to time. But we still have a lot of living to do. Believe it, my dear. Some women burn themselves out by living always on a high. Others, like you, take things steady and still have much to look forward to." He took hold of my hand and gave it a tender kiss.

I smiled. "With you beside me, I can believe anything, Tony."

"Tell me, Alice, did my talk with Roger make any difference?"

I told him what had happened with Roger the week before and he listened with a variety of emotions showing on his face.

"You were very adventurous, but you'll have to take more care of yourself. It's Roger we need to get more active but in more gentle forms of lovemaking."

I gave him a nod. "You are so right, Tony."

"You did a lot for him and it's set the ball rolling but we have to get him to concentrate on you. You know a man can get a lot out of pleasing a woman — the build-up is as exciting as the event."

"I have no doubt he gets something out of the build up. But I doubt it's from pleasing me."

"He hasn't discovered the joy of pleasing you yet. He just sees foreplay as a mere preliminary to the big bang, rather than integral to the whole experience. In a way, he's switched off to your feelings because he's trying to control his own," he said, speaking with the voice of a skilled practitioner.

It was lovely listening to someone who understood the problem. "I do tell him to slow down, Tony, but either he can't or he's just too set on getting there."

"No wonder you're feeling a bit low today. What with your disappointment, your busy week, your friend's doom and gloom, and your painful joints, it's quite a lot to endure all at once. But golly, you certainly have made an effort to get out of it. You look absolutely splendid."

He moved his hand from mine to turn my face to his. The long fingers and soft palm of his hand cupped my chin and cheek so very tenderly.

I smiled with the pleasure of his comforting touch. "You lifted the depression from me, Tony. I will never be able to thank you enough."

He looked into my eyes and whispered, "It really is my pleasure. It's a two-way thing you know — you've done a lot for me too."

He kissed me passionately. My body was so on fire for his touch that my imagination had him slipping his hand inside my dress and working his magic on me. I could almost feel the gentle softness of his hand against my flesh. After a few minutes I was about ready for anything. Thankfully, Tony started the engine and said it was time we had lunch or we would be late for dancing.

We had our meal in a grand little inn. The blazing fire might have been artificial but the welcoming smile was not. The atmosphere was quietly relaxing and the cosy corners, partly enclosed by slatted screens, almost romantic. Mellow lighting was kind to mature skin. Soft background music of Nat King Cole singing old time favourites was easy on the ear. Since we were dancing afterwards, we only had a light meal but it was excellent. All the time we were eating or chatting, a notice on the wall kept attracting my attention. It was advertising three en-suite double bedrooms. My black undies seemed to be burning a hole my skin.

"So, it's to be Roger's special tonight? Better leave some room. I'll give the pudding a miss," Tony said, interrupting my thoughts.

I blinked myself awake from daydreaming; "I'm sorry, what did you say, Tony?"

He realised I had been looking at something over his shoulder. He turned around and saw the notice. "Nothing would give me greater pleasure but I rather think you would have many regrets. Apart from which, we would be missed this afternoon and Roger would hear of it."

I blushed and hung down my head in the shame of having my yearning brought into the open. I had never met anyone as intuitive as Tony. He took my hand and said tenderly, "I'll get you there with Roger. If not, then — well — we'll see."

I looked into his eyes, now sparkling with having been aroused with erotic thoughts. His lips too, seemed fuller and so very kissable. I could see he wanted me as much as I wanted him. I wasn't making it easy for him to resist.

"Thanks, you're a real friend, Tony," I whispered, my eyes still looking deeply into his. "To both of us, of course," I quickly added, but my body was telling me to forget Roger.

He tenderly kissed my hand. "My dear, dear, Alice," he whispered. "I think perhaps we had better leave before I change my mind."

It didn't take long to get to the dance hall. We sat in silence most of the way, with Tony apparently concentrating on driving, and me thinking about how my life had suddenly changed. Before Tony came along, I was always worrying about our sons and their children, but now I just let them get on with their lives; being ready to listen and help if needed. Tony had given me a zest for living. When he was around, even my medical problems became inconsequential.

Roderick and Raymond were at the dance again. Wanting to dance with Tony, I hoped to avoid them but they were both waiting for me to arrive. Roderick walked in front of Raymond and taking my arm led me onto the floor. I was protesting that I was waiting for Tony but he wouldn't take no for an answer.

Rod was chatting away and doing too much bobbing around. I was finding it hard to concentrate and fell over his feet, hurting my ankle.

"So sorry, Alice. I should get arrested for grievous bodily harm," he joked. "Would you like to sit down?"

As we made our way to the tables, Raymond came forward and offered his arm. "I can see you're a wounded soldier, Alice. Need a hand?"

I was flattered by the attention I was getting. The two wives were looking genuinely worried. Rod's wife, Joyce, insisted on getting me a cup of tea, while Joan went down on her knees to look at my ankle. "A bit bruised but it should be all right. Lucky you don't have varicose veins, Alice."

I have, but not near my ankles. The others didn't need to know that. "Please don't fuss," I said, thinking I was being treated like a poor old geriatric.

"What have you been doing to Alice?" It was Tony arriving at the table.

"My fault," said Rod. "Can't keep my plodders off the dear lady's ankle."

"It really is all right. Please don't fuss."

Joan arrived. "Here's a nice cup of tea."

"Please go on dancing," I urged the others, hoping they would clear off and leave me in peace.

The band struck up a barn dance. Rod and Ray looked at their wives, who smiled and nodded. "We've been waiting for this," said Joan. "Do you mind, Alice, if we leave you?"

"Alice won't be alone, I'm here," said Tony.

Before we had chance to talk, Madge and Frank arrived. For the next ten minutes we engaged in pleasant chatter. Madge told us that she had decided to have the biggest party yet. "You must come, Alice, and bring your husband too. Roger isn't it?"

" You remember him?"

"Oh, yes. I think it was a social organised by something Frank belongs to — or was it a lunch? Anyway, I seem to remember him as a very knowledgeable person. Had something to say on just about anything."

"That sounds like Roger."

"I think he said that you were looking after young grandchildren, or some such."

"Quite likely, we do have ten of them. But Roger doesn't need me around, he can talk enough for both of us."

Madge smiled. She knew she had the right person in mind.

"I think you will know some of the ones coming. There's Ray and Joan, Rod and Joyce, and your neighbours, Clive and Barbara. Tony will be on his own — but not for long, if I can help it! Betty and Albert Mayfield, Lorna and Jim Green. Cyril's coming, but I'm not sure about his wife — I hear she doesn't like fun events. There's quite a few others but you probably don't know them."

At the mention of Lorna, I instantly thought of her electric toothbrush and what she might do with it. "Lorna and Jim are coming then? I only saw them yesterday."

"They were not sure if they could make it. It's two weeks tomorrow by the way — fancy dress, of course. The theme is Ancient Greece this time. Simple outfits will do."

I wondered if she intended being a Grecian beauty and wanted the rest of us ladies to look like her slaves. Fair enough — her party. "Thank you. I'm not sure but I'll ask Roger."

"Come with Tony if Roger is tied up," she said with a raised eyebrow and a little smile playing around the corners of her lips.

I looked at Tony. He had been sitting back quietly observing us.

"I rather think Tony will have his own plans," I said, thinking Saturday might be his night for pleasures of the flesh, whether at Madge's house or at a hotel maybe.

Tony grinned. "I think we can get Roger to go. I can just see him swathed in a bed sheet and looking very regal. He can be one of the philosophers; that should get him there."

Madge laughed. "We could give him tan minutes to entertain us."

Frank grinned. "Not the usual floor show. Roger might have to be provided with a few randy jokes to liven it up. Yes, not a bad idea."

I wanted to make sure there would be no hanky-panky going on. "I don't know, I think Roger has heard about odd things happening at the parties. I'm not saying bad things — just odd, that's all."

"But that's what makes a party go! No one goes home disappointed I can assure you," said Frank, sitting back and surreptitiously putting a little whiskey in his tea.

On the whole, it all seemed innocuous enough; after all, Betty Mayfield would hardly be drinking herself silly and throwing herself at another man. Even Glenda had been invited. But did anyone expect her to go? It would be somewhat restrictive for Cyril, poor devil. Thinking of what was involved in fancy dress parties, I decided it might be fun making the costumes. Yes, as long as Roger could be persuaded, I decided to accept.

Tony didn't have chance to talk to me personally again that afternoon. On the way home Cyril was with us, and he didn't leave the car until it pulled into our drive. Roger was waiting with the front door open. He already had the tripe in the oven and we could smell it before we entered the house. Tony looked at me and we both smiled. Roger was soon greeting his guest and whisking him away to talk committee business. I was left to serve up the meal.

We discussed Madge and Frank's party and Roger was surprisingly favourable. I soon found out why. He'd heard that Sam and Vera Bingham were going.

As soon as the meal was over, the men went off to their meeting. With Roger out for the evening, I decided to have one of my little dance sessions. With the curtains closed, I opened the kitchen door to let in sufficient light to dance by in the living room with just a reading lamp on. I put on a Dire Straights disc and got 'with it'. With the lamp correctly angled and my back to the light, I danced with my shadow cast on the wall in front of me. Shadows are better to dance with than reflections in mirrors — a shadow doesn't have wrinkles and we are like two youngsters dancing in perfect unity!

There's something about music and movement that lifts the heart and, no matter how strained my body, makes me feel young again. To the tune of "Walk of Life", I rolled my shoulders and hips sensuously, twisting my arms, hands and neck — pleased to be at one with my shadow. I was walking in tune with life. Aches and pains disappeared. I was alive, vibrant and ready for anything. I couldn't get enough. After dancing to the other tunes, rocking and rolling, I kept returning to walk with life until my flat batteries were completely recharged and I was in harmony within myself.

Afterwards, I went up for my evening bath. I sighed with contentment, and turned my mind to the education Tony might be giving Roger that night. Would Roger want to put theory into practice? A bit too soon after the last event but all things are possible when Roger gets the bit between his teeth!

By the time I stepped out of the water, I was feeling ready for anything. I was about to wrap myself in one of my big soft bath-sheets when I heard Roger coming in through the front door. He came straight upstairs and said that he would use my bath water.

"How about I give you a nice massage afterwards?" I asked him, letting the towel slip to the floor.

"Mm, that would be nice. Stay in the bathroom, you can wash my back," he said in his normal masterful way.

I started putting on my dressing gown.

"Leave that off. I like you as you are."

I thought that a good start — Roger was in the mood!

In the nude, I lovingly smoothed the soap over his neck, shoulders and back — brushing my cheek against his balding head while massaging his tired muscles. As I rinsed off the lather he took me completely by surprise by turning his head and kissing all before him. A most unexpected show of lust! A taste of things to come?

He didn't stay in the bath for long and he left the water for later — a positive indication of what he intended doing. Having other things in mind, he allowed me to massage him with ylang-ylang and lavender oil for about five minutes only. Then pulling me onto the bed he began his erotic love-play.

His kissing started on my lips and gradually drifted lower. I felt a little excitement brewing — tonight would be the night!

"Oh, yes, my darling, mmm, yes, yes," I groaned in response. I must admit it was only a cheerleader encouragement rather than voicing actual delight. But things had only just got started. Roger having been instructed by Tony, there was no telling what I was in for. I soon found out!

Lacking sensitivity and in a hurry to get the job done, he nipped me with his chipped lower tooth. But the resulting "Ahhhh!" from me appeared to be a signal — as far as Roger was concerned — to start the next procedure. He jumped quickly out of bed and swung me around, pulling my legs over the edge of the bed. While I was recovering my breath, he raised my hips and started on the final stage of his planned operation.

He was too soon and too fast for me, but I didn't want to stop his momentum and put him off for good. But I'm not young and lithe, and my hip joints were going into painful spasms.

"Ahh! Roger! Roger! Roger! Ahh!" I yelled, but my dear husband thought I was in a paroxysm of delight and renewed his efforts with even greater vigour.

"Stop, stop! Ahhh!" I yelled again, but Roger thought I was just being coy.

With all his shouting and grunting of, "Oo! Ah! Oo! Ah! Oo! Ah!" there was no doubting the pleasure he was getting!

"No, Roger! My hips, my hips! Ahhh! My leg, my leg, my leg!"

I was in agony as the calf of my right leg began objecting to my trying to ease my hips. I was now in danger of suffering from ferocious cramp. But Roger wasn't hearing what I was saying. With both of us yelling, he must have thought we had complete unison of ecstasy!

It didn't take him long to climax — fortunately for me! He fell on the bed with his eyes closed. "Phew! That was great, really great! You really got going there, old girl — life in the old dog yet, eh?"

I'd already jumped off the bed trying to ease the pain in my leg, but Roger didn't notice. He was so happy, how could I disillusion him? Time for talk later.

"How about a nice cup of tea?" I asked him when I could speak without pain distorting my voice.

"Just what the doctor ordered," he said breathing in deep gasps of air. "You sure are a mover, Alice. The way you were shaking those old legs of yours — don't know how you do it. I wish I had your energy!"

I put on my dressing gown and slippers. With difficulty, I made my way down the stairs to the kitchen wondering how soon we would need to install a stair lift! I took a couple of strong painkillers and had a little weep out of sheer frustration. If Betty and Glenda's husbands were like Roger in that particular department, then I now understand how they felt. Perhaps we should form a club! As I struggled up the stairs with the tea, I hoped I would be able to walk easier in the morning. My pathway to sexual satisfaction was proving far from smooth — in fact, crippling!

Chapter ten

Lunch with afters

I struggled through the weekend with the help of pills. I told myself things could not go on the way they were doing, but then, I had to admit that all that Roger needed was a gentle talking to — not so easy as it sounds — followed by careful practice. More than anything, he needed to be sensitive to what was happening to me.

I tried a few times to bring the subject up but he was too busy planning renovations to the bathroom, preparing old wood he'd salvaged from somebody's skip, and plugging holes in the garage roof — a sudden spell of wet weather was proving his last efforts to be totally inadequate. I had long given up pleading to have the roof replaced — according to Roger our financial reserves had to be kept for a rainy day!

I baked cakes and pies and the family popped in from time to time and scoffed most of them. It pleased me to see the children enjoying decent food. Like so many youngsters, they eat too many junk snacks and visit the golden arches.

At the beginning of the week, while Roger was busy working at his own self-imposed tasks I struggled through my household chores. Somehow, he managed to fit in reading his newspapers and watching his essential TV programmes, but by Wednesday he realised there were minutes to do for the next meeting. Instead of drafting them out first like he usually did, he dictated them while I typed them on the computer. It was absolute agony for me. He kept changing his mind and then arguing that I'd not typed what he'd told me to. I breathed a sigh of relief when he read them through and finally gave his approval. I ran off some copies and addressed the envelopes, grumbling to myself that it was time he gave up at least one of his secretary jobs.

I posted the minutes early afternoon while on my way to work in the charity shop situated along the road from the Coffeepot. Rosemary, who ran the shop, was not very pleased with me. Evidently I'd said I'd help out all day, not just the afternoon. She was not impressed with my excuse and seemed to think I'd been messing about all morning. She suggested I went in on Friday to make up for it. I refused, making the mistake of telling her where I was going. She got very uppity, saying I was always putting myself first, and that I didn't care a jot about the world's starving poor, or the sick and old.

"Tea and dancing? Don't you realise the people we help are starving? You can be so selfish, Alice," she concluded angrily, but not without a hint of jealousy.

That did it! I walked out saying that I'd leave her to be a martyr to the cause. I'd had enough of sorting through the piles of cast-offs, and washing and ironing at the back while they sat drinking tea and chatting to would-be customers.

Amazed at my assertiveness, I went to the Coffeepot to get a pot of tea to calm down and relax my tensed-up nerves. The episode was so unlike me, I was beginning to wonder if I knew myself any more. The renegade within me was getting tired of my being unappreciated and a lackey to the likes of Rosemary.

I wasn't expecting to see anyone I knew at the café that afternoon, so I was surprised when a slightly wavering voice broke through my thoughts, "Hello, Alice, do you mind if I join you?"

"George! Of course not. Sit down — I'll just move my coat," I said, pleased to make room for one of our oldest friends.

George was an elderly widower. His wife had been dead for a year or two and he'd been in and out of hospital ever since. "How are you?" I asked him, genuinely concerned about his health.

"Well, you know — better some days than others," he replied, giving me a sunshine of a smile. "But how are you keeping? I haven't seen Roger for a quite while. Still as busy as ever?"

"We're both quite well, thank you, and yes, Roger is still very active." I smiled at the thought of Roger's more recent activity.

The following half an hour passed by in pleasant talk about our families and friends. No one would have guessed that George had lost most of his guts, that his heart was kept going through bottles of pills and a surgical procedure almost past its sell-by date, or that he had sight and hearing problems. Even his waterworks kept him active day and night through frequent visits to the toilet. George was the most modest, kindest, gentlest and generous person I had ever known. With him, I could relax and be the person I am — warts and all.

When we parted, I felt calmer and more at peace with myself. Never once had George complained about his lot in life; he was grateful for the help he received and for the comfort of his family. It was obvious that he missed his wife — Lily had been the light of his life. But he didn't moan or protest; he was grateful for the sixty years they had spent together and for her unseen presence with him still. Tears of love and thankfulness formed in his eyes as he spoke of his Lily being with him day and night, watching over him and waiting for him.

I walked around town thinking deeply about life and the blessings I shared with Roger. I then returned to the charity shop, apologised to Rosemary and said that just this once I would work in the shop on Friday. I walked home enjoying the feeling of self-sacrifice. But the joy soon disappeared when I told Roger what I'd done.

"You're going to the shop instead of dancing?" He almost bellowed. "You can go there any day. What about Tony? I don't suppose he'll come for his tripe supper now, or go with me to the meeting. Really, Alice, why do you have to ruin things? Does Tony know you won't be going dancing? What a lame excuse. He'll think you're trying to put him off — that you don't want him around. Bad enough his wife's rejected him. He'll think his friends are doing the same."

"Oh, really, Roger, you do exaggerate," I told him calmly. "I doubt that Tony has rejection worries, and I'm sure he'll still come for supper and go with you to the meeting. I'm going to miss the dancing and Tony's company. But there are times when we all have to make little sacrifices."

"Well in future, don't involve other people in your petty acts of self-glory," retorted Roger pompously. So saying, he walked out of the room, muttering that he was going to phone Tony.

It was one of Roger's nights out and he would want an early meal, so I got busy in the kitchen. But I couldn't stop chuntering to myself about the ingratitude of the Rogers of this world while the Georges did their best with the unkind hand Fate had dealt them.

Roger was in a better mood after talking with Tony. "He's coming but I had to reassure him that you wanted him here. He wants a word with you first. Be quick, it's peak rates," he said, always mindful of the pennies.

I hurried into the hall with Roger calling from the kitchen, "And don't put him off!"

I picked up the receiver, "Hello, Tony; I'm sorry about Friday. It's just that I—"

"No problem, Alice. Now don't you worry about it," he cut in. "I'm pleased things are working out for you and Roger. I quite understand, but are you sure you want me to come on Friday?" he asked in his kindly way.

"Yes, please do come, Tony. I want to come dancing with you too. I really do. I'm sorry now that I agreed to go to the shop. I could have put the time in next week. I just got carried away." Dropping my voice, I said, "Things aren't working out with Roger. I need you; you have no idea how much. I'll explain everything when I see you again — if I get the chance, that is."

"Perhaps I'd better see you before I have another talk with Roger. What are you doing tomorrow?" He asked me, sounding quite concerned.

"Nothing planned," I told him. "Roger is going to one of his retired managers' luncheon meetings but I've refused to go with him this week. I'm tired of listening to the twittering of his cronies' wives while the men discuss more interesting things in the hotel bar."

"Suppose I pick you up and we go for lunch where we did last week? According to the weather forecast, it might be raining so we'll decide on other things when I see you."

I was hardly able to keep the excitement out of my voice. "That will be lovely. What time will you pick me up?"

"About ten-thirty. Suppose we make a day of it?"

"How lovely!"

"You'd better tell Roger about it and get his approval."

"Can I tell him you're coming for a meal on Friday?"

"Why not? I'll see you tomorrow then," he said amiably, adding with a hint of double meaning to his voice, "And, Alice, be prepared and dress appropriately."

I didn't think he was just talking about the uncertain weather. Tony had given me reason to believe I was in for a very pleasurable time. I tried to calm the excitement swelling in my breast before going to talk to Roger about my outing.

He was getting ready to go out. I told him the good news. "You'll be pleased to know Tony will be coming for his tripe on Friday. He's also going to pick me up tomorrow to take me to lunch. You don't mind do you?"

"Do I have reason to?"

I was struggling to find a non-incriminating answer when he revealed what was on his mind.

"I don't like him being so free with his money. He's a nice guy. Don't take advantage of his good nature, that's all. By the time Edith's finished with him he won't have two pennies to rub together."

"It is definite then? I mean his divorce — final stages and all that."

"Looks like it. Edith's staying with her sister at present. Nothing unusual in that apparently. She's trying to get the house, the furniture, the lot," he said, shaking his head at the thought of it.

"Sad, isn't it? Married all those years and then to split up," I said, my own situation nagging at me.

"From what I've heard recently, they should have done it years ago." He gave his head another wagging. "It's not all Tony, you know. I've been told Edith's got her eye on a more lucrative meal ticket. Would you believe she's been visiting George Winters several times a week?"

I was surprised but not shocked. "He's much older than she is; I doubt there's anything in it. I saw him this afternoon and I could see he's not a well man — far from it. Perhaps she's just giving him a bit of comfort, he must get very lonely."

"Exactly! Just ripe for picking!" he said vehemently. "He can't have that much longer to live with all his medical problems." I had visions of Roger getting out his black suit in readiness for a wedding followed by a funeral.

"We all have our needs. Perhaps Edith and George might be right for each other," I told him, trying not to be judgmental — I was in no position to be. "Clearly, she wasn't happy with Tony. It's for sure, George won't expect sexual favours — just a bit of company while waiting to join his Lily."

"Poor old George is very vulnerable. I don't trust that woman — she's after something. Edith must have known what Tony was like before they married. Too many women want everything and give nothing in return. They know what to expect when they marry," he said, nodding his head to give solemn weight to his thoughts on the subject. "Women like Edith, just want a meal ticket."

"But Roger, we don't always know what to expect. Some women must be very disappointed for opposite reasons to Edith's problem," I added with feeling. I soon wished I hadn't.

"Are you having a go at me, Alice? You should have told me years ago that you were dissatisfied and we could have fixed it," he muttered, sounding hurt.

"No, my darling, I'm just saying things have to be worked out together, like we are doing. Perhaps—" But Roger didn't let me finish.

He smacked me on the bum, and proclaimed, "Everything's great now — you little she-devil!"

"Roger, darling," I began as he was walking away to get changed, but his mind was elsewhere and he didn't hear me.

It was too late to start discussing my problems anyway. Roger was in a hurry to get a quick meal before dashing off. I heated up a nice bit of beefsteak casserole in the microwave. As he walked through the door to the dining room, it was waiting on the table, complete with a cup of tea and a dish of his favourite pudding. At least, we've managed to get our timing right in the domestic affairs that matter to Roger.

As he went through the front door to his car, he called out, "Be ready tonight — I'll manage a quickie," and he was off, happily whistling his favourite tune.

"That's big of you, darling, but tonight I'm going to bed with a headache!" I muttered to myself, but I couldn't help feeling guilty again.

The following day, Roger had only left the house half an hour before Tony arrived. I was about to put on my button-through dress, over new white lacy underwear I'd bought earlier that morning, when the bell rang. I slipped on my dressing gown and went quickly down the stairs to let him in.

"Sorry, Tony, do come in," I said, looking around outside to make sure I wasn't being observed. "I should have been ready, but I had to nip into town first thing this morning. I've just had a quick bath;

I won't be a minute getting dressed." I quickly closed the door behind him.

"Suppose I come up and help you?" he suggested with a twinkle in his eye.

I gave a little laugh. "I don't think you really mean that, Tony."

He grinned. "Quite right. I only enter a lady's bedroom when I'm invited."

My heart started to beat faster at the thought of him by my bed, touching my flesh and…

He came up very close and his gaze held me spellbound. My imagination felt his hand slipping inside my dressing gown.

"I knew it would be — smooth as silk," he whispered seductively.

"What?" I said, astonished that he could not only read my thoughts, but experience them too!

"Your hair, Alice, it's soft and silky."

I hadn't even noticed he was touching my hair. I had to pull myself together.

"Oh, yes. Thank you. Tony, I—" but before I could say anything else, the bell by the back door rang noisily.

"You answer it please, Tony. I must go upstairs," I said shakily.

While I was dressing, I could hear Clive talking and Tony laughing. After a moment or two, Clive called up the stairs, "I called to see Roger — forgot he's out today. I'll see him at the meeting tomorrow night. Have a good day. I'm sure you will with our Anthony."

Without waiting for a reply, he left the house the way he'd come. I was down the stairs a few minutes later. Knowing my idiotic state of mind, to remove temptation I was wearing trousers and a light jumper instead of the dress.

Tony was waiting for me in the hall. "Just as well he didn't come a few minutes later," he said jovially, helping me on with my blue jacket.

Now what did he mean by that? Did he have it in his mind to seduce me? In the hall?" My bedroom? On the kitchen table? On the stairs?

"I'm not sure what you mean, Tony," I said, my voice unsteady.

"We would have gone, of course. Are you all right, Alice?"

I laughed nervously. "Oh, just a bit of a rough night. I'll be fine when my head clears."

Within a few minutes we were heading for the country lanes. The rain had stopped but it was a bit damp for canoodling in the open air. Tony drove a fair distance from the town and stopped in a gateway down a long winding lane.

"Right, shall we get down to business or do you want to get your problems with Roger out of the way first?" Tony asked in a concerned manner.

"Oh, Tony, if only Roger could be more sensitive to what's happening to me during his experimenting. You know what I mean don't you? You must do — he's never done such things to me before, so it must be from talking to you."

I was feeling rather shy about going into details. But Tony wasn't going to let me off the hook. He took hold of my hand and gently stroked it.

"You really need to tell me what he's been up to, that is, if it isn't too embarrassing for you."

I explained everything that had been going on, leaving nothing out. We both saw the funny side of it and ended up roaring with laughter.

"I'm so sorry," he said, sounding genuinely contrite. "I guess it's my fault really. But it is difficult talking to someone who sees everything in mechanical terms. I try to explain the importance of the woman enjoying love-play but I have to be very careful that I'm not talking specifically about you. You really must talk to him yourself. Don't let him treat you this way. He's going to be even more hurt if it goes on and then later finds out the truth."

"Suppose he's incapable of being sensitive to my feelings? It's great now he wants to try something different; it's lovely to see him enjoying it too, but — well — I want some pleasure and preferably without the pain."

"Of course you do," he said, nodding in sympathy. He kissed the back of my hand; his soft warm lips felt very sensuous. "I think we should get an early lunch and let your mind settle a bit. I have an idea for this afternoon, but we'll see how you feel when we've eaten. Eat well, but keep it light."

A tremor ran through my body in anticipation of what was to come.

We were too early for the pub's serving times, so we had coffee while we were waiting in their small cosy lounge. We made ourselves comfortable in armchairs by the fireplace. A realistic blaze from the artificial logs warmed my mood, making me feel relaxed and contented. Rain was now pouring down outside and lashing against the one small window of the lounge; it seemed to cut us off from the outside world with all of its problems.

Tony smiled at me and said very softly, "I've heard the bedrooms are very cosy here. Just right for what I have in mind."

The thought of a whole afternoon locked in Tony's embrace was intoxicating. I looked into his eyes, alive with reflections from the flickering flames of the fire, and saw the passionate intent of his words. His whole expressive face sent off signals that he wanted to do for me what Roger seemed so incapable of doing — bring me to a complete, enthralling, long lasting orgasmic climax! And that he would enjoy every second of it himself. But of course, I couldn't let it happen.

My heart was racing as I opened my mouth to speak, but words wouldn't come. Desire and longing were battling with fear, shame and guilt.

He took my hand and said tenderly, "You don't have to decide at this very minute. I don't want to rush you, I know how important this is for you."

"I guess it is rather obvious," I said, looking into the flames of the fire.

He squeezed my hand. "There's nothing wrong with you, Alice, I've told you that already. Think about it: the touching, caressing, the oral delights..."

My mind was thinking about it and my body was reacting accordingly.

"A pleasant meal with a bottle of wine. A cosy bedroom out of your normal habitat, and you will be relaxed." His voice was smooth and enticing.

"Oh, Tony, I'm not sure if—"

"Just think about it, my dear, that's all I ask," he cut in. "It would be so romantic and unexpected. Roger would benefit from a change of scene. He would have no planning to do; everything would be worked out for him. You would be in charge of the situation for once. I will be giving him some advice about the touching aspect and the need to take things slowly. As I said, he only needs educating."

"Roger? Book a room and bring him here as a surprise?"

He looked puzzled. "That's what we're talking about, Alice. A romantic weekend away from the everyday scene. Best to book as soon as possible."

I tried not to show my deflated spirit. "Not sure that I can manage the cost, Tony."

"Don't worry about that. That's why I suggested here. I won a raffle and received a voucher for a weekend break in this place. I'm going to be rather tied up for a while, I would like you and Roger to have it."

"Well, fancy seeing you two here!" a voice boomed from the doorway.

In walked Roderick and Raymond with their wives, Joyce and Joan, trailing behind them.

"Rod, I didn't expect to see you here either," said Tony, his dismay being rather obvious.

I quickly withdrew my hand from Tony's and smiled in greeting at the newcomers, but at that moment in time I wished them elsewhere.

"Having lunch here too?" asked Rod. Without waiting for an answer, he said, "We'll join you for coffee while we're waiting."

The four of them pulled chairs around the table. They were blocking out the fire and overcrowding my space. I resented their presence even more.

"Isn't this nice?" Joan said, giving Tony and me a knowing look. "It's quite a while since we were here."

Joyce said mischievously, "The number of times you come here, Tony, they must give you privileged rates.'" Grinning, she added, "Of course, they do have to allow for hard wear and tear on the beds, so perhaps not."

"Well, you know me, ladies," Tony said cheerfully. "But sorry to disappoint you, I've brought Alice here, with her husband's permission I must add, to sample the good food — not the beds."

"Pull the other one!" Joan said, looking at me with a broad grin on her face. She saw I was embarrassed. "Sorry, Alice, just joking. We're always pulling Tony's leg."

"That's why I limp a little," Tony quipped.

"We're here for a little celebration," said Raymond. "Rod and Joyce are celebrating their tenth wedding anniversary."

"Congratulations," said Tony and me together.

I was surprised though. "You know, I really thought you'd been married much longer than that."

"This is a second marriage for both of us," Rod said, as he looked up from a menu the waitress had just handed him.

The rest of us were given menus to look at, and another girl brought the newcomers the coffee they had ordered at the bar.

Joyce didn't open her menu. "I'll have my usual," she said to no one in particular. "We had both come to the end of our first marriage. But I can only speak for myself; Rod will tell you a different story about his ex. I suppose with Ken's retirement on the horizon, we were looking to see how life would change for us. Ken fancied buying a boat and spending most of his time sailing. Not my thing at all. We took stock of our marriage — pretty dull really. We were used to each other. In a way it was comfortable — predictable, I suppose. We were in a rut but inertia prevented us from doing anything about it."

"Are you saying that you no longer loved each other?" I asked her.

"I'm not sure if we truly loved each other in the first place. Possibly we did — something must have made us marry. It was hard to make the decision to go our own ways. I always believed that marriage was for life. What would I do on my own anyway? I was used to being one of a pair."

"I can understand that," I said. "After fifty years with Roger, I don't know how I'd cope without him."

"I thought something similar about Ken. That's the problem with women of our generation — we were brought up to be one of a pair. Single women were almost looked down on. Anyway, Ken bought his boat and I decided to live a little myself. I managed to get a driving licence and took to the road. Drove around Britain, met Rod at a hotel bar, and within a year I became one of a pair again!"

"I'm happy to say," chuckled the laughing policeman.

Joyce looked across at Tony. "You know, I reckon when Edith walked out on you, Tony, she did you a real favour. We all knew your marriage had ended."

Tony smiled and nodded. "But I would not have left her, I was used to having her around. I guess I had a housekeeper more than a wife. I could hardly expect her to put up with my affairs though. Just one of those things."

"Well, we've been together now for forty years, and it don't seem a day too much," sang Ray with Joan joining in half laughing.

"I guess with me teaching as well as Ray—"

"In a higher education headship with salary to go with it," chipped in Ray.

"Yes, quite right. I suppose we had our work to draw us together too. Mutual interest and understanding of job dedication helps. From the start we decided not to have a family — the kids we taught were as much as we could handle. So after retiring we've had a lot of time to spend together; it's been like a long honeymoon."

They grinned at each other. With their laughter lines in their correct positions, and the light of love shining from their eyes, they made a handsome couple.

"Yes, there are many reasons for staying together, as well as for parting after many years," said Rod, nodding. "But enough of that, we are here to celebrate. Let me get you all a drink to go with your lunch."

Lunch was a lively affair with the others telling me about Madge's fancy dress parties, but what Joyce had told me about her marriage was preying on my mind. Was I really in love with Roger or had I become so much part of him I had lost my individual identity? Was the thought of our parting more filled with fear of losing part of myself rather than losing someone I loved? Or was it really the same thing? How can you tell after spending the majority of your life together? I decided to take up Tony's offer. I must not let anyone deflect me from my promise to love, honour and obey until death us do part. Well, at least, the love and honour bit!

But however I was feeling about Roger at the time I made the booking at the inn, being alone with Tony in the car afterwards was a different matter. I was drawn by his charisma. Was it because he was so different to Roger? After a solid diet of nutritious wholemeal bread was I fancying a crispy French stick? Tony broke into my thoughts.

"I have to tell you something, Alice," he said, as he parked the car up a long lane leading to an old mine. You mustn't say anything to anyone or it might cause difficulties with Edith."

"What is it?" I asked him, feeling a sense of foreboding.

"In a few months — it might only be a matter of weeks — I'm going to leave this area to live in Cheshire. It's more central to the work I do."

"Work? I thought you were retired. Living away for good? But why?" I was stunned and already feeling bereft.

"I retired from Finance years ago, when I was fifty-five, but I've dabbled on the Stock Market and have a good sum stashed away in a tax haven. I was lucky; I cashed in most of my shares before the bottom fell out of the market and invested in property and precious metals. Even after what Edith will get, I now have enough money to expand my business without risking my pension."

"Business?"

Tony breathed in deeply before answering. "I already run a small business through the Internet. It's a male escort agency. Now I'm going to expand it into major cities and open up an office in Manchester. I already have a small one in London with an ex-colleague running it. But I want to be more personally involved myself. As you may have noticed, I rather enjoy the company of women."

I was staggered. "Male escorts? For sex?"

"Often women want male company just for a night out. Say, when they are visiting London or wherever. Occasionally it's more than that. I told you that I went to the Bahamas to get myself a tan. Well, it was true, but I was also working. A lady, about your age, won millions on the lottery. She wanted an exotic holiday abroad that caters for active seniors, but not on her own. Her husband died a few years ago. She didn't want some gigolo taking advantage of her, so she came to a reputable agency — ours. Everything was taken care of. To avoid her family she met me at the airport and from then on, I took over. The trip went smoothly and she had a holiday of a lifetime. She actually took her husband's ashes with her to make it *their* holiday. Rather touching really."

"So, it's just for a woman to have a safe and convenient night out, or maybe for companionship and support on a holiday?"

"The men we take on are well vetted. They are smart, well mannered, cultured — the sort of gentleman a woman would be happy to be seen with. Sex is not part of the arrangement but who knows where an evening out might lead? We never get complaints — quite the opposite. A few marriages have lost us both escorts and clients."

I felt tears coming into my eyes. I realised how much I was going to miss him and found it hard to bear.

He looked at me and saw the sadness I was suffering.

"I guess we've formed quite a relationship. I'll make sure you get what you need from Roger," he said gently. "I'll talk very earnestly with him tomorrow evening. Be patient with him though, he's going to need a lot of practice before he gets it right."

"I can't bear to think of you going," I said, tears now streaming down my face.

He took out his hanky and dabbed the wetness from my cheeks. "My dear, I've never broken up a marriage and I can't start now. But I have to tell you, nothing would give me greater pleasure than to take you with me, but somehow I don't think it would work."

I doubt the truth of what he said. He was just being considerate of my feelings. I don't think I was in love with him, but Tony had brought excitement into my rather dull existence and had given me hope of realising my full sexuality. Whatever happened between Roger and me, Tony's leaving was going to leave a big hole in both our lives. I gave him a weak smile and nodded.

He said gently. "Would you prefer that I took you home?"

"No. I want to be with you."

He looked at the back seat. "Do you want to?"

He already knew the answer. This time he folded down the seats and spread a couple of rugs over the huge flat area Volvo's are noted for. He helped me inside and then climbed in himself.

"You will tell me if you get uncomfortable won't you?"

I said that I would and we snuggled up to each other to warm up after being outside in the damp. The windows soon steamed up as our clothes dried.

We kissed and he gently stroked my face, smoothing my cheeks with his thumbs. "You are a gentle creature, Alice. You have given out so much to Roger and your family, time for you to receive a little nourishment."

He pulled me close and rubbed his smoothly shaved face next to mine. "You are adorable," he whispered in my ear.

His hand wandered slowly down my back and came to rest on my bottom. He carefully gripped it and pulled my hips tightly up to him. "Let go, Alice. Use your imagination and enjoy the feelings."

Such was the strength of my pleasure, it was hard to believe that we were both fully dressed. Movement made my clothes rub against my skin. I could feel the texture of the lace on my undies. Awareness of what they covered stimulated my imagination and made my sensitive flesh come alive. He kissed me continually, allowing his soft full lips to wander over my face, neck and throat — no further. I admired his restraint but he knew I would shy off if he went too far. As he pressed me closer to him, waves of intense delight ran through my body. I became hot, moist, and flushed. I wanted to moan with pleasure but years of restraint were holding me back. He was whispering for me to let go and release the ecstasy. He was certainly showing me the way — just to hear him vocalising increased my own measure of pleasurable excitement.

I let out a long, "Ahhhhhh!"

The tension in my legs had brought on painful cramp! Tony immediately summed up the situation and worked to ease the pain in my right calf.

After a couple of minutes, there was a knock on the steamed-up windows and an anxious voice outside was asking, "Are you all right in there, miss?"

Through a little gap in the condensation I could just make out a heavily equipped walker. I gathered my wits and shouted back, "Fine thanks. Just a bit of cramp. Too much exercise this afternoon."

"Easily done," he said, sounding reassured. "Cheerio, sorry to have bothered you."

"Goodbye and thanks. I'm okay now," I shouted to him, still rubbing at my painful muscles.

I looked at Tony and grinned. We both burst out laughing. Soon, tears of pain, joy, and laughter were running down my face unheeded.

As agreed, Tony picked me up from the charity shop the next day and came home with me to eat the meal that Roger so much wanted him to enjoy. I couldn't help but think that it was strange that Tony wanted me to be honest with Roger and yet he hadn't the heart to tell his host that he had an intense dislike for tripe and onions, especially when served with beer.

As we came to the end of the meal, Roger smiled and said, "Nearly everyone says they hate tripe but they enjoy it when they eat it here. It has to be cooked right, that's the important thing. Great stuff! You can keep all your foreign food — nothing like British best! Alice knows just how we men like it."

"I guess she does," Tony said, looking me straight in the eye.

"Well, we must be off — eat up. There's something I want to discuss with you, if you don't mind, Tony," said Roger, giving a brief glance in my direction.

As they were going out, Tony looked at me and nodded, "Thanks, Alice. I'll see you next week sometime." He turned to Roger. "Maybe you'll allow me to take Alice to lunch again in return for the lovely meals I get here?"

"Of course, but don't feel you have to repay us, it's a pleasure to have you here," Roger said with genuine enthusiasm.

They disappeared into Tony's Volvo and set off for their meeting. I went to the kitchen to wash-up while I sorted out my feelings. What lessons would Roger be learning tonight? Was I in for a rough time or pleasurable romance?

I had a bath as usual and lay in the water reliving my afternoon's experience. Surely it was possible for Roger to do the same for me, but far, far better because there would be no restrictions. It would be the real thing — the genuine article — all the way! Tony would be giving him hints and tips on the art of delicate love play, but would Roger listen? If only Roger wasn't such a know-it-all.

Roger was in at his usual time. Finding I wasn't downstairs, he came up to the bedroom saying that he was ready for action. Feeling somewhat apprehensive at his eagerness, I asked him, "Wouldn't it be better to leave it for another night? We could start a bit earlier and we'd be less tired."

But Roger was keen to put into practice what he'd been learning from Tony. He was already pulling off his tie. "Strike while the iron's hot! Get going, old girl."

"Roger, we must talk first," I said urgently, but Roger was throwing off his shoes and trotting off to the bathroom.

"We can talk afterwards," he called back.

I sensed I was in for a rough night. "What has Tony been telling you?"

"Now if I told you that, it wouldn't be a surprise," he said, now back in the bedroom and taking off the rest his clothes.

"Perhaps I don't want a surprise, Roger. Last week was a painful one for me. My arthritis has been pretty bad since then."

"That's because you don't get enough exercise. You're all right when you go dancing. What we do is just stretching you a bit more. Don't worry, you'll enjoy tonight even more than last week," he said, stripping off the last veil to reveal his tool oiled and ready for work.

My eyes were beginning to water. "Be gentle," I begged him. "Take things slowly; I can't cope with being hurried. I don't enjoy it — I really don't."

"Go on. You were great last week — a real dynamo," he said, grinning from ear to ear. "Tony said I should go slowly and test the water with you. I told him you were hot stuff. I could tell by your reactions. Gosh you were yelling your head off!"

"That's because I was in pain! You don't listen. You never listen! You're so busy enjoying yourself you don't give a damn what's happening to me."

Roger stopped admiring his manhood in the mirror. Instead, he stood with his arms akimbo staring at me in disbelief. "That's not true, Alice. You wanted to get more feeling — an orgasm is it called? I've been doing my damnedest to get you there. Tony's been showing me how — did you know that?"

I gave a little nod but felt too guilty to look him in the eye. Instead I was staring at his big toe poking out of a hole in the black sock he was still wearing, and thinking that I must get some mending done. But I still couldn't blot out my guilty erotic thoughts concerning Roger's helpful friend.

"There must be something wrong with you, Alice, it works for all the woman Tony's been with — except his own wife. Perhaps you're like her — lost your hormones or whatever. If you want it, you have to make an effort yourself you know, you can't expect me to do all the work."

"That's it, Roger! You think of it as work but it should be a pleasure — for both of us."

"Pleasure takes working at, you know."

"I only ask you to take things slowly and be gentle. I'm not a chunk of wood that needs chiselling and polishing. Please, Roger — take it easy. We'll practice whatever you like — whatever Tony's taught you — but please be tender with me."

"I'm not sure I want to do anything now. You've put me off. I'm just a rotten bastard — you've made that clear."

He was now sitting disconsolately on the edge of the bed, his head in his hands and his magnificent tool now reduced to a flaccid object forlornly dangling between his legs. I went up to him and put my arms around his shoulders. "I love you, my darling. I've always loved you. Let's go to bed and do things very gently. I want you badly — please believe that. Come now, let me massage your back for you."

I had known my honesty would give him the sulks but I wasn't happy to be proved right. I tenderly massaged his shoulders as he sat on the bed. He soon rolled on to his stomach so as to get the full treatment. I oiled and massaged his back, legs, and down to his feet. By the time I'd finished he was relaxed and sighing with pleasure. I was dead beat and ready for sleep.

"Come here," he said, turning on his back and putting out an arm for me to lie on.

I did as he asked and cuddled up to him. It was, as it always has been, very pleasant and comforting.

"Sorry, Alice. I didn't realise, you know about — well — you know what I mean. But I would like us to do what Tony suggested."

"If that's what you really want, but please, Roger, take it easy."

"I think you'd like it. Just lie there a minute and let me kiss away your hurts."

I was very tired and weary but Roger did his best to please me and I was grateful. After a little while I began responding to his touch. Then he moved his lips down my body and I began to be fearful of him nipping me again. I needn't have worried — he was quite gentle with his titillating. But I knew I wasn't reacting as I should have been. My mood and the expectation of pain were not conducive to feeling euphoric. So for his benefit, I began to fake a fervent response.

Having heard them at it on TV, I was able to put on a good show. When Roger heard my ecstatic groans and felt my back arching with pleasure, he got very excited. I was then worried that he would go overboard. To avoid being nipped in the bud I yelled, "Now! Now! Yes! Yes! Now — do it now!"

He sat me up and faced me. "This way tonight, old girl," he said grinning.

So we had a loving cheek to cheek with arms and legs wrapped around each other type of session. I really loved it. But the position caused my hip joints to start objecting in no time at all. At least with my mouth next to his ear, he couldn't fail to hear me telling him to stop and let me go. He was in no doubt as to why I was groaning this time.

Going back to the method we knew best, Roger heard what he wanted to hear — I made sure of that. He soon reached a climax and I did my best to let him think I was absolutely with him. I told myself that next time I would be. After all, I had been far too tired and aching to expect anything that night. But next time, I would be fresh, ready and eager. More important though — Roger now knew what to do and to feel for my reactions.

I went downstairs to get Roger's hot chocolate and put a little rum in it — a little treat he would not be expecting but which he well deserved.

Chapter eleven

Of love and passion

After taking him his usual cup of tea and biscuit, Roger stayed in bed for an extra half an hour on Saturday morning. This being an unusual event I was a little concerned that he was overdoing things. But when he came down for breakfast he was as chirpy as a bird in spring. Perhaps the previous evening had gone much better for him than I had thought possible. He even insisted that we go out for lunch. When I said that the family might call he said they could come another time — this was to be our day.

In honour of the occasion I put on my fancy underwear. Not that I was expecting him to perform again for at least another week, although with Roger in his present mood anything could happen, but it seemed the right thing to do for the beginning of what seemed like a new relationship.

But first, we went out in the car to do a quick weekly shop. Roger insisted we had coffee in the supermarket cafe — an unusual event indeed. He met a number of his old cronies there but he didn't stop to talk to them — likewise strange for him. And he was giving me his full attention — even more rare! I was certainly enjoying the new Roger.

Saying there was no time to take the groceries home first, he drove straight off from the supermarket to our luncheon appointment, insisting he kept the venue a surprise. With my eyes closed against the cold dull weather outside, I sat relaxed in the car beside a humming husband. What the tune was, I couldn't make out but it seemed to capture his mood.

"Here we are, the greatest little inn for miles around, or so Tony tells me," he said as he slowed the car.

At the mention of our mutual friend, I opened my eyes and was horrified to see we had just drawn into the car park of where I was dining only forty-eight hours previously. Would the proprietor mention the booking I had made for us? I so much wanted it to come as a surprise for Roger nearer the time.

"Hello, hello! Look who's here, Vera. Our old friend Roger and his wife Alice. I do have the name right don't I, my dear?" Sam Bingham added, looking at me and winking in a lecherous manner.

Roger seemed pleased to see them, "You do," he said, answering for me in his normal irritating way. "Well, fancy finding you here, you old buzzard, with your wife too, that makes a change." Apparently Snooty Big had a reputation for entertaining ladies.

I was cross. Who gave Snooty the right to spoil our day or, worse, wink at me? I quickly put in, before I was pushed into the background, "Yes, Alice is my name. Do you have a problem with your eye, Mr Bingham? I'm so sorry, how embarrassing for you."

The men looked at me puzzled. But Vera Bingham said, "Sam has some odd habits. Poor man, his eye blinks every time he sees a woman — no matter how old and fraying at the edges. I do believe we met at that stupid lecture — can't remember what it was about. Must have been boring."

I gathered my fraying edges together and looked Mrs Snooty Big in the eye. I couldn't help but notice, in spite of her heavy make-up, that her eyes were red-rimmed and baggy. "We did indeed meet then. How clever of you to remember me, especially as you were rather occupied with Roger. I don't recall much of the lecture itself — I couldn't hear the speaker. But what I heard from where I was sitting was very boring indeed."

Sam Bingham gave me an ear-to-ear smile. "Why don't we see more of you at these events, Alice? It's always good to have the ladies present."

"She's always busy with her charity stuff — time she retired from all that," Roger told them as though I was incapable of speaking for myself.

"We're here for lunch, come and join us," said Bingham. "There's a log fire in the dining room, just the job for this weather."

I inwardly groaned as Roger willingly agreed. This was going to be some day out just for the two of us!

Although we had agreed to split the bill, Roger offered to buy the wine. Snooty Big chose the most expensive on the wine list. To make up for it, I ordered the cheapest main course and refused starters and pudding, making out that I was dieting. Vera Bingham gave me a little curl of her lips and said she understood my need to lose weight. My stomach groaned with the sudden inflow of bile. Mrs Snooty Big may have had a miserly bust, made to look bigger with a squeeze-me bra, and a waist pulled in by a strong corset, but her bum fully occupied her broad-seated chair. Not even her expensive peach silk and mohair two-piece, could hide the fact that she was a pear-shaped middle-aged woman doing her best to look two stones lighter. For Roger's benefit I gave her my best put-on smile. For my own pleasure, I answered her measure for measure.

"Not to do with weight, Roger likes me as I am. I like to keep my good complexion. I find it easier to be natural than have to wear heavy make-up like some women do. Fatty foods and overeating are so bad for one's health. But I'm sure that's not your problem," I told her with a benign smile.

"Poor Vera suffers terribly with her guts. She's a real martyr to the cause of good eating," Bingham said, giving his wife a grin. "Must admit my gall bladder's due to see the light of day, but what the hell, you only have one life to live."

Some good it did in my reducing the bill. Roger, along with the Binghams, decided to have all three courses, even though they had ordered the huge and expensive mixed grill. Coffee and mints followed — I had water. At least, I no longer had a conscience about spending money on my naughty undies.

While slurping down the last of the wine, Bingham said to Roger, "I should be at the annual dinner in Manchester tonight. I can't make it. My deputy can't make it either. Would you like to go and represent the Professionals?"

Roger's eyes lit up like beacons. "I would consider it an honour. Thank you, Sam, just give me the details and we'll set off home to get ready."

Well, that was the rest of our togetherness day accounted for. I made a mental note to cancel our weekend break at that inn. The chances of being shanghaied by the Snooty Bigs were just too off-putting. Sam would only have to snap his fingers and Roger would be there to deputise for him in bed!

But confusing events changed my plan. I was leaving the ladies' toilets when the inn's receptionist spotted me.

"Mrs Bradshaw," she called in my direction. I was surprised and looked around me, expecting to see Edith.

"It is the lady who was here with Anthony Bradshaw, the weekend break winner, isn't it?"

When I booked, they must have copied Tony's name off the voucher. "Oh, yes, that would have been me. But my name isn't Bradshaw, it's—"

"The room is booked in the name of Bradshaw, that's all we need to know." She gave me a knowing smile. "I was just letting you know that the four-poster bedroom is available after all. Just the thing for the romantic weekend you planned."

I couldn't bring myself to cancel the little surprise for Roger now. "Oh, lovely, thank you," I said and turned to find Vera had come up behind me.

"Planning on a dirty weekend, Alice? Enjoy Tony, from what I hear, many women have."

The receptionist quickly turned her back, presumably to hide the silly grin on her face. I was furious with Vera. But just as I was about to put her right, Roger appeared from the gents and was ready to be off. I decided to tell him about the break on the way home. When Vera knew the truth she was going to feel really stupid!

The sun was shining brightly as we started off home. Roger was happily humming to himself. He turned into the main road, now busy with tourist traffic. He glanced quickly in my direction. "You're quiet. I'm assuming you'll be coming tonight as well as me. We'll take over the booking that Sam made at the hotel for him and Vera."

"Sorry, Roger, not my thing. Anyway, I'm reading one of the lessons in church tomorrow morning."

"Anyone can do that. You won't be missed. They have people falling over themselves to get to the front. Come on, Alice, you'd enjoy it."

"What? A big meal I can't possibly eat, and after-dinner speeches I can't stomach? No thanks, Roger. You know as well as I do, that you will be happier on your own. I would just hinder you from spreading yourself amongst your chums. No, I'll stay at home. But thanks for wanting me there."

He knew I was right, so he didn't argue.

"Since it's supposed to be our day, I'll tell you what I would like, Roger."

"Anything, my love."

"There's a little lane just around the corner, suppose we drive up it and have a little cuddle in the car. Just a romantic cuddle, nothing more."

Roger glanced at the clock on the dashboard. "It will have to be a quickie cuddle — no shenanigans."

I knew I was playing on his guilty conscience for ruining our day out, but so what? I was determined we would have at least ten minutes of mutual pleasure. It was just the time and place to announce our little break — something to look forward to.

Roger drove the Vectra carefully up the rutted lane. "How on earth did you know about this track, Alice? Can't remember us coming this way."

Now that was something I had not thought of. I decided it was best to be truthful.

"Tony drove up here, there's a pleasant view at the end. He's shown me all sorts of out-of-the-way places."

The car suddenly hit a rut, the wheel skidded and we bumped down into a bit of a hole. Something underneath the Vectra went clonk!

"Oh, damn! That will be the exhaust. Really, Alice, why on earth come down here? I'd better see what the damage is."

I could hear him moaning and groaning. He climbed back into his seat. "It wasn't the exhaust. A rock threw up inside the wheel arch — bloody big dent! I'll have to get it seen to next week. I'm not going up this dirt track any further. I'll turn around in that gateway just ahead."

It was where I had planned for us to stop. I decided to say nothing — Roger was muttering to himself. Suddenly, behind us, a Land Rover came into view followed by others. Roger started up the car to move to the gateway but his wheels skidded on mud and rocks. Meanwhile, a tractor appeared in the gateway, intent on coming our way.

"Bloody hell!" yelled Roger.

Very rarely have I heard my husband swear. It just was not him. Clearly, he was greatly troubled and it was my entire fault. I felt very bad about it.

Fifteen minutes later we were back on the main road — courtesy of the Land Rover brigade. I sat quiet, feeling utterly miserable. Roger was concentrating on his driving. He suddenly said, "It's not too bad. Might be able to fix it myself."

That was a relief. "Sorry, Roger, I shouldn't have suggested going up there."

"Too late now. Forget about it."

"Tony has given us a voucher he won in a raffle. It's for a weekend break at the inn we've just left. Quite a coincidence. I've booked us in for the beginning of next month. It's in Tony Bradshaw's name by the way. There'll be log fires and good food, and we'll have a room with a four-poster bed. Won't that be romantic?"

He was obviously stunned. "Why didn't you tell me before? I might have wanted a different time. Oh, well, I suppose it will make a change. A four-poster bed? What's special about that? Do they provide thongs to tie your wrists and ankles up? Kinky!"

To think Roger actually had such thoughts! Things were brightening up along with the weather. Golden light filled the car as we travelled under spreading beach trees in their late summer-come-autumn glory. My heart lifted. It was a beautiful day. Everything was going to be all right.

"I think the room is used a lot by newly-weds. En-suite, television and the usual facilities. Full English breakfast and an evening dinner thrown in too."

"That's very kind of Tony. But why give it to us?"

"He can't use it himself. Perhaps he wants you to make the most of those little tips he gives you."

"Mm, I'm beginning to like the idea. It'll make a change from being crowded out with kids at the weekend."

He must have done some serious thinking on the way home. "Sorry, Alice, things didn't go according to plan. I'll make up for it — promise," he said, as he parked the car in our drive. I turned to him and smiled. He gave me a quick peck on the cheek. "We'd better get cracking or I'll be late."

We pulled ourselves out of the car and collected the groceries from the boot. All the time I was thinking about the change in Roger — he'd actually apologised again!

I made sure that Roger looked immaculate before he set off — giving his jacket a last minute brush and his shoes a final polish with my best yellow duster. Having waved him off, I sat down in the kitchen to eat a sandwich, pondering whether to have a sneaky look at my porn magazine. I needed to make up my mind whether or not to show it to Roger. Just as I was on my way to retrieve it from its hiding place, the phone rang. It was Tony wanting a word with Roger.

"Sorry, Tony, Roger is out for the night. Can I help?"

"I need to see his notes of the last meeting. I want to check on a date. Could you find them, Alice?"

"You should have received a copy of them. Maybe they were delayed in the post. I'll run you one off. I'll just go and check the date for you."

"Hang on, Alice. I could do with other information too, I'm going out shortly, do you mind if I call in for the copy you're running off?"

"Not at all. I'll be here. I'm on my own tonight. We put the kids off coming because Roger and I are supposed to be having a togetherness day. It's a long story and I won't bother you with it. I'll do the copy now."

Tony turned up at the door twenty minutes later. Wearing a dinner jacket, bow tie and a finely striped shirt, he looked very smart and elegant. I wondered if he had an escort appointment that evening. I could quite see why women hired men to take them out — especially guys like suave and handsome Tony. It must be difficult for women on their own. I wondered if I would ever go out at night if I lost Roger — no, definitely not.

I showed Tony into the sitting room. My magazine was under the sofa where he had decided to sit. I couldn't help but smile. In my imagination I could see erotic vibes rising to Tony's nether region. When I came back to the room with his notes and a coffee, my smile disappeared. Having taken off his jacket and tie, he was sitting relaxed with the magazine in his hand, turning its pages with a raised eyebrow.

"Yours, I take it. Do you mind if I have a look?"

"How did you find it?"

The corners of his mouth twisted into a little smile. "I dropped a coin on the floor. Not a very good hiding place — that is, if you meant to hide it."

I put his coffee down on a little table by his elbow, and sat myself down in an armchair at a distance from him. Unbearable heat seemed to radiate from that book while he was looking at it. They were no longer just pink and tan anonymous bodies sexually entwined on those pages. I felt myself entering Tony's mind as he was imagining himself experiencing those erotic delights, and my voyeurism was awakening my primitive urges. I felt drawn to him — wanting to be his imaginary partner.

He looked up and saw me watching him. There was a pregnant silence as our eyes met. I could feel my chest heaving as it coped with my panting breath. My heart rate was increasing by the second. My lips became dry and thirsting for moisture. I licked them with the tip of my tongue. He smiled and a huge thrill ran through my body. It showed in the way two hard peaks had pushed their way through my bra and thin blue jersey. I quickly crossed my arms.

"Come over here, Alice," he said softy.

The tone of his voice was deep and mysterious, and it was drawing me like filings to a magnet. I could not resist. I stood up and walked slowly to the sofa as though in a dream. My clothes — jersey, trousers, bra and knickers, felt alive on my body. I looked down and saw the page of erotic kissing. I blushed and turned my head away. He tossed the magazine aside, took hold of my hand and pulled me down beside him. He put an arm around me, and with his mouth on mine we slowly went down on the sofa — his body half across mine. I felt his hand move up my jersey and I caught my breath in delightful, but fearful, anticipation.

The phone rang, breaking the spell. What the hell was I doing? Preparing to — to what? To eventually commit adultery in my own home with my husband's best friend? Surely not! I dared not think of where things were leading. I was only too conscious of my body on fire with lustful desire — and, oh, to have that desire fulfilled! Wicked, wicked Alice!

The phone continued to ring. I pulled myself away from Tony and rushed from the room to answer it in the hall.

"Mum? Is that you?" It was my youngest son speaking. He sounded very upset.

"What's the matter, Richard? Has something happened?"

"Oh, Mum, Karen's been taken into hospital. She's having a miscarriage. We didn't even know she was pregnant. There's some sort of complication. She's lost pints of blood," he said jerkily. "We need you, Mum. Can you look after the children for a few days? Please, Mum, please, I…" His voice trailed away into sobs.

His pain was tearing me apart but I tried to keep calm. "I'll come straight away, Rich. Don't worry; try to be strong for the children. Where are you?"

"At the local hospital — Emergency. Karen is waiting to go into theatre. I've had to bring the kids with me. You can probably hear them crying," he said, trying to control his voice but not succeeding.

"I'll pick them up and bring them home with me. We can sort out what's best for them later. Get back to Karen now. See you soon, my darling." I put down the phone.

For a few seconds, my mind flashed back to my own complicated miscarriage, five years after Richard was born. The pain, fear and anxiety may well have been passed on to my youngest son. And now it was happening all over again but this time to his dear Karen. How I felt for my poor dear child, and for his lovely Karen, and especially for their little ones.

I went back to the sitting room and looked at Tony with tears in my eyes. "I have to get to the hospital and pick up my grandchildren, their mother's very poorly. Richard is dreadfully distraught — he needs me."

Tony's face creased with concern. "I'll help you. Would you like me to drive you there?"

"Thank you, you're an angel. I'll pick up the children, collect some of their things and bring them here. They can stay with us until we know what's happening. But you were going somewhere tonight, Tony. You only need drop me off at the hospital, I can take a taxi afterwards."

"What I was going to do later can wait. I'll look after you first."

After sending a text on his mobile, he concentrated on my problems. With Roger away for the night, I was glad of all the help I could get.

In less than two hours, I was tucking the weary kids into bed. Tony, after giving me a hand with them, was making us a cup of tea. How the situation had changed in so short a time. Instead of the seducer, Tony had become a concerned 'uncle' and was fantastic with the children as well as being a support to me.

"I like Uncle Tony," said little Sarah sleepily. "He told me a cool story about a bear with no teeth. Will he come up and kiss me goodnight?"

I covered her with the old faded teddy quilt that had once belonged to her daddy. "He'll have to kiss you some other time, darling. Get to sleep now," I said, giving her a little kiss myself.

"Is Mummy going to die?" Sarah suddenly asked, her voice wavering.

"No, my treasure. Mummy is poorly but the doctor says she'll be better soon," I answered truthfully, trying to reassure her troubled mind. "Don't worry, she'll be all right. Daddy phoned from the hospital just a few minutes ago. He said you can see her very soon."

"Can I take Barney with me, he'll make my mummy better," she said, holding up her favourite little bear for me to see.

"I think your mummy would like that very much," I told her, tucking the worn out toy back into bed with her.

She sucked on the bear's paw for a moment or two. "Granny, you won't ever go away and leave us will you?"

The question pulled at my heartstrings and I wrapped my arms around her little body with tears in my eyes. "I'll be here for as long as you need me, my darling."

She whispered sleepily, "I love you, Gran," and within a minute she was fast asleep.

I looked around the bedroom, still filled with the old but good furniture we bought for Richard. Memories of his chubby dimpled face and curly golden hair, just like Sarah's, filled my mind. So long ago and yet it seemed no time at all. I checked the two boys were asleep in their bunk beds — the ones their uncles had slept in — and marvelled how much they looked like Roger in his youth. I kissed their cheeks, soft and downy like peaches, and wondered how long it would be before they would be using a razor. I smiled at thoughts of my sons and their teenage problems, and then sighed as I recalled the accidents they had with their first bicycles, motorbikes and then cars. Nothing very serious — thank God!

I went downstairs to join Tony. He'd placed a pot of tea on a low table, and was sitting by the gas fire looking calm and relaxed, cup in hand. I went over to him and kissed him on the cheek. "Thank you for making things so much easier for me. What a lovely man you are." I was feeling tearful and it showed in my voice.

"Lovely man? I don't know about that, Alice. If you hadn't had that phone call, I'm not sure how things would have gone — in Roger's home too. I'm sorry; I don't know what came over me. Kissing and cuddling in the car is one thing but—"

"Don't say any more, Tony. Nothing did happen and I doubt it was going to."

But we both knew different. The pull for sexual union had not gone away.

His blue eyes were penetrating mine. When he spoke his voice was gentle and appealing. "I guess you know I'm very fond of you, Alice — very fond."

I adored the way he spoke my name; it was spellbinding, as though he had my soul in his grasp. A thrill ran through me. I knew he was being genuine and it moved me deeply. The attraction was mutual. In another time, perhaps fifty-plus years ago, I would have called it love. But surely, what we felt was a kind of love. I loved him in a different way to which I loved Roger, but it was love just the same. Before that night, I might have thought the feeling was mere sexual attraction, lust even, but having seen him with the children, playing with them and telling them stories, I saw him in a new light and my heart warmed to him. It seemed to me that the real Tony Bradshaw had been hidden for years behind a protective mask of sexual prowess, made easier by a reputation built on exaggerated stories, which he himself had fostered. Was it to hide a broken heart — grieving for the children he never had?

He must have read my thoughts.

"You know, Alice, I really envy what you have. I always wanted a family. If only Edith…" His words trailed off as he appeared to sink into thought. "Lucky Roger — a family and you for a wife."

Poor Tony. That, which he most wanted from life, had been denied him. The woman he'd married had refused to bear him children, not only that, but she had considered it a personal sacrifice to allow him his conjugal rights. With so much love and sexual energy to dissipate, it was hardly surprising if he eventually spread his assets around where they were willingly received.

The phone rang. It was Roger.

"Alice, are you all right?" We've had our starters and are about to eat the main course. I've decided to come home tonight. I'll be a bit late."

"But if you've been drinking, Roger—"

"I've only had a sherry and I'll drink nothing else. I want to be with you tonight. See you just after midnight."

I was deeply touched. Was this the new Roger or the old one resurrected? I nearly forgot about the kids.

"Roger, just a minute. Karen is in hospital — emergency. The kids are here. Don't worry, she's going to be all right in a few days."

There was a brief silence. "You know I felt something was wrong. Are you coping?"

"Tony happened to be here — he came for his minutes. I'll tell you about that when you get back. Anyway, he's been driving me around. He's been a real friend. The kids are in bed now. Tony is going soon. But I'll be all right until you get here. Don't rush, take things steady."

I went back to Tony, feeling highly emotional. Roger was missing me. He loved me enough to sense something was wrong. Of course, he might have just been making an excuse to come home having found it was a boring do, but I didn't think so. He might take me for granted, without doubt he's an arrogant chauvinist, he can be an insensitive lover, but he is my husband and we love each other.

I said to Tony, "Roger's coming home tonight after all."

Tony looked at me and smiled ironically. "As I said, lucky Roger."

"Are you going on to wherever you were going tonight?"

"Do you want me to go?"

"No — yes — no. I want you to stay, but I'm afraid."

He nodded. "I understand." He stood up. "I don't want to go, but I too, am afraid."

We looked into each other's eyes. There were tears forming in his, just as they were in mine. He suddenly turned, picked up his jacket and tie, and forced his lips into his most devastating of smiles. "I'll be off. See if I can retrieve that date."

Tony left the house, no doubt to dull that inner pain of loneliness in the only way he knew how.

Torn by so many emotions, I wept. For Tony? Roger? Myself? My family? Our fleeting lives? Or for all humanity's sense of grief and loss? I was beyond knowledge or caring. Exhausted, I lay down on the sofa and was healed by sleep.

Chapter twelve

To love and to cherish

The day of Madge's party dawned. With Karen out of hospital and Richard taking time off work, the grandchildren had returned home and things were back to normal. Roger was attempting to patch the garage roof once more, prune the shrubs that had finished flowering, draw up plans to build a shed out of scrap wood washed up on the beach a few miles away, and arrange for a lecture on behalf of one of his societies. I had caught up with his secretarial needs. Now I was putting together our costumes for that special evening.

I found an old pale blue polyester and cotton sheet that had become devoid of most of its cotton. Being quite thin in places, it draped rather nicely. Since the sheet was king size, I was able to make both our tunics out of it. Roger preferred to have his tunic short. He said he didn't want to be fiddling about when he used the men's room. With only a bit of trimming to stitch around the edges, half an hour and his costume was finished. He had a nice bit of brown soft woollen material to throw over his shoulders where it was fastened to the right with a brooch. With having muscular arms and legs, he looked a virile old codger. Now concentrating on my dress, I stood in front of my bedroom mirror trying to decide how much of my body I wanted to reveal — at my age, not a lot!

I was wearing my lacy white undies. Having already run the piece of sheet into a tube, I pinned the top of it to my bra straps and along for a few inches to hide part of my shoulders. Abandoning the idea of drawing in the garment at the waist — it made me look as if I had breasts swinging down to meet their doom — I wrapped and tied a long silk cord closely under my bust line. With a bit of fiddling and draping, I obtained the desired provocative effect. I looped a length of pretty deep blue material loosely under an arm to fasten with a brooch at my right shoulder, leaving the ends hanging freely. I tied a band of the same material around my head to hold up my silver hair.

"You shall go to the orgy," I told myself in the mirror. The reflection in the mirror told me I wasn't in bad shape for an ancient Greek.

"You didn't say we were in for an orgy," said Roger, grinning. "Will they have dancing girls too?"

"We're all dancing, including you, Roger. Clive's band is going to be there. It's going to be quite a do."

"You know me, Alice. If you're wearing sandals, you'd better take some plasters and that ointment for bruises."

He wasn't jesting.

When we arrived at Madge and Frank's palatial residence, we were amazed at the scene before us. Coloured lights were hanging from the trees that bordered the drive and white statues of naked Greeks were spotlighted amongst the exotic topiary near the doorway. Loud Greek music, which had more to do with tourist Greece than ancient times, hit us head on as we entered the house. In the large hall, realistic columns of cardboard, plaster statues, and swathes of laurel helped create an atmosphere compatible with the party theme. Through open double doors we saw tables laden with food in the dining room. In the impressive lounge, jumbo cushions were spread around the walls. I mused on the purpose of them — to collapse on after the party? Clive's band was waiting to play in the huge conservatory where space had been made for dancing. But at that moment, music was coming from a disc player in the lounge. A merry bunch of golden oldies, dressed in tunics or draped in colourful fabric, were dancing with fluttering handkerchiefs around the furniture, to a version of "Zorba the Greek". I couldn't be certain, but through the glass at the end of the large hall, I thought I saw near-naked bodies preparing to jump into an indoor swimming pool. It was quite a merry throng and the party had barely started. Even as we were about to close the door behind us, taxis were drawing into the circular drive to spill out more party-goers.

I heard a group of women shrieking with laughter and, turning to the dining room door, I saw the gaggling geese I'd last met in the Coffeepot. They were just entering the hall, dancing and waving their handkerchiefs in time with the music. One of them, a shapely-legged woman in her late fifties dressed in a very short orange-red shift, left the others to come and speak to us.

"Hi, Roger; brought your dibber with you? I fancy a bit of gardening tonight — got something to plant?" she shouted, giving my husband a cheeky smirk.

"Hello, Lucy, as lovely as ever," said Roger gallantly, ignoring her questions. "Looks like you're having fun."

"Is she always like that?" I whispered in Roger's ear as Lucy went off to greet Tony who had just entered the hall.

"Always. Just likes a bit of fun, nothing more."

Madge came into the hall and flung her arms around both of us in greeting. There was a heavy smell of alcohol on her breath; obviously the party had started some time ago for her. She didn't stop to chat, others had come through the front door and she was doing her greeting routine. Frank wasn't far behind her and he was quite wobbly on his legs.

We had just said hello to Raymond, Joan, Rod and Joyce as they were making their way to the dining room, and Roger had just shunted sideways to speak to an ex-colleague, when a magnificent tall muscular Greek warrior came along and stood in front of me. He looked incredibly macho. He was wearing a white tunic that left his right shoulder and arm free to wield his sword, which was presently in a scabbard attached to a wide belt. The skirt was short and full enough not to hinder his fiercest athletic movements. The tunic also revealed his well-tanned legs and arms to good effect. His blue eyes seemed to sparkle like icicles caught in sunlight. When he opened his mouth to speak, his smiling lips revealed his beautiful white teeth.

"So, you both made it. You look lovely, Alice; very elegant."

My heart began a tango. Memories of our last meeting were clouding my vision. I felt myself blushing. "You look pretty good yourself, Tony."

"I can hear Clive starting up. Would you like to go to the conservatory for a quickstep?"

My nerves were tingling. I took a deep breath and tried to calm myself. "Yes, I'd love to. I'll just tell Roger where I'm going."

Roger turned around at that very moment, saw Tony and came over to chat. We all moved over to the lounge and found ourselves chairs. Cyril joined us, followed by Roderick and Joyce. With all the noise, I could only sit back and guess the conversation. Every so often, Tony glanced my way and smiled. I wanted to be on the dance floor with him and I knew he was waiting for the right moment to whisk me away from the group.

Lorna and Jim Green, both dressed in garments to match their name, passed by our chairs. Lorna bent over and whispered, "You look lovely, Alice. Teeth are looking white — using your electric toothbrush?"

She gave a little tinkling laugh and hurried on to join Jim for dancing. Tony heard what she'd said. He glanced at me and smiled. What did they all know that I didn't?

I was surprised to see Betty Mayfield and her husband making their way to the dance floor. She was looking very happy. I was pleased things had turned out well for her. With her alleged physical problems, to be dancing at all must surely mean that she was getting healthier. Were Tony's tips to Albert the reason for the improvement? Quite possibly, mutual contentment must bring about very real benefits.

A shrill voice sounded. "Well, Mrs Bradshaw, nice to see you again."

A smirking Vera Bingham was standing over me. Her ugly leer was deepening her wrinkles into deep channels that even plastered make-up failed to hide.

Tony looked at Vera in complete puzzlement. Everyone else at the table stopped talking and glanced from Vera to me. Roger was the first to speak.

"Edith isn't at the party, Mrs Bingham. You're talking to my wife. Have you forgotten her name is—"

"Oh, I haven't forgotten anything, Roger darling. Come on, you're dancing with me — Sam's orders!"

I smiled. Mrs Snooty Big was in for some very unpleasant surprises.

Tony stood up and offered me his magnificent tanned arm. "Shall we?"

Finding a spare space on the temporary dance floor, we started off with Tony holding me close. Roger was not far away and judging by the agonised expression on Vera's face, she was not appreciating his attempt to do a waltz to the rhythm of the rumba. What's more, she had probably heard from Roger the truth of my hotel booking. Poor woman, part of me thought kindly, while another side of me was giggling like a schoolgirl at Vera's discomfort.

Dancing with Tony was the highlight of my evening. His sword might have got in the way a bit, but dancing with a gorgeous male dressed in a short cotton tunic was powerfully erotic. I was sorry when it was announced that games were about to begin. Tony walked me back to where we had been sitting. He smiled, almost sadly, and said that he had someone to see. We didn't see him again that night.

We arrived home at two in the morning absolutely dead beat. Cyril and Clive had organised most of the games. They were all old favourites: passing the balloon between legs, oranges under chins, matchboxes at the end of noses, wheelbarrow races and other nonsense party movers — some of them with rules that lent themselves to serious sexual connotations. Less vigourous games were played too, including passing-the-parcel. Prizes were astonishing — a gold watch, gold cufflinks, diamond encrusted articles of jewellery that were either copies of those worn by Madge or the articles themselves. Madge and Frank were not around to be asked. It was assumed that being the worse for drink, they were resting. Food had kept appearing and drink flowing. Individuals, including Roger, had entertained while others flopped down on the cushions provided — too drunk or tired to go on, or to go home. On our way out, we had been given a gift to take home with us. When we opened it, we found a splendid silver photograph frame. Did everyone receive such an expensive gift?

We stayed in bed until ten-thirty the following morning. We might well have stayed longer were it not for the incessant ringing of the telephone. I stretched out my hand to the bedside table and wearily picked up the receiver.

"Hello?"

"Alice?"

"That's me. Barbara? Up already? You were still at it when we left the party."

"Keep calm, Alice, I have bad news for you."

Roger opened his eyes. "Who the hell is it? The kids knew we were out late."

"Shush, Roger. Barbara's trying to tell me something." I pressed the receiver to my ear to cut out Roger's mumbling. "I'm sorry, Barbara, I didn't catch it, Roger was grunting."

"Madge and Frank have been found dead. Evidently a suicide pact. They left a note to that effect. Don't be surprised if the Police call. Sorry, must go, I think we have a policeman at the door."

Utterly shocked, I put down the receiver and rocked back on the pillow. "Madge and Frank are dead. Suicide pact."

Roger suddenly became alert. "Suicide? But we were at their party a few hours ago."

"Yes."

"But how?"

"I don't know. Barbara didn't say."

"But why?"

"I don't know. Barbara didn't say."

"Don't keep repeating yourself, woman. What did Barbara say?"

"Madge and Frank were found dead. They had left a note."

Roger sank back on his pillow. For once he was speechless.

I lay my head on his chest. "Oh, Roger, it's so sad. They had disappeared halfway through the evening. We were all enjoying ourselves while they were planning to kill themselves."

"Must be what they wanted. But who'd have thought it? In the midst of all that bubbling life we were already in the midst of death." He felt my tears soaking his pyjamas. "Come on, old girl, cheer up, it was what they wanted. Go get us a cup of tea. Then we'd better get up; the Police might give us a call."

Roger wasn't being heartless, I knew it was the only way he could cope with his feelings. When I brought him his tea, he was already out of bed.

"No use stinking in bed when there's work to be done," he said, pulling on his socks.

"It's Sunday, Roger, and there is nothing we have to do that can't wait. Drink your tea. We need to talk."

We did talk, but not then — the doorbell rang! I looked out of the window. An anxious-looking Cyril was outside. And so it went on for the rest of that day. Eventually, we even had reporters from the local rag trying to get details of the so-called orgy that resulted in the deaths of an elderly couple!

Of course, it was a great shock to all of Madge and Frank's friends. Until their sudden deaths, no one had realised just how ill they were. Apparently, Madge was on borrowed time and Frank had been diagnosed with advanced cancer on top of his heart and arthritic problems. They decided to go out with a bang rather than a whimper — each struggling to look after the other. And, of course, one would have been left behind to cope with grief as well as their own physical pain. They were found together on the back seat of their ancient Rolls with their arms around each other. A pipe through the window was linked to the exhaust and an empty bottle of painkillers lay on the floor. A note, written by Madge and signed also by Frank, was found on the front seat. Tony Bradshaw, being the last one to see them alive was questioned by the Police and required to give a statement, but no evidence had been found to suggest he was in any way involved.

Neither of them had close relatives. They had already arranged with funeral directors what they required when the time came and had paid up front. They had considered the party to be their funeral feast and wanted nothing more — no mourning, no service and no graves. Ashes were to be scattered in the local woodland. Much of the money remaining from high living and medical bills was used on the party and, apart from a few small bequests to charities, the rest of their estate was left to Anthony Bradshaw for "helping to make their lives more tolerable" during their last two years. With the house heavily mortgaged, the remaining cash, after settlement of accounts and bequests, amounted to a few thousand. Even so, eyebrows were raised as to why Tony should get it. Remembering something Tony had told me a few weeks earlier, I couldn't help but think they were the couple he had obliged with his own inimitable skills. If so, it was a gift he well deserved. Even so, we heard he was giving the money to buy memorial seats along the local footpaths. Knowing what these seats often get used for at night, it seemed a fitting gesture.

The deaths of Madge and Frank made Roger and me seriously think about our own mortality. We took stock of what we did — day in, day out — wondering if we would do things differently if we knew we would not live out the week. The thought of life without Roger was unbearable and Roger refused to even consider the prospect of living on without me. But we knew it would have to come one day. Before we went to sleep on the day Madge and Frank were cremated, we had a little talk.

"Roger, we have to face it, we aren't going to live forever. And it's quite likely that one, or both, of us will eventually need a lot of care."

"You don't have to remind me, Alice."

"You need to be reminded, Roger. Life's too short to waste a second of it. We should be sharing together what there is left to us."

He sighed deeply. "Maybe."

"There's no maybe about it. With so many relatives and friends ill, disabled or bereaved, we should be thankful that we still have each other, and that we are fit enough to enjoy life as we do."

He sighed again and nodded his head. The suicide of Madge and Frank had really got to him.

"We have to give up a lot of what we do — we'll have to one day anyway. We must make the most of what is left to us."

"Yes, you're right. We'll sort it out tomorrow."

I rolled over to kiss him. "I love you, Roger," and my tears once again wet his pyjamas.

He held my face with his large rough hands and pulled my lips to his. I placed my hands over his and felt the wiry hairs on the backs of his fingers. My man was all-male and I was drawn to him just like the first time I met him. There was deep passion flowing between us and we both knew what we wanted. It might have been a quickie but somehow it had a deep earthy meaning to it. With all the energy he put into it, Roger was soon spent, but it didn't matter — we had performed what man is programmed to do and, at that time, it was enough for me. We were lifetime mates and no one would ever come between us.

In the morning, after breakfast, we sat down and talked about us and our life together. We decided to live every moment of our life in thankfulness for each other. To start with, we each gave up two thirds of our commitments. Oddly enough, our places were soon filled. We were not as irreplaceable as we had imagined ourselves to be. I strongly suspect, in some cases, our organisations were pleased to be able to bring in younger people. Rosemary, for all her huffing and puffing, had me replaced by the following week! In a way, it hurt to know I wasn't needed. Roger was feeling the same. At the end of a committee meeting after most of the members had gone, Mr Snooty Big casually thanked him for his secretarial work. He was instantly replaced. I strongly suspect, with a sigh of relief. Roger was a stickler to points of order and having the meetings reported in fine detail and with absolute accuracy. Snooty Big liked to do things his way.

I managed to persuade Roger to use a large chunk of our savings to get the essential work done on the house. There's still enough work planned to keep him going until he's ninety, but nothing really pressing. So we have much more time to ourselves and loving every moment we spend together. We still do our own thing for part of each week, but now I join Roger in the garden and he comes into town with me several days a week. We walk hand in hand like a couple of young lovers. On Market Day, we shop a little at the stalls and tap our feet to the music of the Town Band. The Old Bakehouse, an inexpensive and very friendly café — never used by the blue-rinse pensioners or the gaggling geese — has become our regular port of call.

"Hello, folks! Your usual?" the cafe owner greets us cheerfully, and within minutes we are brought a coffee with hot milk for me, and a coffee with cream plus a bacon sandwich for Roger — he needs the extra energy.

But we haven't given in to old age; we are as active as we have ever been. As far as our love-life goes, it could not be better. It's as if we've had a new beginning to our marriage and doing the things we should have done so many years ago — if only we had been aware of what we were missing. Sex is integral to our relationship. Fulfilment eventually came from our mutual desire to be wholly part of each other.

Each morning begins with an unhurried kiss. No expectations of anything more, although sometimes one thing leads to another! Each day ends with Roger doing his little act of love for me by putting in my eye drops before we kiss goodnight. If either of us is angry we admit it — no holding back. But a long drawn out kiss restores our humour and we can rest in our love. Well, not always rest straight away; making up may well move us to experience the joy of sex. For it is certain that Roger is tickled pink how I am able to react to his unhurried love play. He has found immense pleasure in giving as well as in the receiving.

A lot of this change took place on that romantic weekend by courtesy of Tony.

Before leaving the area, Tony gave Roger a tool box, complete with instructions, to use on that little holiday. It contained an assortment of feathers, to be used with sensitive care; a miniature of cherry brandy, to be applied sparingly; a small box of high quality chocolates, to be shared one at a time; a tube of exotic gel, to be spread as needed. There was also a little book revealing ancient secrets on the art of making love. Since Roger takes instructions seriously, he followed them to the letter. The feathers applied slowly, were particularly erotic and to be recommended to any serious lovers.

What a night that was! Being so late getting to sleep and then doing a bit more practising in the morning, we only just managed to get downstairs in time for breakfast. With me wearing a new blue dress and Roger wearing his casual country clothes, we went downstairs to the small breakfast room at the back of the inn. The room oozed with atmosphere. The ceiling boards had been stripped away to reveal the original oak beams on which were hanging a multitude of horse brasses. The dark oak furniture, the crackling log fire, the smell of bacon cooking in the kitchen, heightened the feeling of cosiness and welcome. But the congeniality of the place soon dissipated.

All the other residents, who happened to be young couples, had just about finished their meal when we arrived for breakfast. They stared at us, almost with open mouths. Some of them were giggling.

"Do I look funny, Roger?"

"No more than usual."

"Why are they all grinning and giggling?"

"Perhaps something they ate. Kipper bones tickling their tummies."

"I'm being serious, Roger. People keep giving us sneaky looks; even the waitress is grinning."

"Grin back at them, I am."

A young woman, dressed in a tight jumper and low-cut jeans that deliberately revealed a slice of her peachy bottom, was sitting at the next table accompanied by a well-tattooed male with a similar dress habit. She asked us, "Are you on your honeymoon?"

I was worried Roger would tell her to mind her own business. So I quickly answered, "Nice thought. Why do you ask?"

"Oh, just wondered," she said, giving me a rather smirky smile. Her partner turned his head away, a hand over his mouth.

Roger suddenly remembered he'd left his wallet on the bedside table. He nipped upstairs to get it. I heard every footstep and creak of the floorboards. The four-poster bed must have been directly over the breakfast room! The other diners looked at me as if to say, "That's what's funny!" I guess young people find it hilarious that seniors can enjoy sex too.

Apart from Tony's tool kit, another thing happened to put a bright smile on my face. Lorna's Jim told Roger what the grins over the electric toothbrush were about. He soon bought me one — with a rechargeable battery! When needed, the toothbrush moves things along nicely.

We, along with a few others, had dinner with Tony before he left. We spoke very little to each other but our eyes told us all we needed to know. When he took my hand in farewell, a kind of love flowed between us. He kissed me on the cheek. Unbidden, a tear rose to my eye. I saw Roger observing us and felt sure that he realised our very real fondness for each other. Of course, he knew he had no reason to be jealous; I am his and he is mine — a simple truth he has never once questioned. Roger shook Tony by the hand and, much to my amazement, embraced him — something I had never seen him do to any man.

Roger often speaks of how much we are indebted to Tony Bradshaw and I have to agree with him — that man revolutionised our marriage. Some of that which attracted me to Tony has rubbed off onto Roger. We are both revitalised by the superior sex we are now getting. Life could not be sweeter, or more adventurous for a pair of ageing wrinklies. Roger finds far more orgasmic rapture in our coming on together than he ever did when he experienced it alone. We are both convinced that seeking the other's happiness during such times — as in any mutual activity — deepens true love. In spite of the grappling hooks Roger has for hands, by taking things slowly, we have both discovered little nuances of delight along the path to fulfilment. Perhaps things can't always be this way, but we are making hay while the sun still shines. My days are constantly blessed. For that I am so very grateful that Anthony Bradshaw walked into my life on that bright summer morning.

Also from Magpies Nest Publishing

Red Boxes

When Phones Were Immobile and Lived in Red Boxes

Gladys Hobson, fully illustrated by Gladys Hobson and Gary Lyons.
ISBN 0-9548885-0-2

"the author reminisces about her childhood years between 1939 & 1953. ... She covers a multitude of things she experienced (or not) from the NHS, WWII, Sex Education, Boys, Family Affairs ... The book has some very funny anecdotes, but it also shows how people had to 'make do & mend', and how life was much simpler then. It shows a different way of life, but it is a very entertaining book, I could not put it down."

Gwen Green, Westmorland Gazette, Sept 2004

When Angels Lie
When angels lie, all hell is let loose and demons fly!

Richard L Gray.
ISBN 0-9548885-1-0

When Angels Lie follows the emotional and spiritual struggles of two gay clerics. It is set within country parishes coping with the tensions of challenging situations and controversial changes. Dramatic and strange events involving powerful and memorable characters carry the story along to a dynamic climax.

"Set against the backdrop of the church, one would expect a rather restrained expose of love. Richard Gray, however, has done no such thing! Gray's novel dares us to confront prejudice and bigotry and challenges our understanding of the strength of Christianity in a modern world. The love affair between Nick and Paul, two men of the cloth — one settled in a heterosexual marriage, is exactly that ... a love affair.

Gray's three main characters, Paul, Nick and Lucy try to live ordinary lives in an extraordinary situation — a situation that calls for choices to be made and decisions to be taken. In all of this, there is Paul's unconditional love for the church — a love that is tested to the limit."

Sue de Gruyther (Tutor of Sociology and Media Studies)

"... moves along at a good pace ... I really did want to know what happened in the end. Would make the general public look at the Anglican Church, its clergy, and its adherents with new eyes"

John Imlach (Churchwarden)

Coming in 2005 from Magpies Nest Publishing

Designer Love

Angela Ashley.
ISBN 0-9548885-3-7

"A tale of passionate love conflicting with burning ambition, set in the Midlands of post-war Britain."